Praise for *Sparks and Shadows*

"Snyder has a unique voice and her work is almost instantly recognisable ... It's rare to encounter a writer who so loves words and the changes that can be rung and the tricks that can be played. Rare and precious. But because of Snyder's versatility, it's difficult to give an overview of this collection. Every piece is different, and every piece demands attention ... Dark, funny, and romantic by turns, *Sparks and Shadows* is a must read. Go! Buy! Read!"
— *Greatest Uncommon Denominator Magazine*

"(N)ot only does Lucy A. Snyder write truly intelligent horror that is both witty and political but her stories and poems tap the feminist potential of horror to illuminate the shadowy extremes of both love and hate... Whether you are looking for dark fantasy or horror or just something to tickle your funny bone, I recommend you pick up a copy."
— *The Green Man Review*

"The short stories and poems in Lucy Snyder's debut collection range from dark to very dark to sexy to hopeful, often with a wry twist of humor ... Highly recommended..."
— *Sequential Tart*

"At times poignant, witty, erotic, thoughtful, chilling and maniacally gleeful, *Sparks and Shadows* is a delightful collection and book length introduction to an author to watch."
— *Horror Reader*

"Lucy Snyder's *Sparks and Shadows* is everything you could want in a short story collection. Elegant, beautiful prose, deep emotional writing and powerful stories. Do yourself a favor and grab this one!"
— James A. Moore, author of *Serenity Falls*

SPARKS AND SHADOWS

LUCY A. SNYDER

Sparks and Shadows

by Lucy A. Snyder

Creative Guy Publishing
Vancouver British Columbia Canada

Trade paperback edition
CGP-5007
ISBN-10 1-894953-65-7
ISBN-13 978-1-894953-65-8
Second edition–first edition originally published 2007 by HW Press.
First CGP Printing April 2010

Cover art by Malcolm McClinton
©2010 Malcolm McClinton

Cover design ©2010 Lucy A. Snyder

Library and Archives Canada Cataloguing in Publication

Snyder, Lucy A., 1971-
Sparks and shadow / Lucy A. Snyder.

Short stories.
Issued also in electronic version.
ISBN 978-1-894953-65-8

I. Title.

PS3619.N944S63 2010 813'.6 C2010-901956-3

SPARKS AND SHADOWS

LUCY A. SNYDER

CREATIVE GUY PUBLISHING

Author's Note

I want to thank my husband, Gary A. Braunbeck, for his love, faith, support, and advice. I would also like to thank Pete Allen (for taking on this project), Nanci Kalanta (for her work on the first edition of this book), Malcolm McClinton (for his wonderful artwork), Mark Lancaster (for his eagle-eyed proofreading), Jerry Robinette and the members of Writeshop (for their story critiques), David Wyatt and Carol Seiler (for all their encouragement over the years), Caitlín R. Kiernan (for inspiring "Sara and the Telecats" via her musings about chaos magic and politics on her blog), and all the editors who first ran these stories and poems in their publications.

And finally, I'd like to thank the snakes of the San Angelo Nature Center for providing the inspiration for "Darwin's Children" without actually giving me tetanus.

For Henrietta Snyder
(1929 - 2004)
I hope that now you know what Ocean really means.

Table of Contents

Introduction: The Surprising Pain and Joy of Lucy A. Snyder
or, Kill Gump

I hate *Forrest Gump*. Let's get that out of the way right off. The movie has its charming moments, but there's too much treacle to go along with it, and too many of its genuine moments have become—through no fault of its own—cultural touchstones, taking all of the power out of them. Any sentimental wisdom or sweetness evident in the "Life is like a box of chocolates" scene has been drained away by that dreaded disease, Catch-Phrase Fever. Fucking Gump. It's no *Titanic*—by which I mean it actually has some decent acting—but it bugs the hell out of me.

All of which is by way of apology for my regretful surrender to the impulse to say this: Lucy A. Snyder's short stories really *are* like a box of chocolates. The absolute best thing about the experience of reading *Sparks and Shadows* is that as you begin each story, you really have no idea what you're going to get. Some of the chocolates are sweet and some are sour. Some are full of poison and others hide razor blades that will leave you raw and bloody. Quite a few have an aphrodisiac quality... even some of the poison ones.

The metaphor is overworked. I know. But if you're rolling your eyes about it, I have one reply—read the book. Seriously. Maybe, like those scenes in the movie, the metaphor has lost its power through overuse, but it is nevertheless the most apt comparison.

So, what will you find on the following pages?

Pain and joy, often surprising, though not in equal measure.

Snyder writes with an unwavering confidence and purpose. There is madness in these pages. There is profound regret and lingering melancholy to be found in "As Lonely as the Grave" and "Darwin's Children." Much has been made about the eroticism present in some of these tales—including "Boxlunch," "The Roses of Gomorrah," and the phenomenal "The Sheets Were Clean and Dry"—yet I believe that instead of breathless eroticism you will find an admirably honest sexuality that is just one of Snyder's keenly-honed tools.

Within these pages, you will find women who demand their dignity, even if only instinct has ever told them they deserve it. You will encounter twists that work even if you've managed to see them coming. (One of those is in my favorite story in the book, but I can't tell you which without giving it away.) There is grotesquerie here, there are ugly consequences, and there is sadness. There are sinister powers lurking just beyond the curtains of our perception.

And there are other worlds.

Perhaps more than anything else, it is Lucy A. Snyder's science-fiction that truly surprises me. I confess I am not a great reader of science-fiction, but I would consume it voraciously if all of its practitioners brought the kind of dark imagination to their work that Snyder does to hers. Some of the stories are shocking in that they culminate in at least a version of happiness [as do several of the non-SF tales in the book], and hope. Others, however, are full of dread. "A Preference for Silence" and "Through thy Bounty" are two of the best stories in the entire volume, and "Burning Bright" reads like the prelude to a series of novels I would love to read.

"The Dogs of Summer," on the other hand, is not science-fiction but urban fantasy, full of compassion and the woman-striving-for-dignity element that echoes so convincingly and powerfully in a number of these stories. It is also the only story in the book that seems written by the same author as Snyder's excellent first novel, *Spellbent*.

Yet there are things other than stories within these pages. Snyder offers a small handful of pieces that might be essays or arch asides, as well as a number of her excellent poems. There is an elegance to these poems that is inescapable, and they share the same sense of purpose as the collection's prose stories. Lest you be tempted to skip these pieces, let me warn you how foolhardy that would be. Snyder's poems—in particular "The Jarred Heart"—are as effective and affecting as her prose tales.

It was my great pleasure to read these stories, and I'm certain you'll enjoy them as much as I did, and be haunted by them, just as I was. I'm also certain that you will come away from them with the same inescapable conclusion—that Lucy A. Snyder is a writer whose stories deserve to be savored.

Sort of like a box of chocolates.

Fucking Gump.

—Christopher Golden
February 9, 2010
Bradford, MA

Dime Novel

"Nothin' but a one-horse twin,"
disparages sexy Sheriff Dyslexia,
staring arrogant at the Dustbite Boys
astride their poor swaybacked pony.

At low noon, a Siamese centaur gallops down,
mythic hooves rolling with the tumbleweeds,
corded torsos backed like Janus,
arrows raised in a riot of elbows.

The Sheriff hears "raw!" instead of "draw!"
and while she scans in confusion
for sores in the absence of saddle
the hostile horsey Cupids pierce her heart.

They steal her star and hit the bar,
sling whiskey, then twinnish insults
about who's the horse's ass.
One shoots: they're both scored.

When the monster's cold, the ichor dried,
enter the janitors: the Dustbite Boys,
boots and guns shined like Sunday,
swayback pony snorting proud.

They'll hire a yellow Yankee paperman
and clean up as pulpbound heroes
instead of star-stuck survivors who simply
skipped to the end of the horse opera's libretto.

A Preference For Silence

VERONICA WAS a spaceworthy lass with a definite preference for silence and a great sensitivity to detail. She'd never lost her tea in zero gee and had always been the first to note when the coffee maker needed cleaning or when the fluorescent lights would flick-flicker in signal of the bulbs' impending death. Furthermore, she seemed to genuinely relish freeze-dried food.

When the other colonists asked her to take the long watch over *The Doubtful Guest* as it hurtled through space to their new home, she was quietly enthused and declared she'd always meant to read the world's Great Literature.

But they worried that she would get lonely with nothing but books and the hum of the cryopods to keep her company over those dark decades. And, more important, who would watch the ship's systems while she slept?

So they chose a lad named Melvin to be her companion. He matched Veronica in most important aspects: religious affiliation, political outlook, favorite dessert, air freshener preference. While not as attuned to detail as she, he did seem like a fairly alert fellow, respected quiet, and was easily amused by a variety of odd hobbies.

The voyage started well, with Veronica reading the Bronte sisters and Melvin building tiny Spanish galleons out of toothpicks, glue and dental floss. They traded shifts, she awake while he slept, and so they seldom saw one another. When they did, they attempted sex a few times, quietly groping each other beside his mother's cryopod, but it never seemed as satisfying as their respective pastimes.

The trouble began two years into the trip, when Veronica had started on the Russians and Melvin had begun knitting long, itchy black-and-blond scarves from all the hair they'd shed. It was not the aesthetic qualities of the scarves that upset her, for she approved of creative approaches to waste management. Nor did the click-clack of his needles bother her as she slept. It was his snoring.

His snore developed slowly, like cancer. When she began *The*

Brothers Karamazov, it was just a soft, throaty purr like the breathing of an asthmatic cat. Barely noticeable. A few months later, when she was on *Notes from the Underground*, the purr became punctuated with the occasional grunt or snort, and by the time she finished the ship's store of Dostoyevsky and started *Anna Karenina*, his snore had risen in volume to resemble the revving of a small motorcycle with a bad cylinder.

Veronica, who read slowly because she liked to savor every word, could not concentrate with all that infernal noise. She wrestled with issues of politeness and protocol for a few days, then woke Melvin and suggested they re-synchronize their schedules so that they were awake at the same time. He reluctantly agreed after she promised to program an extra set of monitors to sound an alarm if anything should happen while they slept.

With the snoring gone, Veronica happily resumed her normal reading rate of ten pages a day. But then she started to notice other things about Melvin that disturbed her. The click-clack of his knitting needles made it hard for her to focus on all the nuances of Tolstoy's use of the verb "to be," and the sound of him gargling in the morning broke her concentration entirely.

She did not approach him with her complaints because she felt a bit sheepish for making him adjust his sleeping schedule to salve her sensibilities. After all, he'd taken her imposition with such good spirit. And, as her dear departed mother had always taught her, it simply wasn't polite to comment on others' personal habits.

So she tried to concentrate on her text. But more malignant Melvinisms arose. The crunching of him eating his daily ration of vegetable flakes. The wet slurping sound he made when he drank his coffee. The way the air whistled through his nose when he sighed. The low, animal grunts he made when he whipped himself with one of his scarves behind his mother's cryopod.

Finally, one morning when Melvin was drinking his coffee and knitting in the nude, he belched. Not a mild little burp, but an eructation that shook the whole ship, thundering like the Four Horsemen of the Apocalypse.

Her patience snapped along with her concentration. She threw down *War and Peace*, launched herself across the room and started to strangle Melvin with his scarf. He made quite a lot of noise, but only for a little while. When he was unconscious, she stabbed him fifty-three times with the knitting needles, then hauled him and his scarves, toothpick ships, fungus sculptures and rotifer farm to the airlock and ejected everything into the cold silence of outer space.

Feeling exquisitely relieved, she washed her hands, carefully dried them and resumed her reading.

But then she started to notice the low hum of the cryopods, the periodic hiss of the cooling units. The flutter of the air vents. The raggedness of her own breathing. The lub-dup of her own heart.

Her hands began to shake.

Boxlunch

O N THE sixth day the Libertarian People's Army had the city under terrorist siege, Wendy Banks and her husband Juan Petrov ran out of orange juice, beer, hummus, and condoms.

Wendy, who'd reluctantly resorted to drinking some generic-brand diet soda someone had abandoned at their last party, continued to rummage vainly through the pile of ROM disks, computer cables, socks, and sundry debris around their bed in search of contraceptives.

"Just one condom," she muttered. "My left tit for one lousy condom."

She spotted a thin patch in a promisingly white medical wrapper peeking from beneath a pair of sunglasses. A hormone transderm? Oh, that would be entirely too sweet!

"Come to mama!" She snatched up the wrapper, only to have her hopes dashed. "Dammit! You're a band-aid!"

Disgusted, she crumpled the Curad and threw it back in the pile.

"Hey honey," Juan called from his perch on the couch in the other room. "Any luck?"

"*No.*" Wendy stomped into the living room. "We are entirely out of anything even remotely resembling birth control."

"Well, there's always your sparkling personality," Juan replied, then dove for the meager cover of the throw pillows at the other end of the couch.

"Die!" Wendy leaped onto the couch, grabbed her husband by the waistband of his jeans and bit him on the ass.

"Ow! Hey, no teeth, no teeth!"

Wendy sat up, scowling.

"That was a mean thing to say," she pouted.

"But highly accurate," he pointed out, rubbing his rump.

Wendy growled and buried her face in her hands. "You *know* I'm PMS. I'm so horny I could die, and with my luck I'd get pregnant if a sperm were to jump up and yell 'Boo!' at me. And I've been stuck here all week because the freaking Libbies blew up the freaking *gas company*, killing dozens of poor freaks working third shift and leaving me freaking *unemployed.* And my vibrator's burned out. And I can't even spend any time with my own husband because your stupid bosses decided they need two backup sysadmins on premises at all times. Though I *don't* see how your pulling double-shifts for them is gonna help if the Libbies do their normal thing and blow shit up.

"And when they finally let you take a day off...WE HAVE NO FREAKING CONDOMS!"

She began to weep.

"Aw, don't cry, honey." Juan scooted over beside his wife, slipped his arm around her and began to nuzzle her neck. He'd recently trimmed his black goatee and the bristles tickled. "Maybe Penny has some in her apartment upstairs?"

"Maybe," Wendy sniffled. "She always did take that 'Be Prepared' thing she learned in Kid Scouts pretty seriously."

"Computer," Juan announced. "Connect to Penny's smartwall."

The big flatscreen monitor on the wall facing their couch clicked on. Onscreen, an image resolved of a young dreadlocked woman with pink plastic snakes wound through her black hair.

"Hi, I'm the avatar for Penny Lucas. In this, our sixth day of chaos, the hot conversation topic remains: the Libertarian People's Army. Neither Libertarian, nor for the people, nor an army? You decide. Let's look at the evidence. So far, they seem to be a bunch of unwashed *dorks* who figured out how to make bombs–"

"Avatar," Wendy broke in, rolling her eyes. Penny had it programmed to talk endlessly to foil marketers. "Is Penny home?"

"Mmmm, I dunno, sugar. You got the magic word?" The avatar crossed her arms and cocked her head to one side.

"The magic word is 'weenie-roast'." Wendy replied.

The avatar's image froze for the briefest beat while the password authenticated. "Voice and data match!" the avatar exclaimed. "Hi Wendy, hi Juan. How you lovebirds doing? Sadly, Miss Penny is not at home right now; she's pulling double shifts at St. Anne's. She won't be home for another 14 hours, and after that she's gonna be asleep."

Juan sighed. "Okay, thanks, avatar. Computer, break connection. Find us a music server playing some light trance."

The stereo came on. Wendy recognized the music as being an old Massive Attack remix.

S P A R K S A N D S H A D O W S

Juan wrapped his arms around Wendy and began to kiss the sensitive spot behind her left ear. Shivers of pleasure ran down her spine.

"Oh, Juan, don't start," she moaned. "We can't–"

"Yes, we can," he whispered. "You just don't get any man meat."

"But I *want* man meat," she whispered back. "So let's go hit the convenience store, huh?"

⁂

The streets were a stinking mess; garbage service had been suspended three weeks earlier because the Libbies had taken to firing surface-to-surface missiles at city waste collection vehicles. A pair of National Guardsmen were patrolling the street on foot, automatic rifles held at the ready.

Wendy and Juan picked their way through ruptured bags of garbage fermenting on the sidewalk in the spring sun and entered Halfmann's Deli & Grocery. They split up, Wendy to seek condoms and Juan for orange juice.

Wendy found a single $30 3-pack of lambskins still on the rack in the toiletries aisle. They had expired the previous month. She was still staring at the pack when Juan came up beside her with an elderly-looking quart carton of grapefruit juice.

"They want $15 for this, can you believe it?" he whispered. "They're out of everything else except a bottle of Clamato."

She tapped the price tag above the condoms.

"Jee-sus," he said. "I guess it's tap water and oral sex for us until this mess is over with, huh?"

Wendy's eyes narrowed. "Ve should not giff up on ze condom mission so soon, Comrade Petrov. Ve still haff Thorn's Pharmacy to infiltrate–"

"I told you I need butter for my kittens!" someone shouted.

Wendy and Juan turned. A street person had come into the store while they were shopping. His gray hair and beard were a wild mane around his grimy face. He wore a stained, peeling raincoat over a mismatched exercise suit.

"Sir, please, we're all out of butter–" the girl at the cash register said.

"Liar!" the man shrieked. "The lady in the colander helmet told me I should butter the kittens to ensure their acceptance into Vishnu's secret garden. She said you would have the butter, but you would *hide* it from me, because you don't want poor deserving kittens to reach nirvana!"

"We don't have any butter...really," the girl pleaded, glancing out the door past the man. Wendy suspected she was hoping the Guardsmen were within earshot.

"Liar! Liarliarliaaaaar!" The man scrabbled at the pocket of his coat and pulled out a machine pistol. It looked to be one of the cheap Chinese models, but that made it no less lethal.

"Oh shit," Juan muttered. "I bet one of the Libbies gave him that. It's just the kind of uncontrolled chaos that really turns their crank."

The old man was waving the pistol in the air, and the cashier was cowering behind the counter. "Vishnu wants the butter now! Now now now!"

Before Wendy could stop him, Juan had grabbed one of the two remaining jars of petroleum jelly and stepped to the front of the aisle.

"I have butter of the earth," Juan said, holding out the jar. "The dinosaurs made it long ago, and it is very pure. I think Vishnu would be pleased to have it on his kittens."

"Earth butter?" The old man looked puzzled, but he lowered the pistol to waist level.

"Yes, earth butter. Take it. It's all yours."

The man reached for the jar.

Wendy saw movement in the corner of her eye. A Guardsman had stepped into the store, raising his rifle.

A pop and flash from the rifle's barrel.

The old man's shoulder exploded in a crimson mist. He shrieked, his gun hand jerking up reflexively. His pistol vomited bullets right at her husband.

Juan fell.

✳

The ambulances got to the store surprisingly fast. Wendy refused to leave her husband's side, so the medics reluctantly let her ride with him on the way to the hospital.

She gripped his hand while the EMTs worked to control the bleeding. His belly had been nearly ripped to shreds by the two bullets the old man had managed to fire directly into him. She'd never seen so much blood in her life. Juan's face was paper-white, and his fingers were like ice.

"Wendy?" Juan asked weakly.

"I'm here, Juan," she said.

"Can't...can't feel my legs..." he trailed off, his eyes rolling up into his skull.

"Get me another unit of plasma, his pressure's dropping fast," the lead EMT said.

"We're out, man," the other said.

"Shit! Well, his microchip says he's covered for resurrection. Pass me the cerebral recorder."

"Oh God, he's not–" she began.

"I'm afraid so, ma'am. Please stay clear," the first EMT replied. The second passed him a fat steel cylinder with a handle and a cable leading to what looked like a hairnet made up of wires and electrodes. The first EMT put the net over her husband's head and flipped a switch on the top of the cylinder.

"Push 9 milligrams of epinephrine; he's gotta be conscious for a good read," the EMT continued.

The second medic injected the drug into her husband. His eyes fluttered open, and the heart monitor started beeping madly.

"He's taching bad," the second said, pulling out a pair of defibrillator paddles.

"No, don't," the first said. "His heart's pumping air. You shock him now, it'll screw up the recording and he'll be gone for good."

Her husband went into a spasm of coughing, bright pink foam spilling from his lips. Then he went limp.

The heart monitor flatlined.

Wendy stared at the cerebral recorder. "Did – did you get him?"

The EMT checked the monitor on the side of the cylinder. "Yep. Got him. Your husband's alive and well in softcopy, ma'am."

After a nerve-wracking hour-long wait, Wendy was met by a doctor from Community General Hospital's cloning department.

"Wendy Banks?" he asked as he approached her in the waiting room. He carried an odd-looking black computer drive attached to a fabric shoulder strap. "I'm Dr. Smythe."

She stood and shook his hand. "What's happened?"

"Well, your husband is fortunate to have an employer who provides for such excellent resurrection benefits. The EMTs were able to do a full, clean download of your husband's mind in the ambulance. We've extracted his DNA, and have begun culturing a clone that will be ready in about 5 years. According to the terms of his insurance, he must stay with his company for at least a year after he is able to return to work, or he loses the right to be downloaded into the clone."

Wendy nodded, waiting for him to continue.

"Unfortunately, due to the recent trouble with the terrorists, there have been an unusually large number of deaths of people with resurrection benefits. As a result, this hospital currently does not have any temporary bodies to download your husband into. Also–" the doctor took a deep breath "–we are out of the more modern quantum storage units, so we had to put his dynamic data into a Dirac drive."

Wendy stared at the unit in the doctor's hands. The Dirac quantum drives were painfully obsolete and tended to lose data like a cat sheds hair.

"The drive's lead shielded to make it as resistant as possible to data loss from stray cosmic rays, but our cyberneurologist estimates you have 5 hours to get him to a downloadable body before his data starts getting corrupted. I called around, and there's a replacement body available at St. Anne's. Unfortunately, all our ambulances have been called to the scene of a suicide bombing out in Grandview. I've called you a cab; it should take less than an hour to get across town, so there should be plenty of time to get your husband taken care of."

Smythe pulled a mini-headset out of the pocket of his white lab coat and a small plastic zip bag containing a microchip. "The Dirac is always on, so your husband is conscious in a virtual reality environment inside it. To talk to him and hear him, plug in this headset. The drive also has standard input/output ports if you have a camera or digital device you want to hook up to communicate with him. And here's his ID chip; they'll need to scan it at St. Anne's before he can be processed."

Wendy took the items and thanked the doctor – while inwardly cringing at the thought that they'd stored him in a medium slightly less durable than toilet paper – and he escorted her out to the front doors.

While she waited for the cab, Wendy slipped the microchip into her pocket. She clipped on the headset's earpiece and swiveled the matchstick-thin steel microphone arm into place above her lips. She plugged the cord into the Dirac unit.

She heard a click. "Hello?"

"Juan, is that you?" she asked. "Are you okay?"

"Yeah, I'm fine...a little dizzy." The voice was a flat, generic voice-synth, nothing like her husband's warm baritone. "Where are you? I came to in this hospital room, but the door's locked and the phone's dead. Or it *was*, until you called just now. It feels like I've been in here for *hours*."

A green cab pulled up. Wendy pushed through the glass revolving doors. "I'm on my way to St. Anne's," she told her husband.

The cabbie rolled down the passenger window. "Are you Wendy Banks?" he asked.

"Yes," she replied.

The cabbie smiled and nodded at the back seat. "Hop on in and we'll get you to St. Anne's in a jiffy."

"Who's that I hear in the background," Juan asked.

"Just the cabbie," Wendy said as she climbed into the car.

"Am I at St. Anne's?" Juan asked.

"Uh...sort of..."

"Sort of? What does *that* mean?" he asked, then paused. "Wait a minute. I remember you were with me in the ambulance, and I...oh God. I got shot, and I'm not shot anymore. Even if they'd used the fastgrow gel on me, I'd still be hurting right about now."

Another long pause. "Oh crap. I *died*, didn't I? I've been boxlunched."

"It's not so bad. *Really,*" she said, trying to sound cheerful. "They got a full download in the ambulance. No detected memory loss. And there's a new body waiting for you at St. Anne's."

"The company will be pleased, I'm sure," he replied dryly. "So what kind of a box did they put me in?"

"Uh." Wendy considered lying to her husband, but they'd long ago promised never to keep the truth from each other. "A Dirac 20 terrabyte."

"A D-dirac?" he stammered. "What, were they all out of papyrus and stone tablets?"

"It'll be okay," she insisted, hugging the unit to her chest. "We have hours before the expected drive failure point."

"*Hours!* Woo! Be still my beating heart," he said, his sick desperation clear even through the synth's mechanical tones.

"Is that your husband in there?" the cabbie asked.

"Yes," she replied.

"Lucky man, gettin' a second chance like this."

"Yeah," she admitted. "But he'd have been luckier not to have gotten shot today."

L U C Y   A   S N Y D E R

"Was it a Libbie thing?" the cabbie asked. "Not to be pryin' or nothin'."

"Maybe. This crazy homeless guy had a machine pistol, and a National Guardsman got trigger-happy. I can't think of many places the old guy could've picked up a gun like that unless the terrorists gave it to him."

"Sounds like a Libbie trick," the cabbie agreed. "Heard they were doing shit like putting explosives in kids' toys and stuff. And they still haven't made any money demands or nothin'! They're just fucking stuff up to fuck it up. They're not even anarchists, they're, like–" the cabbie snapped his fingers, seemingly trying to coax the word from his mind.

"Nihilists?" she prompted.

"Yeah! That! Fucked up fucks, ya ask me. I mean, if it was the Indians trying to reclaim California or something, *that* I could maybe understand, but this trying to destroy society stuff...totally wacko. And they've got a rich guy bankrolling them – what's up with that?"

"I heard he's an extreme environmentalist," Wendy replied. "He decided the only solution to save the rest of the Earth is to wipe out as much of the human race as possible. Funding the Libbies is just a local means to a global end for him."

The cabbie shook his head. "Buncha wackos."

"Well, human overpopulation and overconsumption *has* caused the extinction of 75% of the species on the planet," her husband commented inside her left ear. "There *is* something to be said for reducing the population as quickly as possible."

Wendy frowned. "Are you saying you'd rather be dead? I mean, you're population, too."

"No, no," her husband said quickly. "I'm a man of enlightened self-interest, and I very much want to continue living, if for no other reason than to be able to make love to you every night for the next fifty years. At least."

She smiled and hugged the unit tighter. *Nice save, honey,* she thought. They'd had some of their worst arguments over ecopolitical issues. Wendy was all for trying to save the environment, but she couldn't agree with the notion of killing people, even indirectly, to save animals. There had been a time when Juan would argue a point until they were both close to tears. They'd both learned a lot about agreeing to disagree in the two years they'd been married.

He paused. "It's gonna take them how long to get my clone up to

S P A R K S   A N D   S H A D O W S

size?"

"Five years, the doctor said," Wendy replied.

"You wouldn't happen to know what my 'temporary' body looks like, do you?" he asked. "I mean, what if it's got buck teeth and no chin? Or massive amounts of body hair? Or a microscopic dick?"

Wendy sighed. "Honey, what's that they say about beggars and choosers?"

"I know, I know," he replied. "I suppose I should just be glad I'm still virtually alive."

They were on the city's interior loop around downtown. Only a few cars besides theirs were on the road; well over half the city's population had fled or been evacuated, and the rest had been officially discouraged from unnecessary travel. Abandoned and wrecked cars lined the sides of the freeway. Wendy could see that at least half of the big glass-and-steel high-rises showed some form of rocket or bomb damage. In the first few days of the siege, the terrorists had bombed buildings containing offices for credit card companies, banks, insurance agencies, utility companies, and the like. *Collateral infrastructure damage,* the Libbie spokesman had called it in his video to the news sites. *Take out the financial underpinnings of society, and society will fall. We will destroy the corrupt and rebuild in the ashes of the old.*

Wendy counted herself and her husband lucky that his company's insurance was based in Canada.

"Oh crap, what's that?" she heard the cabbie say, craning his neck up at the sky.

Then he was slamming on the brakes, tires shrieking, the car slewing sideways on the dry pavement. Wendy held onto the quantum drive for dear life as she was thrown sideways in her seatbelt. A car behind them honked frantically and Wendy heard the squeal of tires as it swerved to avoid a collision.

Then the mortar hit not twenty yards in front of the cab. There was a tremendous boom and mushroom of orange fire. Hunks of concrete and asphalt rained down on the cab, cracking the windshield.

"What was that? What's happening?" her husband shouted in her ear.

"M-mortar attack," Wendy stammered. "W-we're okay. I think."

"You okay back there, lady?" the cabbie asked.

She could only nod in reply.

The cabbie pulled a shotgun from beneath the front seat and got out of the car. Wendy fumbled with her seatbelt, got it unlatched, and pushed open the door to follow the cabbie.

He was standing in front of the car, staring at the smoking hole in the highway. A ten-foot-diameter section had been knocked out, sending huge hunks of rebarred concrete crashing to the road below the highway. Fortunately, it didn't look as if anyone had been crushed beneath the rubble.

"I'm going to have to turn back," the cabbie said. He nodded towards a section of the city outside the loop, beyond the downtown area. "St. Anne's is to the southwest of here; I'd say it's about four miles on foot."

"On foot?" Wendy could feel the blood draining from her face.

"I'm real sorry, lady," the cabbie said. "But I've got to go back. Company rules; a cab gets damaged like this, I gotta take it back to the garage. You could come with me and get another cab, but now that the loop's trashed, it might take a real long time to get back down to the hospital. I think you can get there quicker on your own."

The man went back to his cab and opened up the trunk. He pulled out a big coil of rope and a pistol.

"Here, take this," he said, offering her the gun. "You should be out of Libbie territory where you're going, but you never know. Go on, take it; I got lots more at home."

Wendy accepted the pistol, hefting it in her hand.

"If you gotta shoot it, hold it with both hands, 'cause it's got a mother of a kick. You look like a pretty strong lady, so it shouldn't be a problem. The clip holds nine rounds, and there's a round in the chamber. Safety's on."

The cabbie began to unwind the rope coil. Wendy tucked the pistol into the waistband of her jeans. The cabbie tossed her an end of the rope.

"Tie this around your waist," he said, "and I'll tie the other to the bumper and help lower you down through the hole..."

✳

Once Wendy was on the ground and the cabbie had shouted his goodbye and disappeared, Wendy said to her husband, "Well, *this* is going well. I have no ride, you have no body, and we never *did* find any condoms."

"Though the whole condom problem is moot 'til I get a new body,"

S P A R K S   A N D   S H A D O W S

he pointed out. "But, look on the bright side...you also have a gun."

"And I have the sense of direction of a donut," she said, looking up and down the deserted streets. Off in the distance, she could hear someone firing a gun. "I have no idea how to get to the hospital. It looked kind of easy from up there, but now that I'm down here..."

"You have your PDA, right? Just look the directions up on the 'Net," he said.

She checked her back pocket; the slim, playing card-sized PDA was still there. She pulled it out and flipped it open, then began to unspool the thin uplink cable stored in the edge of its case. "I have a better idea," she said, plugging the PDA cable into the Dirac and tucking the PDA into her shirt pocket. "Why don't *you* look up the directions, and read them off to me? I hate trying to read detailed stuff on this little screen."

"But how do I–" he began, then paused. "Wait, there's a video monitor over here in the corner. I tried it before and it didn't work. Maybe...bingo! Works now. We have 'Net. Where you at, honey?"

Wendy glanced at the nearest street sign. "I'm at the corner of 33rd and Hudson."

"Looks like you just go left down 33rd for about a mile and a half, then hang a right onto Riverside until you reach the hospital."

"Sounds easy enough," she replied. "Hey, could you find some dirty stories online and read to me while I walk? It's awful quiet out here."

"Sure," Juan replied. "Anything for my little nymphomaniac."

*

Wendy had been tromping down 33rd for a half hour when a National Guard truck rumbled onto the road toward her. She was in a commercial section of town; there was a Chinese restaurant, a small motel, an office supply store and an office strip nearby. All were boarded up and seemed entirely deserted.

"Ooh, it's the cavalry," Wendy told her husband, readjusting the Dirac's shoulder strap for the umpteenth time. The drive had seemed to double in weight since she'd been carrying it. "Maybe they'll give me a ride to the hospital. These boots were *not* made for walking."

"Just be careful, honey...these guys do seem to be in the 'shoot first, questions later' mode."

"I'll be careful." Wendy began to wave her arms and jump up and down.

The truck ground to a stop a dozen yards away. Wendy ran up to the

L U C Y   A   S N Y D E R

driver's window.

"Hi, guys, I was wondering if you could..." Her voice failed and her heart dropped to the bottom of her stomach when she saw that the two men inside the cab were unshaven and wore ragged Army surplus combat fatigues re-dyed an off-gray and plain black baseball caps. Libbies. She stepped away from the truck, her pulse pounding in her ears.

"Say, that's a real nice quantum drive you got there. Think I want me one of those for target practice," the driver drawled.

Wendy shook her head. "This one's not for sale," she said, voice shaking, still backing up.

"I didn't *ask* if it was for sale, now did I, bitch?"

Wendy pulled the pistol out of her waistband and pointed it at the driver. "Mr. Smith and Mr. Wesson say back the fuck off!"

The Libbie in the passenger seat raised a machine gun. "And Mr. Tommy here says hand us your stuff, and we'll consider not wasting your ass."

Wendy fired two wild shots into the cab, nearly dropping the gun from the force of its recoil. She sprinted for the cover of the boarded-up motel across the street. She heard an angry yell from the men in the cab, then the rattle of the machine gun. Bullets whanged into the pavement near her feet. She pelted into the nearest breezeway, stumbled rounding the corner, and took refuge in the doorway of one of the courtyard-facing rooms.

"I'm guessing they weren't Guard," Juan said. "How much trouble are we in?"

"Tons," Wendy squeaked, getting a better grip on the pistol. "Dial out on my PDA and call the Guard. Maybe they can do something," she whispered.

Wendy heard the truck's doors slam and then the sound of booted feet hitting pavement.

"Ah, just let it go, bro. We gotta get the stuff back to camp," one man said.

"Fuck that," the other said. "She *shot* me! Her fuckin' head's gonna be my new hood ornament."

"She *grazed* you. This is a waste of time."

"Shuddup. She could be anywhere around here."

Wendy held her breath. She heard their footsteps come through the breezway, then turn in her direction–

Anger and panic got the better of her. She jumped out of the doorway, firing the pistol. The men jumped back, surprised, weapons falling from their hands as Wendy's bullets slammed into their chests and bellies.

In seconds it was over. Wendy's pistol was empty and the men lay dead on the motel sidewalk. A wide pool of dark blood was spreading beneath their bodies.

"What's going on? What's going on?" Juan was hollering.

"Oh...oh God," Wendy said, her whole body quivering. "I killed them. There's blood everywhere. I think I'm gonna be sick."

"Deep breaths, honey, deep breaths," Juan said. "You better make sure there aren't any more."

"Right. Make sure there aren't any more," she repeated numbly. She dropped the spent pistol and picked up one of the automatic rifles, grimacing at the sticky blood on the barrel and stock.

Holding the gun at the ready, she crept back out of the courtyard through the breezeway toward the truck. The men had left it running. No one else seemed to be in the cab. She circled around back, raising the rifle, expecting a half-dozen terrorists to come leaping out from beneath the camouflage canopy–

–but the back of the truck was empty.

Except for several dozen cases of ammunition and what looked like long crates of rockets and rifles.

Wendy stared at the idling vehicle and its valuable contents. A smile crept across her face. "Honey, do you have the Guard on the phone?"

"They put me on *hold*," he replied grumpily.

"When you do get through to them, please inform them that I have liberated one of their missing vehicles and have retrieved a nontrivial quantity of munitions. They can pick up said munitions and truck at St. Anne's hospital. Whenever they can get around to it, of course.

"In the meantime, honey, we've got a *ride!*"

Wendy spent three hours in St. Anne's fifth floor waiting room, alternately dozing and reading magazines until Penny came down from the nurses' station on her break. The two women chatted for a while, and then Penny sneaked Wendy into an unused hospital room so she could catch a proper nap while she waited for the doctors to finish downloading and neurologically imprinting Juan into his new body.

Four hours later, Penny gently shook Wendy awake.

"Wha–?" Wendy groggily asked.

"Husband is served!" Penny's broad smile stood out a stark white against her dark face in the dimness. "Juan's D&I went smooth as butter. He's awake, and ready to see you now."

Wendy laced her boots back on, ran her fingers through her hair, and followed Penny down the hall.

Penny stopped just in front of Juan's hospital room. "He's going to be partly paralyzed for the next few days until he can teach his new spinal cord what it's supposed to do. He'll have to be in physical therapy for several weeks before he can function more or less normally. In the meantime, he'll need your help to learn how to use his new body."

Penny pressed a small plastic package into Wendy's hand and ushered her into the room. "Think of it as a new honeymoon. I'll make sure you lovebirds aren't disturbed for the next few hours."

Penny closed the door behind Wendy. Wendy heard the click of the lock. She lifted her hand and looked at the package her friend had given her. Condoms.

Smiling, Wendy approached her husband's hospital bed. A completely strange body lay there, hairless and skin still shiny as all fresh tank-grown bodies were. The new body was smaller, younger and thinner than Juan's old body, his fingers long and elegant. He wore only a thin hospital gown and an ID bracelet around his wrist. There was a small band-aid on the back of his hand where they'd reinserted his microchip.

"How are you feeling, honey?" she asked.

The man turned his head toward her but did not otherwise move. "I feel so weird," he said. His voice was softer and mellower than Juan's. "This body feels completely wrong in a thousand little ways. I can't get over how my teeth feel; I keep running my tongue over them. And...I can't move much below my neck. That's got me a little freaked out."

"Penny said all that's normal. And you'll only have to live with it for a couple of years. In the meantime, it's time for your first physical therapy session." Smirking, she held up the condoms.

"Ah, I see our mission was successful after all, Comrade," he said. "But I don't know that I *can*..."

"We'll see about that," she smiled.

Wendy set the condoms on the foot of the bed. She started to dance, doing a slow striptease for her husband. When she was completely naked, her nipples hardening in the cold hospital air, she saw that Juan had made a tent of his hospital gown.

"Looks like you're gonna do just fine," she said. She crawled up onto the bed and pushed the gown up around his chest.

"But how am I down there...?" he asked, looking worried.

She smiled and gave him a long, slow kiss.

"Like I said," she replied, "You're gonna do just fine."

The Monster Between The Sparks

I am the death you cannot see
when you gaze upon your starry skies.
Your telescopes, they lie to you
when they show a cosmos glittering
with a million fiery gems;
I lurk unseen between those sparks,
swelling, growing larger and smarter
with every sun I swallow whole.

I've grown tired of passive fare;
worlds and stars and dust,
all spiral to my maw
with no effort, just the force
of my immense dark gravity. I want
prey that thinks itself a predator,
a victim that will find its way to me
carried on the silver wings of mortal pride,
prey that fights and feels the terror of my bite.

I know you'll fly to me; babies can't resist
the shiny, pretty things, reaching for a bauble
lying near the snake, grasping at the flame
that burns soft flesh. You'll try for worlds
to replace the one you broke
and when you come I'll crush you
to my frozen breast and take you to my heart
of darkness, and your pain will keep me warm.

I am the death you cannot see,
I am all you cannot bear
to know about your universe,
because to know that I am real
is to know there's no escape
from this, your fragile world,
your tiny azure ember burning down
in the cold of an endless night.

Through Thy Bounty

I STARE down at the naked body of the boy on the butcher block as my mother's nightmare washes through me. She is ill. Last night's dreams were filled with fever-warped images of shrouded doctors, knives and needles, tubes and dark blood. The doctors of the Resistance will do their very best for her, but she is an old lady now, her body fragile. The thought that she might die turns my guts to ice.

Her life is my only hope in this Hell. But at least I know she is safe from the Jagaren. For now.

The boy is maybe eight or nine, redheaded, skinny and bruised. His ankles are purple and rope-burned. The gash in his neck is pale as raw bacon; they've drained the blood from his body. Sometimes, depending on the menu du jour, they leave the chilled blood for me in a stainless steel thermos jug beside the corpse's head. But not today.

He has the look of a child who's been in captivity for a long time. But he has to be the flesh and blood of somebody important in the Resistance, else he would not be here in my kitchen. The Jagaren always have their most precious catches flown in fresh from the battlefields, concentration camps, and torture chambers.

As always, the menu instructions are printed on stiff paper tucked in the corpse's mouth. The Jagaren have been sampling every aspect of Terran cuisine, each day a new ethnic menu. Today they want to taste the Deep South: sweet barbecue, collard greens, chicken fried steak with gravy, chitlins, sausage, watermelon, corn on the cob, fried green tomatoes, and apple pie. Dinner for twelve. I have but eight hours to prepare this meal.

I touch the boy's forehead, close my eyes and say a brief prayer for him. I don't know what religion he had, if any, but we all live under the same God. Maybe someday He'll remember us. Prayer finished, I pick up my curved knife and begin to skin him.

The boy's left hand has the calluses that come from years of throwing a baseball. A lefty Little League pitcher. As I work, I imagine him playing ball in a sunny Midwestern field, jeans stained with grass and dirt. His grin is the very definition of childhood joy, and he goes home victorious to a hot bath and hugs from his proud father. He spends the evening catching fireflies with his friends until his mother calls him home to be tucked in and read to sleep.

I have been alone here for over a year, all my waking hours spent in this huge, beautiful, damnable kitchen. It has a walk-in refrigerator that is stocked every night as I sleep, an immense pantry of dry goods, racks of jars of dried spices from every corner of the Earth. In case I ever face an unfamiliar menu, the back wall is lined with hundreds of cookbooks selected by the Jagaren; undesirable recipes have been cut out. The side door leads to a room with rows and rows of herbs under grow lights. There's an open-pit barbecue and spit big enough to roast a whole ox, a man-sized oven, wok, industrial meat grinder, and on and on. No kitchen I ever worked in as a chef in Los Angeles and Dallas was even half as well-equipped.

The Jagaren picked their torture well.

I always loved the kitchen, even as a child, and everything I know about cooking, about life, is but a pale shadow of what my mother knows. Her mind, her *will*, is astonishing. When the Jagaren came to take our planet, my mother turned from managing her restaurant empire to managing the covert movement of arms and soldiers around the world. Some of the military leaders would not believe (at first) that a master chef could have so sharp a mind, would not believe she could turn from butter to guns, but she would not be denied. Later, when the Jagaren found the secret tactical bunker in Montana and killed most of our generals, she kept the Resistance from falling apart. Ever since, she's been leading most of the war efforts in North America.

I have no wartime talents. I'm a good cook, but nothing more. I was helpless to do anything to save myself or my friends when Dallas fell.

My friends are dead by now, tortured to death to amuse their captors. Everything seems to be for the Jagaren's amusement, even the war to take the planet. I have no doubt that they could have used a biological weapon to wipe us all out from the safety of their spaceships. But that wouldn't have been any *fun* for them. They *like* seeing their slave troops clash in bloody, primitive conflict with our people. I suspect that the Jagaren are their world's spoiled, sadistic rich children who've been sent off to vent their twisted aggressions in war games well away from home. Or maybe they've come on their own, like the boys who used to wander my neighborhood in search of stray cats to set on fire, their apathetic parents oblivious to their misdeeds. I can't imagine how their civilization evolved if they're *all* like this.

I have not been physically abused much. They know I need my strength to cook for them. And they want to keep me alive because I am my mother's only child, and there is the chance she will try to rescue me.

Every day, I try to warn her away. I know she gets my messages. When I was very small, we learned that if one of us slept while the other was awake, the sleeper would dream of the other's activities. If we both slept at the same time, we shared the same dreams. My connection to her has weakened as I've grown older, but she's told me her connection to my mind has remained as strong as the day I was born. Almost all my dreams have followed her life, though I can't always see it clearly. She is my only window to the free world. I can only imagine that it is the same for her, that now she must dream of dismembering and cooking little boys.

I finish skinning the corpse. I set the skin aside for chopping and deep-frying, pick up the bone saw and survey his stripped flesh with my butcher's eye. He smells like raw lamb meat. His arms, ribs, and most of his legs will have to become barbecue. I pull a stout knife from the block and start to separate his joints. Very little of him can be made into steak, but I will try with his glutes and quadriceps. I have to try to meet the menu, or I will be punished, and my punishment will be my mother's nightmares.

I tried to commit suicide my very first day as the Jagaren's cook. Loudspeakers ordered me into the kitchen from my cell that first morning. I found seven babies lined up on the counter, with instructions to roast them like suckling pigs. I stared at the menu for a while, then got a knife and cut my own throat.

The Jagaren kept me from dying, of course. While my body healed, they walled my mind in a VR hell, piping in the recorded final memories of people they'd tortured to death. By all rights, the experience should have shattered my sanity, but my mother's stability saved me.

But I dare not try suicide again, for I cannot bear to inflict such nightmares on her. Furthermore, in my dreams she *orders* me to do their bidding, to do whatever I must to survive. That's always been our family's way. My ancestors survived every sort of war and atrocity. My great-great-grandmother, as a little girl, survived the massacres in Rwanda by hiding in a pile of corpses for three days. Two hundred years ago during WWII, one of my Jewish ancestors was put in the camps in Poland. They set him to work prying the gold out of the mouths of the people they gassed or shot. He survived, and afterward moved to the U.S. where he became a very successful dentist. Just to spite the Nazis, no doubt, because I'm sure he had no real desire to touch a tooth ever again. Even if he'd been a sadist, he'd have hated the work.

I wonder if I will be able to cook again, if I ever get out of here alive. I wonder if I will ever be able to hold a child or lover in my arms without my fingers automatically seeking the places a knife should be inserted to crack apart their joints.

The boy is completely dismembered now. I lay his hands, arms, and shins on a rack for the barbecue. Then I slice open his abdomen to figure out what will be sausage, and what will be chitlins.

I wonder if I and my mother are the first in our family to have shared minds, shared souls. It's hard to tell, because we've kept our connection an utter and complete secret for fear that we'd be locked up for examination. No doubt any others would do the same. But such a thing has to be as much a matter of genes as it is a matter of spirit. How can a four-year-old girl find the courage to stay still and silent, without food or water, in the midst of stinking corpses for half a week? How can a young man be made to rob the corpses of his friends and neighbors for five years and survive sane and unbroken? Perhaps they, too, dreamed of freedom through a loved one's eyes.

I work hard and fast the rest of the day (if it is in fact day; all the clocks in here tell me how much time I *have*, not what time it *is*). I make the pie crust, chop the apples and tomatoes, stew the collards. The boy's large muscles are breaded and fried and covered in cream gravy, his limbs and ribs coal-smoked for hours and drowned in sweet barbecue sauce, stomach and large intestine chopped and stewed for chitterlings, skin chopped and deep fried into puffy rinds. The rest of him becomes sausage.

I never taste the meat dishes directly, only the sauces and the vegetable dishes. I have a good knowledge of spices and how they blend, so if I'm careful with my measurements I don't make mistakes.

Not that I really have any idea of how the Jagaren's sense of taste works. They aren't human, after all. Though they are warm-blooded, they don't resemble any Earth mammal in the least.

It took the Resistance some time to capture a Jagaren for study and vivisection. The Jagaren's slave troops are composed of species from many other worlds, including humans and even some Earth animals now that the Jagaren have had a few years to study the mammalian brain. All their slaves are turned into murderous automatons via viral reprogramming of their brains and are fitted with bioelectronic radio receivers in case their orders should change. No officers, just the soldiers in battle 'til they die and the Jagaren well away from the fighting.

But the Resistance captured a tourist in the rubble of Boston: one of the Jagaren had apparently wanted to see a little blood and thunder up close. Mother, knowing full well the risk of telepathy, made sure it was kept in a dark, soundless chamber until they found an anaesthetic that would keep it under.

I saw some of the inspections and vivisections through my mother's eyes. I suspect I may have appreciated the procedures more than she, since I studied quit a bit of biology in college. A squat creature it was, beautiful and hideous at the same time, its tentacled body covered in bright green and blue feathery scales. I wondered how they managed to capture it; the Jagaren was radially symmetrical, with an eye pointing out at each corner of its square skull. It's hard to sneak up on something with 360-degree vision. I guess they ran it down; the Jagaren's four stout legs were good for kicking and climbing, but too short for speed.

When they cut it open, the fleshy steam smelled like fish. The vivisection revealed an incredible digestive system: a multi-chambered stomach, with colonies of bacteria to break down cellulose, bone, even some types of rock. And it could probably eat just about anything; the mouth was a wide, sphincter-lipped cavity at the top of its head (the brain was set out of harm's way in the torso). The muscular oral cavity was lined with circular rows of grinding teeth, and in between were millions of taste buds. Far more than we poor mammals have, and far more specialized.

So even if I prepare everything to taste exactly as it should to humans, the Jagaren might hate it and punish me. Of course, they might like it, and punish me anyway.

✳

When the meal is ready, I prepare the twelve dinner plates and dessert dishes and set them on the conveyor belt that carries the food away to be eaten. The conveyor belt door is maybe just barely big enough for me to try to squeeze through (I've lost a lot of weight since I've been here), but the thought of being in the Jagaren's dining hall is unspeakably terrifying. They would devour me, I'm sure, gourmands gobbling down a bit of sushi. To feel my arms and legs being sucked into those grinding maws, my bone and flesh shredding as surely as if my limbs had been thrust down a garbage disposal...no. I stay as far from the door as I can.

There is only one other way out of the kitchen: the door to the hallway that leads to my cell. Or *cells*, I should say. I go into the hallway, sit down on the concrete floor, and wait. There are three doors in front of me. The one on the right leads to a room with a soft hotel bed, a toilet, a shower, soap, and a change of clean clothes; I will get this room if the Jagaren enjoy their meal. Behind the middle door is a bare concrete room with a futon, sink and toilet; I get this if the meal is indifferent. If the meal is unsatisfactory, I get the last room, a cold, cramped, brightly-lit cell with nothing but a sink and toilet. The Jagaren do not want their cook to be contaminated with excrement.

I cannot simply spend the night in the hallway or the kitchen. Once, when I refused to respond to the loudspeakers, they sent knock-out gas through the vents. The corpse-movers carried me to the small cold cell. I woke with a headache that lasted three days.

I wait for one hour, two. Finally, the buzzer sounds, and the right door swings open. The Jagaren were pleased. I should sleep well tonight.

I enter the room, and find the concrete shard I've hidden beneath the bed. I pull off my shirt, and stare down at my scarred chest and belly. One cut for each man, woman, and child I've butchered for the Jagaren; almost every inch of my torso is engraved. I find a smooth place, right above my sternum. I push the sharp end of the shard into my flesh and slowly rake it down, again and again, until blood washes dark and soap-slick over my pale skin.

I dream of my mother. She is feverish. Lances of fire arc through her veins with every step she takes down the dark corridors of the bunker. Her generals take her to a briefing room, where they tell her of an island in the Caribbean. They have found where the Jagaren are holding me, and are going to stage a rescue mission.

My mother will go with them.

They are treating it as a suicide mission. I desperately want to tell her to stop. I'm not worth it; she is dying, yes, but her last days could surely be spent better than *this*. But I can be nothing more than a mute observer.

And all the while, my mother thinks: *300 degrees, 300 degrees, don't go over 300 degrees. You will know what to do.*

I wake up crying, bile in my throat. My mother is going to kill herself for me. She is everything to the fate of the human race, and she is going to *waste* herself, just because I am her child. Her helpless, useless child.

Soon, the morning alarm blares through the room, and the door slides open. The loudspeakers order me into the kitchen. It's always like this; the whole thing is automated.

In the kitchen, I find two young women and an order for French fare. The recipes are demanding, and I cannot concentrate on my work. I burn the bread and scorch the sauces, and at the end of the day I am sent to the tiny, cold concrete room where it is nearly impossible to sleep. I do not dream much, and that is a mercy.

I walk through my work a tear-stained zombie, half awake and half asleep. I feel as though I've been wrapped in an invisible shroud. Sound, light, touch, all my senses are muffled. My fingers are clumsy and numb. I spill more food on the floor than I get into the pots.

Just as I set the last of the poorly-cooked fajitas and enchiladas on the conveyor belt, a searing pain shoots through my thigh. Suddenly, my blood races with adrenaline. Gunfire and screams ring inside my head. A stabbing pain rips into my chest, and I pass out.

Later, I come to in my small cold cell. My heart is beating strong, and I realize what I felt was my mother's death.

The human race is lost. I sit huddled with my head on my knees for a long time, unable to even cry. Finally, I drift off to a dreamless, black sleep.

The next morning, on the butcher block I find my mother and two young men with Marine Corps tattoos on their forearms. Stark against their pale skin are purpling, quarter-sized bullet holes. My mother has been shot through her right thigh and between her breasts.

My whole body is shaking, a tic in my eyelid making my vision twitch. But my mind is dead and cold. I can feel nothing, no rage, no grief, nothing. This is my waking nightmare, and everything I see and touch has taken on the distant, insubstantial sheen of dream.

Only my work is left; everything else is gone. I pull the paper from my mother's mouth. The Jagaren want an Ethiopian meal today. Dinner for sixty. This is twice the number I've ever had to serve before. Apparently, they've all come out to devour her.

I will have to work fast, and my mother's flesh will have to go a long way. I pick up my skinning knife and start to prepare the corpses. As I start to skin one Marine, I realize that his flesh looks strange. His fat is ever so slightly bluish, and his blood vessels are thickened. How can such a young, fit man have arteriosclerosis? I turn to my mother, and slice open her leg. She has the same blued fat, the same hardened veins.

I dig deeper and cut open her femoral artery with my knife. Inside the plaque that is almost blocking the vessel I see the shine of minute blue crystals. If the plaque showed up on a CAT scan or MRI, it would simply look like advanced cardiovascular disease.

My mother's thoughts echo in my memory: *300 degrees, don't go above 300 degrees. You will know what to do.*

The realization hits me, and I curse myself for not catching on sooner, for letting my grief blind me to what my mother has planned. Virus. The plaques contain crystallized clumps of virus, resistant to denaturing up to 300 degrees.

I stare at their exposed flesh. They're absolutely *loaded* with the virus. Suddenly, the cause of my mother's fevers and surgeries is clear to me – she's been letting the doctors turn her into a walking bioweapon.

I cut out some of their arteries and leave them to soak in a cauldron of warm water; I will use this to make the batter for the thin pancakes used to scoop up the food. The pancakes cook at about 200 degrees, and with luck the artery-water will render them virulent. I take several pounds of fat from my mother and the Marines and pulverize it in the food processor until it's a fine paste. This will enrich the sauces and the lentil paste, after they have cooked and cooled down a bit.

I work constantly, sweating from the heat of the kitchen and my own anticipation. The cut over my heart breaks open, staining the front of my shirt with blood.

I get the banquet prepared barely in time. It's beautiful; I haven't done this well in weeks. There's enough food for half of them to have seconds.

As I set the plates on the conveyor belt, I say grace.

"We thank thee, Lord, for these Thy gifts which they are about to receive, through Thy bounty and Christ, our Lord, amen."

My mother is standing beside me. She squeezes my shoulder gently.

"It's a very good dinner, dear," she tells me. "I wouldn't have put quite so much pepper in the lentils, but a very good dinner just the same."

"Thanks, Mom." I pause, not knowing how to express how terribly sorry I am for what I've just done to her. When I look over, I realize she's not really there. She'll never be there again.

❋

After the wait in the hallway, I am sent to the best room. I cut myself for a while, carving a cross into my chest, then take a long, hot shower and lie down. I'm still shaking, my heart pounding. Will it work? What will they do to me if it doesn't?

Whatever happens, this is the end of my career as a cook.

I lie awake, mind churning. I've cooked my own mother. Sliced her, and diced her, and made her into a beautiful gravy-covered communion for our new lords. Will I be freed, when so many better people have suffered and died? Or will I join them in a horrible death? Which fate do I really prefer?

And I can't stand this God-damned *waiting*! If I am to die, then I want to *die* already! If I am to live, then I want *out*!

My thoughts wind me so tight I can't stay still. I get up, pace, babble nonsense rhymes to myself, anything to drown out the roar in the back of my head.

When the timed alarm finally sounds and the door opens, I race into the kitchen, my skin prickling with manic fear.

The carving block is bare. I have no corpse, no instructions. The refrigerator hasn't been re-stocked.

"What?" I scream at the loudspeakers. "No meat? How can I make your pudding when you won't leave me any meat!"

I run to the conveyor belt and peer down the ten-foot-long shaft. I see dim light, but no movement.

"Allee allee out's in free!" I call.

No response, no sound. The thought of crawling through this thing to the dining room is unspeakably terrifying. But what's terror worth when you've cooked your mommy?

L U C Y   A   S N Y D E R

I climb onto the conveyor belt. Sensing my weight, the motor starts automatically and slowly carries me into the shaft. The heat lamps lining the ceiling come on, filling the shaft with red-orange light. Almost instantly, the shaft is sweltering. The light burns into my back, my scalp, my face. Sweat pours off me, and my itchy cuts start leaking blood again. I'm stewing in my own skin. It suddenly occurs to me that I should be on a platter with a nice side of cranberry sauce. The thought makes me giggle, and for a long time I can't stop.

An eternity later, I come out of the shaft into the huge, airy dining room. The breeze hitting my roasted face is wonderfully cool, feels like the breath of God.

The room is filled with rows and rows of long wooden tables without chairs. There are a few dirty plates still scattered on the tables. The place is dead quiet, abandoned. Dull light from the overcast sky filters through high bay windows. Even this weak radiance makes me squint like a newborn baby; it's been years since I've seen the sun.

"Hey! Come and eat me, already!" My voice echoes hollowly.

I turn around, and see a set of double doors. One is ajar, swinging gently in the breeze. I jump off the conveyor belt and run to the door, my arms raised as if I am a dove about to take flight. I push out into the warm Caribbean air. I smell the ocean, and flowers.

And something rotting. I nearly trip over a Jagaren that lies just outside the door. I squat, and stare at the corpse for a bit. The stout body is covered with deep, oozing ulcers, and the ground is littered with its molt of feathery scales. The flies have found it, and are bustling for a sip of ichor and a chance to lay eggs in the fishy flesh. The maggots will have quite a feast.

I leave the corpse, and walk down the path to a gazebo that overlooks the ocean. The sun is a red orb just above the horizon, lighting the streaked clouds with delicate purples and pinks. I don't know whether it's rising or setting.

In the distance, I hear helicopters.

The Fish and the Bicycle

Consider the physics:
how could she pedal
with fragile fanning fins,
sit with slippery tail,
steer with gasping mouth?

She breaks the surface,
peeks up goggle-eyed
at his bold chrome frame,
his knobby cocked handlebar,
his rugged hunky tires.

Dory knows that Schwinns can't swim.
Undersea, the salt and wet
would rot his shapely seat,
rust his shining chain,
blister his pearly paint.

But she'd be happy to drown in the air,
flip and flop on the gritty boardwalk,
shake to flakes in the stinking heat
for just a single slimy ride
on her Adonis machine.

Camp Songs:
Innocent Fun or Diabolical Brainwashing Plot?

PICTURE, IF you will, a road trip to attend New Year's Eve festivities in Philadelphia. It was late at night, and it was my turn to drive. Our car was stuffed to the brim with goth chicks. I thought everyone else was asleep. I couldn't reach the CD case. So, to keep myself awake, I started singing the first thing that popped into my head:

> I've got something in my pocket
> That belongs across my face
> I keep it very close at hand
> In a most convenient place
> I'm sure you couldn't guess it
> If you guessed a long, long while
> So I'll take it out and put it on
> It's a great big Brownie smile!

"You've got *what* in your pocket?" Drea asked, cracking one mascaraed eyelid and peering at me.

"A smile?" I replied.

She started giggling. "Substitute 'ball gag' or 'throbbing cock' and you've got one of the filthiest songs known to humanity. Where did you learn that?"

"Summer scout camp," I said. "It's the 'Smile Song'; every Girl Scout knows it."

She broke into louder peals of laughter that awakened the rest of the car, and she was eager to share the joke. The meme spread amongst my friends:

"Is that a great big Brownie smile in your pocket, or are you just happy to see me?"

Part of me was appalled at the treatment this sweet little childhood song was getting at the hands of my barbaric goth friends. But I soon realized that the kink in that song was built-in: it never sounds innocent when it's coming from the lips of an adult.

Girl Scout songs are a kind of indoctrination; they're supposed to be a fun way of teaching little girls positive values and good citizenship. But did they have a subtext that was teaching us something quite different?

I started thinking about all the other camp songs that were firmly wedged in my memory. And then I remembered Rhino.

Rhino was the nickname of one of the counselors at one of the camps I attended. She was, in retrospect, butch as fuck. After a long day of horseback riding, this is the song she taught us all under her buzzcut supervision:

> I know a Weenie Man
> He owns a weenie stand
> He sells most everything
> From hot dogs on down!
> Someday I'll be his wife
> His lit-tle weenie wife
> Hot Dog, I love that Weenie Ma-a-an!
> Weenie Man!
> Weenie Man!
> Yaaaaay Weenie Man!

God only knows what this song did to our tender, impressionable young minds. True, I know of no girls who actually took the exhortation to marry a hot dog vendor or bratwurst meister to heart. But one can only shudder to imagine these blossoming girls casting secret glances at the virile vendors slapping meat into the soft buns, growing flushed from the smell of grilling mystery meat and weenie steam, their hearts a-flutter and their loins a-quiver as they step up to the counter and say, "I'd like a footlong, please."

Because this song will lead to the worst sorts of carnal desires. Desires that will spawn unspeakable fetishes involving relish and hot mustard. And they won't be satisfied with just hot dogs, oh no. Because once a young woman gets a taste for sausage, she'll inevitably try bulging kielbasas and hard salamis behind the Elk Lodge. She'll want to move to Germany. Or worse, she'll move into the blood sausage demimonde, start wearing black and smoking cloves and be lost to decent society forever.

But those little songs weren't just preparing us for a life of kink. Some songs were filled with nihilism and raw violence. Consider "The Window Song," in which almost any nursery rhyme or children's song can be turned into a seemingly-gleeful chant about rampant defenestration:

> Mary had a little lamb,
> Whose fleece was white as snow.
> And everywhere that Mary went
> She threw it out the window!
> The window, the window!
> The second-story window!
> High low, low high
> Throw it out the window!

> Humpty Dumpty sat on a wall
> Humpty Dumpty had a great fall
> All the king's horses and all the king's men
> Threw him out the window!
> The window, the window
> The second-story window!
> High low, low high
> Throw him out the window!

> It's raining, it's pouring,
> The old man is snoring,
> Got out of bed
> And bumped his head
> And threw it out the window!
> The window, the window
> The second-story window!
> High low, low high
> Throw it out the window!

Note the repetition of the song, and the repeated exhortation to "Throw it out the window." Seems almost like brainwashing, doesn't it? I suspect – but cannot yet prove – that our camp counselors were really part of a diabolical black operations plot to secretly convert young girls into assassin moles, ready to commit the worst violence upon hearing just the right bars of music.

Imagine: legions of upstanding American women could be Nymphomaniacal Puppets of Death in the hands of the dark forces controlling our government. I can see the newspaper reports now:

"I don't know why I seduced the Armenian ambassador and threw him out the window," sobbed Judy Baker, a registered nurse now held without bond at the local jail while she awaits transfer to federal facilities. "I was giving him a sponge bath, when...when, I don't know. I think there was music. I couldn't control myself. Does anyone have a hot dog?"

Why I Can't Stay Out of My Husband's Pants

IREMEMBER the first time I got into my husband's pants. That morning, all my work-suitable pants had problems: a stray red sock had bled on one in the wash, another pair had shrunk, and a third was fraying around the hem.

My kingdom for a lousy pair of khakis, I thought.

Then I spied with my little eye a pair of crisp olive-drab khakis hanging on his side of the closet. I touched them. The material was soft and substantial, and smelled faintly of his cologne. If I wore them, I'd think of him all day. Would they fit? I pulled them off their hanger. The zipper was strong, much sturdier than the zips on my own women's trousers.

I pulled on his pants, and I faintly heard an angelic chorus somewhere down the block. His pants fit, fit better than many of my own clothes. Better yet, they were even rather flattering; the material was thick enough to not show off my every last figure flaw.

And, oh, the pockets! Deep, capacious pockets! I could keep all my hopes and dreams in pockets like those.

My husband came in from his morning shower, toweling off his hair.

"Can I borrow your pants today?" I asked.

"Ew, but you'll get girl cooties all over them!"

I stuck my tongue out at him. "So where did you get these? I want them. I want your pants."

"I got them at Target...they were $18."

"So UNFAIR!" I wailed. "These are made better than chick pants! And way cheaper! And they fit better!"

"Huh." He scrutinized my rear. "Yeah, they look better on you than they do on me. Weird. 'Cause you're built all girly and stuff."

"Well, not so girly," I sighed. "It's been a while since I've even been able to fit into a size 14, and all the interesting clothes stop there. It's like us big girls aren't supposed to ever buy clothes. And most of the stuff in the Women's section is all nasty synthetics and fits about as nicely as a gunny sack. And let's face it, oh-so-low jeans just don't look good if you're not built like a 16-year-old."

I was warming to my rant. "And have you ever noticed how they stick the Women's section right by the Petites? It's like they're taunting us: 'Neener, neener, look at all the cool stuff you could buy if you weren't such a great big cow!'"

"I think you've got a persecution complex," he said.

"You try finding decent clothes in the Women's section sometime," I replied.

He shook his head. "Those polyester florals frighten me. Maybe you should just buy guy pants."

"But that would make me a transvestite, wouldn't it? I mean, I'd still have to try stuff on. We're in Ohio! I'll be shunned as a freak. I'm not trying to push the gender envelope; I just want clothes that will fit."

He paused. "Well, we've established that you can get in my pants. So, I'll buy the clothes, and you can be my little pants bandit, my little trouser rustler..." He dropped his towel and backed me up against the bed.

"Your Jean Genie?" I asked, just as he was about to kiss me.

He winced. "I'll be glad when this 70s fad has died out."

The Dickification of the American Female

THERE ARE eight million dicks in the Naked City. And chicks are some of them. Here are two of their stories.

Cassandra's Story

It all started when I was twelve, and saw *Blade Runner* down at the mall. It completely blew my mind, and so I ran right out to Waldenbooks to look for the novelization.

I had no idea who this Dick person was. *Do Androids Dream of Electric Sheep?* was a lot different than the movie...and the more I read it, the more I realized it was even cooler.

I got *The Man in the High Castle* next, and after that *Confessions of a Crap Artist*. By the time I was 16 I started on *The VALIS Trilogy*.

I started to seriously question the nature of reality and memory, and I began to distrust the government. When all the other girls were reading *Seventeen* and writing fan letters to the Backstreet Boys, I was reading the Philip K. Dick Society newsletter and engaging in intermittent correspondence with Tim Powers.

When it came time to go to college, I enrolled at Cal State Fullerton, just so I'd have the chance to read all his personal papers. I was a total dickhead.

Right now I'm working on my PhD at Stanford and doing experiments on the nature of time. If I can build the machine, maybe I can go back and save him...and then he will be mine, all mine.

Randi's Story

I used to think that having a pussy was pretty cool. G-spots rock, plain and simple. And being able to have a baby and create a whole new human life – how awesome is that? And if you aren't the baby type, you can keep your pot stash in there; if you wrap it up good and wear enough Chanel No. 5, the drug dogs are none the wiser.

Umm. Forget what I said about the stash – that's just an example. My point is, the pussy is handier than most people realize.

And if you're turned on, nobody has to know, right? That's why guys don't wear skirts, you know, except for Scotsmen and they've got a sporran to hide behind and keep their dignity intact.

But then I started camping with my boyfriend, and damn, the first time you gotta go pee in the mountains when it's freezing outside, you really wish you had that dick. Then, of course, I met that hippie chick in Sonoma who showed me how to pee standing up. All you gotta do is get one of those hollow medicine spoons and cut the end off and press the spoon end against your bits – instant pee tube! No frozen butt on the mountaintop! And you can do it without; you just gotta learn to pull your lips up with your fingers and practice in the shower for a while, and you can get pretty good aim. I even learned how to write my name in the snow! It freaked my old boyfriend out something fierce, but then I figured it's better to have a pussy than *be* one so I dumped him.

The pee thing aside, it wasn't until I started reading Freud that I really got on the dick trip. I mean, here's this doctor with all these women coming to him with stories of molestation and societal oppression...and he goes and decides they're all crazy and have penis envy instead.

At first I was thinking, "Man, this Freud dude is such a *dick* for dismissing their abuse and thinking it was all about them wanting the Mad Powah of the High Holy Man Meat."

But then I realized, for him to ignore all their stories...the cock must be pretty compelling, you know? He must have thought that his dick was just the most wicked thing *ever*.

And so I started noticing the inherent coolness of the almighty cock...and I began to seriously respect the cock, though sometimes not the guy it happened to be attached to.

I decided I wanted my own dick. First I got a functional red rubber number from the local fetish shop – I felt like Mick Jagger strutting around my bedroom with that thing strapped to my hips. So I went back and got this mighty 15-incher – you could hit homers with that baby. I felt like John Wayne and Sammy Sosa all rolled up into one petite package.

But wearing those rods under my clothes...well, I do have some sense of ladylike discretion. So I bought a couple of soft, wibbly pack-and-play numbers that wouldn't show under my dresses. I could be a chick with a dick all day long! I felt powerful and confident.

But as time went on, and I got passed over for promotion after promotion at work, I realized it wasn't enough to have the dick...you have to *be* the dick.

So I started extending my dick. I started smoking cigars, and I bought a cell phone with an extra-long antenna. I saved my money and bought a Hummer that I ram through every traffic opening I can find on the freeway. I use my cell phone as much as possible, antenna up, and talk loudly so that people know I'm more important than they are.

Am I a complete dick? I don't think so, but I try harder every day.

Menstruation For Men

IT'S HARD to properly imagine an uncomfortable, aggravating biological condition that affects organs you simply don't have. It's probably as hard for your average guy to imagine what it would be like to menstruate as it is for the average gal to imagine what it's like to suffer from a fractured penis.

Pain is part of the human condition, and we can all relate to plain ol' pain. It's the particulars that get real fuzzy real quick, especially for something that creates such a sticky mess of symptoms as menstruation.

So. We'll have to use the organs at hand for this descriptive exercise. If you have a penis, and want to know what menstruation might be like for your girlfriend, sister, or mom, read on!

Start by imagining that your urethra is quite a bit larger than it is now. Now, imagine that you have a magical prostate gland that holds back urine but does nothing to hold back blood and tissue.

Yes, that's right, boys...you're going to be bleeding through your dick for the next several days! This is fun already, isn't it?

Now, imagine that, overnight, a mass roughly the size of a ping-pong ball or a hen's egg has grown inside your bladder. This mass is free-floating, and has a hard surface much like that of a cheese grater. On the third day or so, your hormones will work another feat of magic and the mass will rapidly shrink down to a size you can easily pass.

Because this mass has taken up ¼ to ½ the normal volume of your bladder, you have to pee more often than usual. Sometimes, a lot more than usual. And while it's bouncing around in there, it starts to grate off the inner lining of your bladder. Painful!

So when you're not having to run to the bathroom to pee, you're bleeding. You have to wear a pad, sometimes two if you're bleeding quite a lot. They chafe the inside of your thighs and your balls, and sometimes your pubic hair gets caught in the adhesive backing.

You decide that pads suck, so you stick a cotton wad in your urethra to stop the blood. It can chafe quite a lot if there's not much blood flowing when you put it in, and if often chafes coming back out if you have to remove it to pee.

If you're lucky, you can't feel the wad in there, even if you get an erection, but if you have a smaller penis, you almost always feel it. It doesn't hurt exactly, but when you sit down you're aware that you've got a foreign object lodged in your dick, and it's not an awesome sensation. Also, it seems to make the cramping from the little landmine in your bladder worse.

And when you pull it out, there's sometimes a lovely little backlog of tissue in there. Clots of blood and reamed-off bladder lining come slithering out of you like warm slugs. In that moment, you so love your body, and just feel ever-so-sexy.

Your girlfriend, if she deals well with blood, is quite keen to have sex with you, since you're infertile while all this bleeding is going on. Otherwise, she's avoiding intimate contact with you on the grounds that you smell weird or you'll get blood all over her sheets.

If you're especially unlucky, your girlfriend will be totally unsympathetic to your situation: *You go through this every month, John, I'd have thought you'd have learned to deal with it by now. It's only a little pain, go take some Advil and be a man about it!*

Meanwhile, you feel run-down and mostly want to sleep, the inside of your dick is chafed, two pairs of your drawers are stained with blood, the inside of one of your internal organs is peeling off, and sometimes the pain meds just don't do the job.

And that, my friends, is what it's like to menstruate.

Permian Basin Blues

The sky's the color of my old blue jeans,
and the land is pulled tight by drought.
All the fields are perfectly smooth,
planed and drawn and quartered
by old farmers and good ol' boys
in their diesel-smoking tractors,
and everything is boxed off
into barbed-wire squares.

They say the air is clean and pure,
but there's an overwhelming smell
coming from every corner of the town:
it reeks of sheep piss and cheap booze,
smoldering hostility and burning books,
dirty laundry and minimum-wage sweat.
People say they can't smell it at all,
but I can't take a single rotten breath.

My neighbors' bodies are neat and clean,
but their brains are caked with the dust
of generations of low hopes and ignorant fear;
their lives were fossilized well before birth.
The tight minds of the old men who run
this town are walled in Biblical rock;
their thoughts are locked against the chaotic
joys of the weird, the wild and the young.

This place is little more than a roadcut,
and the stratification is plain to see.
Little white people live in big white houses
that stretch out like blank limestone slabs
bleaching on the sunny southern side of town.
But on the north side, peeling clapboard shacks
that contain the unfortunate children of Spain
sit like worn and crumbling sandstone fragments.

And here I sit, trapped between the strata,
a misplaced bit of flint or gneiss or granite,
an arrowhead from some alien tribe lodged
mysteriously amid these prehistoric layers
that bear down with unrelenting pressure
until keen edges are ground into gray sand.

So I'll drive out to some big, flat ranch,
strip down to the pink to let my skin breathe,
and I'll dance for pleasure, I'll dance for rain,
I will dance for lightning, I will dance for pain,
I'll scream out at the emptiness until my lungs bleed
and try for the volume that will make the fossils stir
deep in the sterile ground and rise to the surface,
hard skeletal denizens of a long-dried ocean swimming
through layers of rock, wreaking a tectonic tsunami
that will shock the city from its flatland coma.

And if the rancher drives out, armed
with a shotgun and a look of confusion,
then I will just smile at him and say
that I'm just trying to make some waves.

Feel the Love

IT WAS a beautiful Saturday morning, and the protest outside the women's clinic had taken on an almost carnival atmosphere. The usual Scary Guys In Camouflage were out with their bullhorns and full-color battleflag posters of dismembered 3rd-trimester fetuses. Preacher Bob had come out, too, apparently taking a break from the college campus circuit where he soapboxed in central greens and called girls in miniskirts "whores of the Devil." That morning, he'd been calling most of the patients coming into the clinic "bare-breasted harlots of Satan" through his bullhorn. The festivity was making him more eloquent than usual.

There was also a group of a dozen or so little kids – probably a Sunday School class on a field outing – holding up crayoned signs that read "Don't Kill Babies" and singing "Jesus Loves You." A group of initiates from the seminary north of the city had come down in a bus and were singing along with the children. The priests-in-training had beautiful voices; it was too bad they were being drowned out by the bullhorns. And to top it all off, a couple of teenage girls dressed like mimes were acting out the Birth of Jesus.

Judy Greene, the clinic's director, wondered when someone was going to set up a lemonade stand with a sign that read "TEARS OF CHRIST – 25 cents." All the hollering was bound to make the Scary Guys work up a powerful thirst.

She glanced down the street at the black-and-white Crown Victoria police cruiser parked in the shade of a broad oak. The two cops inside were engrossed in a handheld TV. The local police department made the gesture of protecting the clinic's patients and staff from being terrorized, but most of the cops were firmly on the side of the protesters and wouldn't lift a finger unless something extreme happened.

Rubbing her temples, she turned away from the barred, shatterproof window and surveyed the women and girls in the waiting room. Most of the patients were looking absolutely miserable, whether from their own personal disasters or from the harassment they'd received coming into the clinic Judy couldn't know for sure. But at least a third of the souls she saw wore black eyes and threadbare clothes; misery was no stranger to these women.

Betty, the clinic's coordinating nurse, came up to Judy with a clipboard. "You feeling okay this morning? You look pretty pale."

"I've been working on a migraine all morning. Took some meds, they haven't kicked in yet. The boys with the bullhorns aren't helping. But I'll be okay," Judy replied. The budding migraine was a dull, tightening band of pain across her forehead. She was already seeing rainbow auras around the fluorescent lights and little flashes in her peripheral vision. The pattern in the gray clinic carpet seemed to be crawling, little ants marching in circles.

"What have we got today?" Judy asked.

Betty ran her finger down the list on her clipboard. "Well, five are in for regular pelvic exams; I think at least two are worried they have STDs. Two have come for blood tests. One's here for a mammogram. Three are here for birth control counseling. Two are here for first-trimester terminations. And Dr. Darby is running late – someone slashed his tires."

"Swell. Have you–" Judy began.

CLANG!

Both women jumped. A Scary Guy in a John Deere cap had run up to the window and tried to smash in the steel bars with an aluminum baseball bat.

"Jesus hates you!" he screamed at them through the window.

CLANG!

"Jesus hates you!"

CLANG!

"Ginger, call the police," Betty called to the receptionist.

"No, call Agent Beverley Joseph at the FBI," Judy replied. "The local cops did fuck-all when the place got sprayed with butyric acid last month. All the two Barney Fifes down the street will do is pull him off the bars and shoo him away. He'll be right back at batting practice this afternoon. Bev'll send someone out here right away to get this jerk to a padded cell someplace."

CLANG!

The impact rang inside Judy's head, and the band spasmed tighter around her skull; the headache bloomed, brightened, felt like someone was driving a power drill into her left temple; the overhead lights seemed to turn red, and bile rose in her throat; her knees turned to pudding, and she had to steady herself against her gray metal desk.

CLANG!

"JESUS HATES YOOOOOOO!"

The drill bit deeper, hit resistance, broke through. Her nerve endings sizzled in synaptic fire. Judy doubled over in agony, pressing her forehead into the cold desktop, sure she was on the edge of a blackout.

This couldn't happen, not today, if she got hit with this migraine she'd be down the rest of the day and she had to pick her cat Bennie up at the vet and call the restaurant to set up the surprise birthday party for her brother Joe and oh dammit she forgot to approve Ginger's leave for next week the poor girl had been working himself to the bone and –

– then a sudden, unexpected bloom of euphoria that took her breath away. Judy was floating. She felt no pain, no pressure, no fear, no anger, no frustration. She straightened up and turned to the window.

CLANG!

The string of obscenities from the man at the window sounded like the barking of a rabid dog.

"Are you okay?" Betty asked.

"He's going to stop doing that," Judy heard herself say.

Before she quite realized what she was doing, Judy had walked through the waiting room and pulled open the heavy, concrete-reinforced front door.

"No Judy, for God's sake don't go out there–" The door swung shut behind her, and Judy could hear Betty no more.

She marched around the corner. The young man was still screaming and leaping up to whack the bars with his bat. Judy could smell tobacco and whiskey. She was surprised he hadn't hollered himself hoarse yet.

"EXCUSE ME!" Judy yelled. "You're breaking Federal Law, and furthermore, you're behaving like a brain-damaged caveman, and on behalf of myself and everyone inside, we'd like you to cordially invite you to SHUT THE FUCK UP."

"My wife is inside there with you butchering whores, and I ain't leaving until she comes out and gets what's comin' to her!" He delivered another ringing blow to the bars.

Judy stepped closer, her voice low. "Did your mother raise you to act like this?"

"Don't you say nothin' about my mother!" The man charged her and slammed his bat into her belly.

Judy was knocked off her feet and slammed back-first into the cinderblock clinic wall. She felt something inside her crack and something else burst, but there was no pain.

"Do you know how many women I've seen with broken faces and bodies and hearts?" she asked him. "Do you know how many women I've seen whose wombs are rotting with disease their husbands gave them and then refused to let them get help for? Do you know how many women I've seen with clitorises cut or burned away by the people who were supposed to love them? They all end up here, because this place is free, and they at the very least are owed a little peace and quiet and freedom from having to listen to an idiot like you having a macho-psycho tantrum."

"God hates you, you murdering cunt!" he screamed in her face, spraying a thin line of saliva across her cheek.

He reached inside his camouflage hunting jacket and pulled out something shiny.

She raised her hands. "Hey, put that down, you don't want to—"

Two bangs, two flashes of fire. Judy felt the bullets punch into her chest and belly. As the shock passed through her, she felt no pain, only... *love*.

She felt a great, blissful warmth filling her, and suddenly she knew everything about this young man, this young Simon McGee, who'd been raised by an alcoholic, violent father in a rural Michigan trailer park and who'd never graduated high school, never learned to love, never learned to think. Judy saw through his bloodshot eyes to the hurt, confused little boy hiding under the layers of machismo and hate. Tears rose in her eyes. She felt his lost dreams and frustrations and wasted potential, saw right through him to the core of his soul, and...she loved him.

Her new love for him didn't waver a bit as she felt her lungs and throat filling with hot, salty blood.

'Nothing so becomes a man as modest stillness and humility', Judy thought.

In the corner of her eye, she saw that the two police officers were running toward her and Simon, their revolvers and riot clubs drawn. They were shouting something, but she couldn't hear them.

She lunged forward, caught Simon by his shoulders, and clamped her mouth over his. She forced his lips and teeth apart with her tongue and let the suffocating blood flow into his mouth, down his throat.

Feel my love, she thought. *And in the name of God, learn to be still.*

"Hey! Break it up!" The first policeman pulled her off Simon.

"Dammit, he shot her. Hands in the air, buddy! Put 'em up where I can see 'em," shouted the second, training his revolver on Simon.

Judy gasped and let her knees buckle. She had only seen this policeman at a distance, but now she knew him: his name was Andrew Peterson. He'd been on the force for five years, and had a wife and toddler at home. He couldn't understand why anyone would want to murder a little baby before it had even had the chance to be born, but he also couldn't stand to see a pretty young woman die.

She knew this honest, simple policeman deep in her blood. And soon he would know her in his.

She let herself choke on her own blood and fall back on the grass. Officer Peterson knelt beside her, pulled her jaw down and sealed his mouth over hers to do CPR.

Judy grabbed his head and coughed her sweet blood deep into his throat. Peterson gave a muffled shout and tried to push her away, but she was much too strong for him. She rolled over on top of him, letting gravity help her bleed into him.

"Hey! Get off him!" The second policeman grabbed her neck in a sleeper hold in the crook of his arm. She let herself go limp, let the officer drag her away from his gagging comrade.

This officer was named Jimmy Zebedee, and he was angry, so terribly angry. He was supposed to have gone to the racetrack today with his buddies, but Peterson's regular partner got sick with the flu and the captain made *him* come in and babysit the feminist cunts and their fucking meat grinder masquerading as a clinic–

Jimmy Zee's hate burned bright inside his heart. Even though she was limp, he tightened his arm around her neck, threatening to crush her trachea.

She remembered one of the last things Jimmy's mother had said to him on her deathbed. "'I love you, Jimmy-boy. Never forget that,'" Judy whispered. "'But promise me you'll try to do something about that *temper* of yours...'"

She felt shock extinguish his anger, and his grip went slack. It was enough: she turned in his embrace and kissed him deeply, bloodily.

I love you, Jimmy-boy, she thought.

S P A R K S   A N D   S H A D O W S

He squealed in her embrace and beat her head and shoulders with the butt of his pistol, but she'd locked her arms tight around his neck. He tumbled down onto his back as her heart shuddered and stopped, and the world went black...

✳

"...but the jerkoff who did this to her and the two cops who rescued her are upstairs in critical condition, can you believe it?" said one male voice in the darkness.

"How'd she manage to defend herself against a guy with a club and a gun?" asked another. She heard the clink of metal surgical tools.

"She laid a big ol' kiss on the asshole and puked a pint of blood into his lungs before she died. The cops aspirated her blood doing CPR. And it's stayed alive in their systems. Graft-vs.-host reaction. Freakiest thing anyone's seen," the first replied. "Doc said their kidneys are dog food. Their spleens are gone, too. Her lymphocytes are just tearing through them. Only way they're gonna make it is if they can get a heart-lung transplant in the next couple of days."

"Damn. No way they're going to come up with just one set of organs, much less all three."

"Hey, more work for us, right?"

Judy opened her eyes and sat bolt upright on the cold steel autopsy table.

"What day is it?" she asked.

The two morgue technicians screamed and stumbled backward, knocking over a cart covered with instruments. The steel tools clattered across the concrete floor. She caught a glimpse of herself in the mirror above a nearby wash basin. Swollen, cracked skull, bruised shoulders, purpling, quarter-sized bullet holes in her chest and belly, skin grey and bloodless.

She looked away from the mirror and smiled at the white-uniformed techs cowering by the refrigerated corpse drawers. Without saying a word, they told her how long she'd been in the morgue: two whole days. They'd been shorthanded and very busy lately.

"Don't be scared. God loves you," she told them. "And so do I."

✳

Judy walked upstairs, naked and blood-smeared, oblivious to the sea of panicked people parting before her. She knew exactly where to go; the essence of the men who had drunk her blood lingered inside her, and she in them.

She reached the ICU on the first floor and stood at the foot of Simon's bed. The young EMT in the room was pissing himself and screaming for the cops, but Andrew just stared at her in fear and wonder through his sunken, feverish eyes.

"Can you feel my love, Simon?" she asked him.

He nodded slowly and pulled the clear respirator tube out of his throat so he could speak. "I was lost before, but now I am found," he croaked.

"Rise, and come with me, Simon," she said, lifting her arms toward him. "Your brothers need to learn to love."

Simon pulled the I.V. drip out of his arm and the heart monitor electrodes off his chest and crawled out of bed to stand by her side, his breath coming in labored, wet gasps. She led him down the hall to the room where Officer Andrew Peterson lay.

"Andrew, wake up," she said.

He opened his sunken, bloodshot eyes. "I knew you would come. I understand everything now."

"I love you, Andrew," she said. "Will you come with me?"

He sat up slowly, painfully, and began to pull off the wires and tubes connecting him to various machines. "Where you go, I will go. Where you sleep, I will sleep. Your blood shall be my blood, and your grace my grace."

Judy helped Andrew rise from his bed, and the trio went down the hall to the room where Jimmy Zee lay dying.

The anger was fighting to survive inside him, lashing out against her love. The anger was all that he had left from a life of frustration and disappointment. He groaned in his fevered sleep.

"Terrible is this anger, so fierce, and his fury, so cruel!" she said. "He clings to his hate even more strongly than you did, dear Simon. But we shall cast it to the shadows where it belongs."

Without being asked, Andrew and Simon took their places at either side of Jimmy's bed and took a firm grip on his arms. Jimmy started awake, and began to struggle against them.

"No, no keep that fucking bitch away from me, no I don't want to go..."

Judy crawled onto his bed and laid her lips on his. She breathed in, pulling out his anger, then turned her head aside and breathed it out. It disappeared like steam into the cool antiseptic air.

He fell back on the bed and gazed up at her, his eyes as unfocused as a newborn's.

"Welcome home, James," she whispered. "With love you will be at peace with the very stones of the Earth, and you will know discontentment no more."

"I love you," he said, weeping.

"I know you do," she replied. "Now rise and help me bring that love to your brothers and sisters."

✳

Under Judy's watchful eye, James and Andrew waylaid the two cops in the hospital lobby, took their uniforms and cruiser keys and left them trussed and unconscious in a linen closet.

Judy drove them all to a peaceful city park with a goldfish pond. The four sat by the pond, and Judy helped them die.

Simon was the first to go. As his labored breathing turned to a wet gurgle, the others held his hands and loved him with all their hearts. His body was wracked with spasms as death overcame him, but he felt no pain; Judy's love had completely banished all the fleshly agony of crossing from life to death. The pain of death gone, his soul was content to stay in his dead shell until his task was complete.

Andrew died next there on the soft grass, basking in the warmth of the sun and Judy's love as his heart shuddered and stopped. She held his hands until the very last beat of his heart, and sealed his crossing over with a gentle kiss.

James followed him just a few minutes later, painlessly retching up all the old bile he'd carried with him for so long. Judy wiped the sweat and blood from his face and sang him a lullaby until his sickness passed.

After their lives had faded, the men stood up on strong, steady legs. Judy beamed at them all.

"My boys. My *men*. You three will be my right hand, my left hand, and my heart from this day forward. You know my mind, and you know what needs to be done in the days to come."

She and Simon got in the back of the cruiser, and Andrew and James, looking quite official in their stolen uniforms, drove them back to the clinic.

The sight of Judy's murder had repulsed the more moderate

protestors, and in their fright and dismay they'd all decided to limit their future activism to writing letters to newspaper editors. The hardcore protestors, however, had been cheered and galvanized by Judy's death on the clinic lawn. They had smelled blood, and with it the heady fragrance of victory.

So there were no initiates and children singing pretty songs outside the clinic that day. Those who remained dressed in camouflage, carried signs nailed to ash baseball bats and wore long knives hidden in their hunting boots. They chanted like soldiers preparing to hit the hill.

There were six police cruisers parked near the demonstrators today. The on-duty cops stood stiffly by their vehicles, faces creased behind their mirrored aviator's sunglasses, hands on their revolvers. None of them paid any attention to the arrival of the seventh cruiser.

Andrew parked the car in the shade of the old oak tree. They were close to the protest, but not so close that any of the cops might immediately recognize their fallen comrades.

When she was sure their cruiser wouldn't be approached, Judy spoke: "These broken souls claim to terrorize and kill on behalf of a God who only ever wanted us to love our fellow human beings."

"We must heal them as you've healed us," said Simon.

"They claim to have the power of God behind them," she said.

"Their only power is human hatred," James replied.

"Are you all ready to show them how far the power of God's love really goes?" she asked.

"Yes," the others said.

"I'll love them until there's nothing left of me," added Andrew.

"Good men," she smiled. "Let's go."

They all got out and began to walk toward the seething mass of protestors.

"People, get ready to feel the love," Judy whispered.

She spread her arms wide and closed her eyes, waiting to embrace them all.

Sara and the Telecats

SARA BAILEY-JONES didn't know why she watched the President's address. Surely it was the same masochistic compulsion that drove her to watch the ever-worsening stream of reality shows on the networks. She'd hit rock bottom the night she stayed glued to "My Big Fat Obnoxious Transvestite Janitor." God only knew how many brain cells that one lost her.

A moth fluttered around the TV screen, and her cats Monte and Peanut batted and leaped at the dusty bug. The dark parts of the curved glass reflected their excited yellow eyes.

"Y'all have any questions?" the President asked.

Dozens of hands shot up amongst the media throng; the President pointed to a young man from *The Dallas Morning News*.

"Mr. President, can you address the comments your aide supposedly made to the *New York Times*?"

Well, this is all kinds of meta, she thought, a reporter asking a question about another reporter's questions. Then she reflected that she hadn't even thought of using the term "meta" since she was in grad school. Studying to become a journalist.

Sara's low mood sank even further. She'd never cottoned to the notion of college as trade school, but grad school was so expensive she switched from environmental science to a masters' program that seemed more likely to keep her gainfully employed.

Ha, she thought. *Shows you what I know.*

She hadn't had work in over two years, not with two college degrees and over five years of experience coding web sites. She couldn't even get temp work as a secretary. When her husband Kevin caught pneumonia and went to the hospital for a week, the bill came to over $40,000, forcing them to file for bankruptcy and move back to her mother's house in Texas where at least they wouldn't have to worry about rent.

And then in the summer before the elections, her mother was diagnosed with advanced liver cancer. She might have lived six or seven more months, but she contracted cryptosporidium, which the doctors–in their disinterest in doing much about a 74-year-old cancer patient–failed to diagnose until her mother was dangerously dehydrated.

"Was this about universal health care or something?" The President asked, unable to keep the boredom out of his voice.

"No sir," the young reporter replied.

Her mother's systems began failing by degrees. The kidneys went first. Sara sat by her mother's side as the woman disintegrated from within, her lungs filling with fluid, the dialysis port in her neck a bloody mess. She held her mother as the old lady doubled over with stomach cramps, helped to get her to the toilet chair so her ruined bowels could bleed into the bowl, her intestines empty except for blood and bacteria because she hadn't been able to keep anything down for almost two weeks.

There was next to nothing left of her mother near the end, just fragile skin over bird-light bones.

The President frowned. "Was it about our War on Terrorism?"

"No sir," the reporter replied.

Sara's mother was just nine when the family fled Nazi Germany; they landed penniless in New Braunsfels, Texas, where there were enough other German immigrants that she never quite lost her accent. But she learned to be unflaggingly cheerful, because they had escaped the worst tyrant in history, and that was worth enough joy for a lifetime.

In the hospital, Sara saw her mother weep for the first time.

And then she saw her die.

After that, Sara couldn't close her eyes without seeing her mother's gaunt, pale face and hearing the terrible bubbling as she suffocated on the fluid in her lungs.

Where were you supposed to go after your own nightmares had come to roost? Sara felt trapped in the darkness, despite her husband's love.

Her mother's death taught her that life was not merely golden but *gold*: a huge hunk of metal that was at times far too heavy to carry, but carry it you must. You dragged it through the desert sands if you had to, because it was all you had that was truly worth anything.

So Sara threw herself behind the other presidential candidate's election campaign. The Candidate promised to stop the endless wars and to do something to make health care affordable; he promised to do something about the economy; he promised to keep the big corporations from trashing the planet. Sara didn't have much faith in politicians, but if the Candidate accomplished a tenth of what he promised, she and

S P A R K S   A N D   S H A D O W S

Kevin would be 100% better off than they'd been during the President's disastrous first term. She spent 12 hours a day on the phones, built the local web site, helped distribute signs, decorated for rallies, anything and everything to help the campaign.

There seemed to be a huge amount of support for the Candidate, and for the first time since her mother died, Sara felt happy and hopeful.

But somehow the President was re-elected anyway.

"Well, can you refresh my memory?" the President asked from the safety of the television screen. "My people have made lots of comments to reporters about one thing and another."

"According to the article, the aide made disparaging reference to your critics being in 'the reality-based community'," the reporter replied. "Can you address whether his comments are representative of current thought in your administration?"

"Well, see, you people worry too much about defining reality," the President replied. He pronounced "reality" like it was something a homeless person threw up on his shoes. "Studyin' it. Doin' a lot of thinking before you dare eat a peach. That ain't how things work anymore. That ain't how a strong country like ours gets led."

"What the fuck?" Sara sat up on the couch. "There's suddenly some alternative to consensual reality? Are you kidding?"

"This country is stronger than ancient Rome," The President said. "We're stronger than the English Empire ever was..."

"That's the *British* Empire, you jerk!" Sara yelled at the TV screen.

"We're the strongest empire there ever was. And when we do things, things an empire should do, we make our own reality. And y'all can study it if y'all want, spend all the time in the world studying and thinking, but we'll be out there making the decisions and making new reality happen. And anyone who won't act with us will just get left in the dust, wondering what happened."

Something broke inside Sara. She started giggling, and was soon howling with hysterical laughter.

Kevin came running into the living room, dishwashing bubbles dripping off his hands. "What's the matter? What's happened?"

"The P-president," Sara giggled. "He said we can make our own r-reality."

"He said what?" Kevin blinked. "Are you sure you heard him right?"

"Oh yes. I heard him fine. We 'make our own reality' just by thinking it's so, and acting accordingly. Who knew we'd elected Erwin Schrödinger for President? Oh, wait, we *didn't* elect him. He just *decided* he'd be President, and that became the reality. Our votes didn't actually mean *shit*."

"Honey, are you okay?"

"I'm fine," Sara smiled. Rage and anguish were rising in her so hard and fast she didn't know how to contain them. "Oh, and he said we're an empire, too. That must make him our Emperor. The Emperor of the Free World just said that we get to make our own reality – just by snapping our fingers! Wow. Isn't that awesome?"

"Honey–"

"Wow. All this time, I've been looking for work, you've been looking for work…hey, screw the resumes and thank-you notes! All I gotta do is act like I've *got* work and suddenly I'll have my *dream job!* And speaking of *dreams*, I've been having all these nightmares because I can't close my eyes without seeing my mother's dead face…who knew all I had to do was just decide I'm not gonna have any nightmares anymore?"

Sara was sobbing now, tears running down her face in hot streaks. She felt like she was going to throw up. "Maybe this create-your-own-reality shit's just for rich Yale cowboys who have the nation's political machine and an Army of kids from Appalachia backing them up? No, wait. I'm being *negative*. We're a *democracy*. If it's good enough for our Emperor Schrödinger, it's good enough for the Common Man, right?"

She stared at her husband through burning eyes. He stared back helplessly, wiping his damp hands on his jeans. "Can I make you some chamomile tea, honey? That always makes you feel better–"

"I don't care for any tea, honey, but gosh, I'd really like my *mom* back. Having my mom back would be *swell*. So drive me out to the cemetery, would you?"

"Honey, I don't think that's–"

"We. Are going. To. The. Cemetery," she said in a hatchet monotone that would have made a drill sergeant tremble. "*Now*, sweetie."

They arrived at Greenhaven Cemetery a little after 10 p.m. Sara hauled the shovels out of the back of the Toyota and began marching up the hill to her mother's gravesite.

"Honey, honey, *please*." Kevin's voice was cracking with anxiety.

"Please don't do this."

"Every day I miss her." Sara could barely see the dark ground through her tears. "Every single day. I feel so *lost* without her. She lived through so much. She knew how to grow corn and slaughter pigs and play the violin. I'm not half the woman she was."

"You know how to do lots of things," Kevin replied. "Your mom didn't know the first thing about computers or graphic design. You're your *own* woman."

"Oh yeah. I know so much that people won't pay me to do any of it, right? But the President, *our* President, said we get to make our own reality now. So I get to have my mom back. End of fucking story."

They reached the grave. Sara held out a shovel. "Help me dig. Please."

"No. This is crazy. I won't—"

"I need help here!"

"I *won't!*"

"Well, then go wait in the car!" Sara threw the shovel at his feet, then lifted hers and stabbed it into the dirt.

Sobbing, she chopped past the sod into the dry Texas earth. Kevin dumbly stood there staring at her.

"I won't stop, dammit," she wept. "Help or go away. Help or go home."

Kevin took a step back, then stopped. Perhaps he was considering whether digging up a corpse was worse than leaving his beloved in a cemetery in the middle of the night. Maybe he was weighing the possibility of jail time against the certainty of divorce.

Regardless, he finally picked up a shovel and began digging.

The town had a dry summer and fall, so the dirt above the casket was still loose. The topsoil in the land was so thin that the gravediggers could only go down a few feet before they hit hard limestone bedrock. They'd jackhammer room for the casket in the living stone and let that suffice as a vault to keep the dead out of the groundwater.

"I knew there was a reason Mom didn't want to be embalmed," Sara said, digging furiously. "She always knew what was coming. She knew our President would decree this whole moratorium on reality and she'd get a second chance. I couldn't save her in the hospital, but I can save her now. Isn't that cool?"

"Sara, she hated the thought of having all those chemicals in her,"

Kevin said carefully, digging much slower and glancing around as if he expected the cops to come screaming down on them any minute. "She *told* us this. She hated the thought of being gutted and filled with cotton batting and turned into this sick parody of a doll."

"Well, sure, that's what she *said*," Sara replied. "But she knew she was gonna get to walk like an Egyptian one day. Yessiree! She didn't escape Hitler's death camps just to die because her doctor couldn't fucking look at her long enough to figure out she had cancer, did she?"

They uncovered the casket, and Sara broke the seal with a strong blow from her shovel. The stench of decay puffed out of the crack.

Sara looked out into the night and, raising her shovel like a torch against the darkness, yelled: "By the power vested in me by the President as a rightful citizen of the United States of America, I declare my mom to be alive and well because that's the reality I declare. So Mom, you can wake up now and arise and come forth and we'll go home and watch the *CSI* marathon on the Spike channel, okay?"

Nothing but silence from the dusty casket.

"I am speaking to Mrs. Gretchen Morgenstern Jones! Arise, Mom, arise! You're alive and you're gonna come forth and that's that!"

There came a rustling and a bumping inside the casket. Kevin gasped and started muttering *OhsweetJesus* over and over under his breath. Sara ignored him and levered the casket door open with her shovel.

Her mother lay grey and desiccated inside, her blue funeral dress covered in vile brown and yellow stains. The leathery eyelids opened, and her mother sat up, taking in a breath that sounded like the wheezing of ancient bellows.

"Mein gott, child, what have you done to me?" her mother croaked.

Kevin reacted to his mother-in-law's resurrection by obsessively cleaning house or burying himself in books. Sara ignored his flinching fear in disgust.

Monte and Peanut hissed and fled from Sara's mother at first, but once the smell of death left her, they accepted her much as they once had. The old woman still opened food when they begged, and still gave them a warm enough lap to sleep on, even if she no longer cooed over them as she used to.

Sara nursed her mother back to relative health with a steady diet of tomato soup, instant breakfast shakes, and old Clint Eastwood movies.

Her mother always had a crush on Eastwood. Now there was a *real* man. He'd surely embrace her mother's rise from the grave for the miracle that it was. Sara considered writing to tell him about it, but discarded the idea as overly fangirly.

In a few months her mother looked much as she had before her cancer diagnosis.

But her cheer was gone.

"What can I do?" Sara asked her mother as they shopped for lemons one day. "Don't you enjoy being alive again?"

"I do. I suppose." Her mother's voice had a dry, papery quality; her clear alto had been left in the dust.

"I tried to be a good woman," her mother continued. "I did my very best, and I thought that after everything I would go to Heaven. I remember nothing from my time in the grave."

"But maybe you forgot," Sara replied. "Maybe Heaven is like a dream, and sometimes people can't remember it when they wake up?"

"No, that's not what I meant. I remember *Nothingness*. I remember eternal blackness, coldness, isolation. There was no Heaven when I died. Everything I was told to believe in was a lie.

"How can I take joy in new life knowing that nothing good can come of all this?"

Sara was determined to make this work. You might be able to lead the dead back to life, but making them drink from the Springs of Happiness was another matter.

And there were more folks dead now than all the Saras in the world could raise. The President poured young soldiers into grinding battles to take control of Afghanistan, Iraq, Iran, and the Sudan, and returning Army planes creaked with caskets that couldn't be shown on national TV.

The Enemy, it seemed, had different ideas about making a new reality for the world.

"I will spare no effort in bringing the terrorist nations of the world to justice," the President told them after the 6 o'clock news. He'd started doing quick morning and evening live telecasts from the White House.

"But America will prevail, because...uh, that's what we do," the President finished.

"This is really messed up," Kevin said from the reading chair.

"Hmm?" Sara turned.

Kevin was reading a thick hardcover the Secretary of State had just published entitled *The Power of God's Chaos*. He shut the book and waved at her. "This thing is *nuts*. Most of it's lifted directly from Aleister Crowley's *Magick Without Tears*, only they've changed words here and there so it *looks* like it's talking about Christian Apocalysm instead of magick...how can they do this? Why isn't anyone *noticing*?"

"So he's plagiarized Crowley's chaos magick and is pretending it's Christianity? Huh. That *would* explain the election."

"Honey, crass demagoguery explains the election just fine. This *isn't* real."

Sara knew he'd dabbled in the occult as a teenager chafing under his strict, unimaginative Lutheran upbringing. But as much as he claimed to value intellectual diversity, he'd become deeply uncomfortable with the idea of magic and the supernatural as an adult. Wiccans were harmless, woolly-headed hippies who were to be smiled at and indulged. Wizards were a fancy for children at Halloween. Getting him to think that real, honest-to-Goddess magicians were in control of the White House was like trying to get a 386 to run Windows 2000. His brain wasn't built to hold an idea like that.

At least he'd managed to mostly get over the heebie-jeebies about his mother-in-law. He still wouldn't talk about it, but he'd stopped avoiding Sara and they'd even made love a few times that month.

Sara was determined to take bright spots whenever she found them.

Her mother shuffled in with a peanut butter sandwich and a glass of Scotch and soda.

"Ach, President Cowboy," she spat. "If I wanted to watch bullshit, I'd go down to the stockyard."

"What would you rather watch, Ma?" Sara dug through the couch cushions to find the remote.

"I don't care. Anything but this." She sourly sipped her Scotch.

Sara flipped through the cable channels until she found an old black-and-white Western.

"Hey, honey, is that Ronald Reagan?" she asked her husband.

He pushed his glasses up his nose. "Yeah, I think so."

"Ach," her mother muttered. "*Another* President Cowboy."

"Do you want me to change it, Ma?" Sara asked.

"No, no." Her mother waved the sandwich at the TV dismissively.

"It's all the same. Cowboys on every channel. Big hats and no cattle."

Sara turned back to the screen. The camera was doing a slow dolly pan across a bustling farmer's market inside a big barn. The market stalls were all separated by high wooden walls. A striped cat was sitting on a bundle of wool in one of the stalls, and it noticed the camera. It jumped up on top of the wall and followed the camera as the pan continued.

"Oops," Sara said to her husband. "That's a bit worse than having a boom mike in the scene. I guess they didn't have enough money for a re-take."

The wall was coming to an end, and the cat leaped up onto the camera platform and stuck his face right in the lens—

—and then he came right through the TV screen.

He plopped out on the living room floor, still in monochrome, shook himself, and mewed as if to say "I'm here! Pet me!"

"Hey guys, we got another cat!" Sara exclaimed.

Sara's mother peered at the newcomer and humphed. "We've got two cats already; we don't need a cat from some lousy 40s western. If we get another cat it should be from a Scorsese or Fassbinder film."

Sara ignored her. She supposed that, having been raised from the dead, her mother was jaded to most forms of miracle and magic.

"I shall name him Ringu!" Sara said.

Ringu hopped up on the couch where her two cats Monte and Peanut were sleeping. They awoke, chirped at the new arrival, and started to play with him.

Kevin stared whitefaced at Ringu.

"You okay, honey?" Sara asked him.

"Is it safe?" he croaked.

"What?"

"Is – is it safe for it to be with our cats like that?" Kevin stammered helplessly. "Maybe it has a disease. Maybe it needs shots."

"The kitty is from Hollywood. It would never get sick in a movie, unless the script made it so," her mother said.

"Ringu looks fine to me, honey," Sara said, "but I'll call the vet first thing in the morning, just to be sure."

Just then, the TV switched to a commercial. A blonde woman in a hunter green pantsuit was petting a huge ginger Persian.

"Everyone loves a fluffy cat...but is your cat a little *too* fluffy?" the blonde asked. "Flava-Chow provides all the nutrients your cat needs, all the taste she craves, and just half the calories!"

The screen switched to a close-up of the Persian eating from a bowl of wet food. The blonde's green shoes were visible a few feet behind.

Ringu sniffed the air, and hopped off the couch and padded to the TV.

The Persian in the commercial raised its head and growled.

"Flava-Chow comes in tuna, chicken, and salmon flavors that are guaranteed to satisfy even the most finicky feline–"

Ringu hissed back, and leaped up into the screen. Cat food scattered as the felines yowled and swatted.

"Oh my god!" the blonde screeched in voiceover, her green shoes tripping backward.

"Ringu, get back in here!" Sara hollered.

Ringu broke off his attack and leaped back into the living room, the Persian hot on his heels.

"Holy Jesus!" Kevin screamed as the two cats tore through the screen. Monte and Peanut fled in terror for the safety of the bedroom closet.

Green shoes approached the abandoned cat food bowl. "Boris? Where did Boris go?"

The TV cut to an obnoxious local car ad.

Boris was growling and stalking toward Ringu, who was fluffed up, his fur cracking with TV static.

"Knock it off! No fighting in the house!" Sara yelled.

Much to her surprise, the cats knocked it off. They sat on the floor, tails curling primly around their toes, staring at her expectantly.

Kevin had pulled his knees up onto the couch and was clutching them to his chest, rocking back and forth. He looked like he was about to have a genuine nervous breakdown, or a stroke, or both.

"You guys wait there a minute," Sara told the cats, then got up and went to her husband.

"Honey, you're having a bad dream," she told him.

"I am? I'm asleep? Yes. Of course. That's the only logical explanation." He went slack.

"Yes. It's all very logical," she agreed. "We're Americans, and I've been thinking too darned small. You just need to go back to bed, sweetie, and when you wake up in the morning, everything will be right with the world. We'll have a brave new domestic policy."

She helped him get up, led him back to their bedroom, and put him under the covers.

When she came back to the living room, her mother was shaking her head. "You shouldn't lie to your own husband like that."

"It's no lie. Things *will* be right with the world come morning. The only reason things go *wrong* is that no one freaking *listens* to me. I ask for a job, I get no job. I ask for my mother to be happy, she's not happy. But these little guys–" Sara pointed at the waiting cats " *–they* listen. They do what I say."

"But what good are a couple of television cats?" her mother asked.

"What good is a newborn baby? What good is a pound of uranium?" Sara countered.

"Eh? You're not making any sense," her mother grumped.

"You're right. I'm not. Why don't you go to bed, Ma? Like you said, there's nothing good on anyhow."

After her mother tottered away, Sara looked down at Boris and Ringu. "Well, my mom's right about one thing – I need more than just the two of you. Wanna help me find the right channels?"

She surfed until she came across some old episodes of "Mr. and Mrs. North". It only took a few minutes to lure Gin, Sherry and Martini away from their sleuthing owners. A visit to a channel showing "The Dick Van Dyke Show" landed Sally's cats Mr. Henderson and Mr. Diefenthaler. Now Ringu had plenty of monochrome company.

The local CBS affiliate was showing re-runs of "Early Edition," and soon Panther was sniffing around the living room. Sara retrieved Jelly Bean from "Malcolm in the Middle" and Lucky from "Alf." The Spike channel was showing a "Star Trek: The Next Generation" marathon, and it didn't take long for Mr. Data's cat Spot to end up on the couch beside Sara.

A few cat food commercials and French movies later, and Sara had a herd of close to thirty telecats.

"Well now," she said. "Pound for pound, you little guys are the deadliest predators on the face of the planet."

She flipped around until she found an edutainment channel. "World's Funniest Pets" was on. Somebody's prize pig, laugh-tracked and dressed in a leather vest and red cowboy hat, was squealing along to "Born in the USA."

"I want that shit *off* my TV," Sara said, pointing at the porker with her remote.

The cats leaped into the TV in waves. They tackled the pig, ripped its ears, tore its throat. The thrashing, pathetic creature never stood a chance. When the cats returned to the living room, their fur was slick with blood.

Ringu hopped up on the couch and dropped the pig's cowboy hat in her lap.

"Good kitties," she said. "*Very* good."

The hat was from a child's Halloween costume, and wasn't nearly big enough. She slapped it on her head anyway.

Small hat, big herd, Sara thought. *Emperor Schrödinger, your subjects have escaped the idiot box.*

She flipped to CNN and settled down to wait for the President's morning telecast.

... And Her Shadow

CHARLIE...

Eleven-year-old Charlotte gave a start and stared over the boat's railing into the sparkling green St. Augustine water. Nobody was there. But as she looked harder, she thought she saw a dark shape moving beneath the waves lapping against the hull.

I can give you what you want, Charlie, the voice said coyly, a little louder. It was a girl's voice, and it was almost as if she heard it inside her head.

Her heart beat fast and her stomach churned, like it had when her father made her take a shower with him. She hated the way he touched her. The stink of his sour sweat and the whisky on his breath made her sick to her stomach, and she threw up on him. She couldn't help it. Furious, he dragged her out of the bathroom and whipped her with his belt.

When her mother came home, he claimed he'd beat Charlie because he caught her stealing change out of his desk. She'd tried to tell her mother what really happened, but her mother slapped her and told her she was bad for making up nasty stories. She sent Charlie to bed without dinner.

Charlie realized she shouldn't be surprised that her mother believed her father instead of her. Whenever her mother was gone on sales trips, her father wouldn't come home until very late, until after Charlie had put herself to bed. She'd hear the front door bang open and he would stumble in, singing off-key to himself. Sometimes she'd hear a strange woman's voice, too.

And sometimes, there'd be makeup stains on the couch the next morning. Her mother would see the lingering spots and ask her father about them. He always said Charlie had been playing in her makeup and got it on the furniture. She'd get smacked for that, too.

If her mother would buy a lie about a lipstick smear, she'd buy a lie about practically anything.

Tell me what you want, Charlie.

"I don't want anything." It was wrong to want things, she knew, because wanting what she didn't have just made her chest ache and her eyes burn. Wanting never helped her get anything.

"What did you say?" her mother asked behind her.

Charlie nearly jumped out of her skin; she hadn't heard her mother walk up.

"Uh, nothing, mama..."

Her mother bent down to whisper in Charlie's ear. Though she still wore the smile she used with her sales clients, her voice and eyes were cold.

"What did I tell you last night?" her mother asked, her voice taking on a nasty edge.

"You told me to act happy, and smile, and play with Mr. Bannister's kids, 'cause you want him to hire you," Charlie stammered.

"So what are you doing over here sulking by yourself, *honey*? Put a *smile* on your face. You'd better not mess this up for me ..."

Letting the threat hang unfinished in the air, her mother turned away and gave the rest of the boat party a bright smile.

"Is she okay?" called Mr. Bannister. He was a huge, hairy man, but he had a nice smile, and he told silly jokes ("What's brown and sticky? A stick!"). Charlie decided she liked him.

"Oh, she's just a little seasick," her mother replied. "She's never been on a boat before."

"Well, how 'bout a swim? That'll help us work up an appetite. Not that some of us need any help," he added, laughing as he patted his belly.

His two little boys shrieked in delight and scampered to the ladder. Mr. Bannister stripped off his bright Hawaiian shirt, and her father slipped off his polo shirt and Bermuda shorts. The sight of him wearing nothing but his Speedos made her feel ill all over again, and she had to look away.

Tell me what you want. She peeked over the railing and saw the dark thing spreading like black ink beneath the waves.

"Are you coming?" her mother asked.

The thing in the water scared her worse than anything her parents might do to her later. But she knew her mother wouldn't believe her if she said she saw something down there. "Can I please just stay up here?"

"Fine." Her mother smiled tightly, the peeled off her tee shirt and

S P A R K S A N D S H A D O W S

went down the ladder.

Charlie moved around the railing to watch the others swim. The Bannister boys giggled as they splashed water on each other. They probably got to go to the beach all the time. She'd lived in Florida all her life, but her parents never took her to see the ocean. *They'd* gone to the beach, but always left her behind with a babysitter. Until today. Today she was finally *convenient*.

A knot of rage tightened in Charlie's chest as she watched her mother laughing and smiling that fake, fake smile of hers as she treaded water and chatted with Mr. Bannister. And there was her father, floating on his back and looking so very unconcerned and happy with himself, but Charlie knew that men who did what he did deserved to go to Hell...

"I want them gone," she whispered through clenched teeth.

Suddenly, the dark shape surged up under her father. He had just enough time to let out a shriek before it dragged him under and tore him apart, staining the water with his blood.

Her mother screamed.

"Oh Jesus, getintheboat, getintheboat!" Mr. Bannister yelled to his kids.

Her mother, who'd always been a strong, graceful swimmer, had already reached the ladder and was almost clear of the water when the thing grabbed her leg. It yanked her down so hard that Charlie heard her bones snap. Then came another furious churning under the waves. The water bloomed red.

Then silence.

Mr. Bannister, who'd stopped when he saw her mother snatched from the ladder, was treading water with his boys a few yards away. The children were crying, and Mr. Bannister's face was a bad gray.

Finally, when it was clear the thing had gone, Mr. Bannister towed his kids to the boat and boosted them onto the ladder. After they'd scrambled up to the deck, he hauled himself up with shaking arms.

Charlie was still staring at the fading bloom of blood, numb with shock. What had she done?

Mr. Bannister put his arm around her and gently pulled her away from the railing.

"Oh, please don't look, you shouldn't see that," he said. "Jesus. It musta been a shark. I had no idea they'd be out this time of year. God, I'm so sorry...you poor kid, nobody should have to see something like that."

She wasn't sorry, but she was terribly afraid.

The Coast Guard never found any trace of her parents' bodies, nor did they manage to catch any sharks. After the memorial service, Charlie left Florida and went to live with her aunt's family in Cuchillo, Texas. It was hot and dry and far, far away from the ocean.

Her mother's sister, Lois Wilson, was a real estate agent, a tall blonde woman in her early forties who'd married the local tennis pro right out of college. They had two teenaged girls, Misty and Jennifer, who were just as tall and pretty as their mother, and like their father they had dazzling smiles, good tans and fearsome overhead volleys.

Charlie, like her father, had bark-brown hair, freckles and a pug nose. And, as her mother had often told her, she was fat. She'd taken a lot of teasing back in St. Augustine Elementary ("Fatty, fatty, two-by-four, can't get through the kitchen door!"), and so she *knew* deep down that she was worthless and ugly, but moving into the Wilson's big limestone house just drove it home.

Summer came and school let out, and Misty and Jennifer went off to sports camps. Mrs. Wilson deemed Charlie too young to be left at home alone. So she was sent along with Mr. Wilson every morning as he went to work at the Swim & Racquet Club at the edge of the city.

They'd arrive early, before the club opened. Mr. Wilson would go off to check the courts and open the pro shop. Charlie would be able to swim by herself for an hour or so, a time when the whole pool was her private blue ocean. She'd pretend she was crossing the English Channel, or she'd throw pebbles in the deep end and pretend she was diving for pearls. Sometimes she wondered about what had really happened at St. Augustine. The voice *couldn't* have been real. Could it?

But when the club opened and people started trickling in, her paradise rapidly turned into Purgatory. By noon the pool was clogged with screaming kids. The poolside became a maze of greased adult bodies basking in the sun. To make matters worse, her breasts were growing, perpetually sore little lumps that made her feel even more self-conscious. At school, she was covered, camouflaged. Here her every flaw lay blazing in the sun.

One boy, a big red-haired thirteen-year-old named Jason, delighted in harassing her. At first, it was just the usual taunts about her weight.

Then his tactics changed alarmingly.

It started when she was in the pool near the 4' mark, mutely watching a group of seven-year-olds play Marco Polo, when Jason grabbed her butt. She whirled around, a protest on her lips which died when she saw he'd pulled down the front of his trunks, just enough to expose his genitals.

"Touch my monkey," he drawled.

The sight made her remember her father. Charlie splashed away from Jason, numb with shock and nausea, and got out of the pool to sit in the cold shade of the snack bar.

Jason was still in the pool, smirking at her. She watched as he called over two of his buddies and whispered something to them. Then all three of them started pointing at her and laughing.

Charlie felt herself blush a deep red. She wished the ground would open up and swallow her. She couldn't tell the lifeguard what had happened, not *now*, because even if Jason got in trouble, he'd just tell all the other kids what a chicken sissy she was.

She prayed that Jason would get bored and find someone else to bother, but he didn't. The very next day, he rubbed up against her in the deep end.

"My big brother said you fat chicks are good fucks," he giggled. "He said it's 'cause you're so ugly, you're grateful to get any dickin' you can."

Charlie fled from the pool and went to the ladies' locker room. She changed back into her shorts, sandals and a dry tee shirt. There was no way she was going back into the pool. She'd just go watch her uncle give tennis lessons.

But when she stepped outside, she saw that Jason and his two friends were standing around on the sidewalk that led to the tennis courts. Charlie bit her lip. There was no way she could avoid the boys.

Then she noticed the back gate was open. There wasn't much to the land beyond, just patchy grass and a winding arroyo obscured by short mesquites and thick brush. The arroyo snaked around the whole West side of the city, a shallow, muddy gash in the arid landscape. Mr. Wilson said that the club owners wanted to turn the land into a golf course, but some local environmentalists had gotten it protected as a wetland. He'd told her not to go back there because people had seen coyotes skulking in the brush.

After St. Augustine, coyotes just didn't seem all that scary. And there would be butterflies and rocks and plants and stuff, much more interesting than tennis.

Charlie went through the back gate and padded across the dry grass toward the arroyo. The sun seemed hotter out here, and now that she was away from the pool and its smells of chlorine and suntan lotion, her head practically buzzed with the bittersharp scent of a thousand weedy wildflowers. She waded into the brush and stopped beside a patch of sunflowers that towered over her. She stared up at the bumblebees fumbling in the heavy, nodding blooms. A beautiful black-and-yellow butterfly flitted past her face and lighted on a small thorny bush a few feet away. Charlie stepped over and bent down to get a better look at the butterfly. Her shadow crossed it, and it flittered away. The stench of rotten meat slid up her nostrils.

She looked down and saw the fresh carcass of a headless jackrabbit just a few inches from her toes. Shiny black ants covered the ragged stump of its neck and crawled through the blood-matted fur. She could do nothing but stare at it, morbidly mesmerized.

"Hey, Fatso!"

Charlie jumped away from the dead rabbit. Jason and his two friends had put on their sneakers and come through the back gate. They were sauntering toward her, grinning. Her heart pounded hard in her ears as she realized the horrible mistake she'd made coming out here where none of the adults could see. The boys would be able to do whatever they wanted if they caught her.

She plunged into the brush, tripping over rocks and fallen branches. Thorns tore at the bare flesh on her arms as she pushed through the mesquites, trying to find a place to hide. Then she broke free of the branches and nearly fell as she stumbled down the muddy red bank into the arroyo. The winding, shallow creek was wide as a road, and the water came up to her knees. Her feet scared away a school of tiny, translucent minnows.

She tried to splash across to the other side, but the red mud sucked at her sandals. Her left foot got stuck when she was halfway across. Her terror turned to frustrated anger as she tried to pull her foot free, only to lose her sandal in the mud.

The mesquites rattled, and the boys appeared on the bank.

"Hey, that creek's too small for a whale like you," laughed Jason.

Charlie's heart was pounding with rage.

These little boys need to be taught a lesson, don't they, Charlie? It was the little girl's voice from the ocean, whispering softly inside her head.

"Yeah, come on out of there," said one of the other boys. "We just wanna play with you."

"What if I don't want to play?" she retorted.

"Then we'll *make* you," Jason replied, not smiling.

Charlie could feel her shadow spreading beneath her, hiding under the red silt, darkening the water to the color of blood. She could feel the beating of the boys' hearts, and she knew that the cruel power they'd wielded in the pool was gone in this living water.

"Then I guess you'll have to come down here and get me, penis breath," she said. "Unless you're scared of the water."

The boys looked at each other, then hopped down the bank and splashed toward her.

"*You're* the only one who's gonna have penis breath," Jason threatened.

"Jason, did you ever think about what it's like to die?" she asked.

He frowned, confused. "No."

"That's too bad. You should've thought about it, 'cause now you're *DEAD!*"

The dark, silty clouds curling around the boy's ankles suddenly turned to hard, razor-sharp jaws that clamped deep into their flesh. They screamed as their legs were ground down into the watery maws like celery sucked into a garbage disposal. In seconds their bodies were liquefied and consumed. The slashed rags of their swim trunks and sneakers were all that remained.

Charlie stared at the bloody water and rags and started to shiver. Dear God, she hadn't really wanted *this*, had she?

Her sandal bobbed to the surface.

Run back to the clubhouse as fast as you can, the voice told her. *Tell them you came out here to play hide-and-seek with Jason and his little friends. Two men grabbed the boys, but you got away because you were hiding.*

She grabbed the sandal, shoved it onto her foot, scrambled up the bank and ran through the brush. Dear God, what had she done, what had she done? By the time she made it back to the gate, she was crying and screaming for help at the top of her lungs. It felt good to scream. A half-dozen people crowded around her, and she haltingly told them what the voice had said to tell. Someone ran to fetch Mr. Wilson and the club manager.

They wrapped her in a beach towel, and Mr. Wilson sat with her and tried to soothe her with kind words and a soda from the snack bar. Charlie drank it, even though she felt sick to her stomach. Her lower belly hurt, too, a weird crampy ache she'd never felt before.

The police arrived and searched the arroyo. Soon, the officers came back with the boys' bloody trunks and sneakers in plastic bags.

✳

When she finally got back to the house, Charlie locked herself in the bathroom and drew a big tub of hot water.

She undressed and eased herself in, wishing that the tub was bigger so that she could get her whole body under the water. The dried mud melted away from her arms and legs, staining the water a brownish red.

Charlie...

Suddenly, there came a bright pain like someone had stabbed her lower belly with an ice pick. She doubled over, bile rising in her throat.

Her eyes widened when she realized she was bleeding. A thin tendril of blood rose from her pudendum and began to spread through the water. The pain was so bad she thought she might faint.

You're a woman now, Charlie. Hurts, doesn't it?

"Please, make it stop," she whimpered.

You'd be hurting a lot worse right now if I hadn't been there today to save you from those boys. I won't take away the blood, but I can take away the pain, if you do something for me.

"Yes, anything," she gasped. It felt as if her womb was trying to turn itself inside out.

Tell your aunt and uncle that you don't want to go back to the club, not after what happened today. Tell them you're old enough to be at the house by yourself...

✳

The Wilsons reluctantly agreed to let her stay at home, and the voice took her for long walks around the city. They visited all the playgrounds and parks in the city, and she learned about all the best places for her shadow: the river, park ponds, drainage pipes, ditches, even the perpetually-muddy ground around the public water fountains.

She also learned to spot the quiet men who lurked near the playgrounds. Sometimes they sat and fed the birds, sometimes they jogged or walked dogs, but they always watched the children. One afternoon, she hung around a merry-go-round until one of the men noticed her. Pretending she didn't see him, she walked off to a deserted alley.

The man followed her in. He offered her a soda, then tried to grab her. She let her shadow devour him in a puddle of fetid water beside a dumpster.

After that, her shadow made her hunt in earnest. She walked all day, sometimes even skipping lunch when her shadow scented a pedophile or a new wet place. By early August, she'd trapped two more men. Hunting was easiest when she was on her period; when she was bleeding, her shadow spoke to her constantly, urging her on. When she wasn't near her period, the shadow spoke rarely, and only near water. When it wasn't there to reassure her, she worried about the hunt, and lay awake at night, wondering if her soul was destined for Hell.

When school started, Charlie had no choice but to abandon her daily walks for the dull routine of books and teachers and bland cafeteria food. She was in junior high school now; she'd hoped it would be better than elementary school, but it was just bigger.

She sat in the back of the classrooms, like always. Almost everyone ignored her. Everyone except her shadow.

It started to whisper ominous suggestions when she was walking to classes:

See that boy? He burned a litter of kittens alive. He's going to the restroom; follow him in and let me have him.

See that girl? She's been trying to poison her baby brother, putting soap in his formula. She'll kill him soon if you don't help me take her.

Charlie knew she couldn't possibly do what her shadow wanted, not at school. Parks and underpasses were one thing; there was lots of space, lots of ways to slip away unnoticed even if people screamed as they were dying. But she was trapped at school. She'd get caught for sure.

She tried to ignore her shadow's exhortations by making up rhymes in her head while she was between classes or by doing anagrams and palindromes in class when the teachers got boring. But when her math class had a young substitute teacher named Mr. Berling, the shadow became unbearable.

Mr. Berling was young and smiled a lot. He explained things a whole lot better than their regular teacher, and Charlie liked him.

He touches little girls, the shadow told her. *Takes them out to see the horsies on his father's farm and feels them up in the stable.*

"Able was I ere I saw Elba," Charlie muttered under her breath. Her hands were shaking so bad she couldn't write.

He's scum, just like the rest of them. Follow him home, let him take you to the farm. He'll fit nicely in the horse trough.

"Stressed desserts." Charlie thought she was going to start crying.

"Charlie, are you okay?" asked Mr. Berling.

"I think I ate something bad at lunch," she stammered. "I think I need to go to the bathroom for a while."

"Please do," he agreed.

Charlie bolted from the classroom, ran downstairs to the girls' restroom in the basement. It was usually empty; Charlie prayed no one else would be in there.

She pushed through the door and found four girls clustered around a pack of Camels. Two were inexpertly puffing on cigarettes as the third showed the fourth how to work the childproof lighter. They all turned to stare at her when she came in.

Charlie, get out of here this instant! the shadow demanded. But it seemed to be growing weaker, recoiling from the smoke. With each breath she took, it slipped farther away.

"Can I try one of those?" she asked, stepping toward the group.

"I guess," said the girl with the pack. She pulled out a cigarette and handed it and the lighter to Charlie.

Charlie lit it and took an experimental drag, then immediately started to cough and gag. This was surely the foulest thing she'd had in her mouth since...since a time she didn't want to remember. Eyes streaming, she took another puff.

It was working, wind and fire canceling water and earth. Her shadow's indignant demands were faint, fading into the rhythmic drip of the leaky faucet.

Charlie soon learned that it only took two cigarettes a day to silence her shadow. She smoked them on the sly in the bathroom at school and in the back yard at home. When the shadow started to talk to her in her dreams, Charlie bought incense and started burning it in her room at night.

She knew she was vulnerable without her shadow. The sick men she'd hunted before were still around. And she had the awful suspicion that she was still attuned to them, and they were attracted to her. She needed a way to protect herself.

So, when her aunt asked her what she wanted for her fifteenth birthday, she asked for martial arts lessons. Her uncle took her to Master Kim's Tae Kwon Do dojang, bought her a white uniform and belt, and enrolled her for a class that started that very night.

✳

Charlie had always hated PE classes, and although taekwondo was several degrees harder than any sport she'd been made to try at school, she liked it instantly. Unlike running stairs or chasing balls, the kicks and strikes had a *point,* a real and practical purpose. Everything she learned was useful; getting into shape was just a happy side effect.

Another happy side effect was David. He was a year older than Charlie, tall and cute but painfully shy. Charlie was attracted to him the moment she saw him. It took her weeks to swallow her own fear and talk to him after class, but once she did they became fast friends. Best friends, and, as far as she could tell, each other's only friends. He already had his driver's license, so they often went out to see movies or go hiking in the low hills north of the city.

Six months after they started going out, Charlie knew that she loved David, even though he'd only hugged her briefly and had never tried to kiss her. He didn't say so, but she suspected it was because of her smoking. His favorite aunt had died of lung cancer, and he hated being around smoke. She cut back as much as she thought she could, and wished she could explain her habit to him. But she knew that her shadow, though quiescent, would not tolerate being exposed.

✳

A year later, David get his red belt, and Charlie got her blue. They were both drenched in sweat by the end of their respective skills tests. Charlie got a quick shower and changed at the dojang, but David never liked showering in the men's room there, since Master Kim had not thought to provide separate stalls for the men.

"I feel way gross," he said as they climbed into his truck. "I probably stink, too, sorry. Let's go back to my place and let me get cleaned up, and then you wanna go get some ice cream?"

"Sure." Charlie suddenly realized that she hadn't had a cigarette all day. She hadn't smoked that morning because she wanted her lungs clean for the test, and she'd forgotten to bring her pack with her for a puff in the ladies' room afterward.

"It's really cool that you've got your blue...now you'll be able to spar with us in tournaments. I heard Master Kim on the phone the other day; he's arranging for all of us to go to Corpus Christi next month for the Tejas Invitational. That will totally kick butt; we'll get to go to the beach. I've never swum in the ocean before."

The ocean. Charlie's skin prickled with dread.

"I – I can't go," she muttered.

"What do you mean? You gotta go, this will be too cool to miss!"

"I can't." Dammit, why had she forgotten her cigarettes?

"Is it because you're nervous about competing? You shouldn't worry about that, you're really good. And you know how to intimidate people, I mean, you should see the look you get on your face when you hit the heavy bag–"

"Look, don't bug me about this!" she snapped. "I said I can't go, end of discussion!"

"Okay, okay, sorry."

They drove on in silence until they got to David's house. The place was empty; his father was probably off on a sales trip, and his mother was probably working another 14-hour nursing shift at the hospital. David didn't like to talk about his parents much.

She followed him into the house and to his bedroom. David kept his room excruciatingly tidy; Charlie doubted she'd even be able to find dust on the tops of his bookshelves.

"You wanna just hang out here while I shower?" he asked as he pulled fresh clothes out of his dresser. "If you want a Coke or anything, just help yourself."

"Okay."

David padded off to the bathroom, and she sat down on the edge of his bed, trying not to muss the perfectly smooth green bedspread. She stared around at the neat rows of kung fu movie posters on the walls.

I wonder what David keeps under his bed?

Charlie's breath caught in her throat. Had that been her own thought, or her shadow's?

"Are you there?" she whispered, aching for a cigarette. "Damn you,

David's a good guy, there's nothing bad under his bed."

Are you sure?

Charlie sat very still, muttering anagrams to herself while she tried to ignore the dreadful curiosity building inside her. She could hear the hiss and spatter of water from the shower.

Are you afraid? If you don't look, you'll always wonder.

"Damn you." Charlie slid off the bed, got down on her hands and knees and peeked under the bed. She pushed aside a baseball mitt and a pair of cleats and saw a wide, flat cardboard box. She pulled it out and opened it up. Inside was a stack of comic books in plastic sleeves.

"See, it's just comics," she said, starting to riffle through them. "Batman, and Nighthawk, and the Hulk, and...oh shit."

At the bottom was a Swedish magazine, unsleeved. She couldn't understand the words, but the pictures of naked prepubescent boys were clear enough. The center spread showed an elevenish boy giving a slightly older boy a blow job. And tucked inside the back cover were three Polaroids of a naked boy in different poses on David's bed. On the same green bedspread she'd tried not to wrinkle.

Charlie felt completely and utterly numb. Defeated. She put everything back exactly the way she'd found it and reassumed her perch on the bed. A few minutes later, David came in, freshly dressed and toweling off his short brown hair.

"You're right, I shouldn't be nervous about Corpus Christi," she announced. "I changed my mind; I'll go to the tournament."

His face broke into a broad grin, and he leaned over and gave her a quick hug. "That's great! We'll have a terrific time, I bet."

In her mind, Charlie could see David, the only real friend she'd ever had, being torn apart in the waves. Her shadow felt smug, satisfied.

Was her whole life going to be like this?

✳

Despite her depression, Charlie did well at the tournament, placed tenth in her belt class out of a field of seventy competitors. David did even better, placing third. In fact, most of Master Kim's students did quite well, so he took all eight of them out for pizza that night, and drove them to the beach in his big van the next morning.

The sky was overcast, and though it was a hot day, the strong, salt-greasy wind from the ocean carried a chilly bite.

"Watch out for undertow!" Master Kim admonished as they piled out of the van in their flip-flops and big T-shirts. "It take you down like *that*." He hit his palm with his fist for emphasis. "And watch out for what lifeguard say. If he yell 'shark,' get out of water, fast as you can."

Charlie walked across the sand and set down her beach bag. She pulled out the single-edged razor blade she'd hidden in the folds of her towel. Hiding it in her hand, she kicked off her flip-flops and headed out to meet the waves.

David had run ahead of her and was already paddling around, happy as an otter. The water was dark, a green-gray like moss on a headstone. The Charlie waded out away from the others until she was in chest-deep.

He's in over his head, her shadow whispered. *Let me have him.*

"No."

For a moment, nothing happened as her shadow considered this new rebellion. Then Charlie felt a sharp cramp, deep in her womb.

Give him to me. The shadow's little-girl voice was ominous.

The cramp got worse, and bile rose in Charlie's throat. "No."

I saved you! the shadow shrieked inside her head. *Without me, you'd be less than nothing, and* this *is how you repay me?*

"Maybe I *am* nothing. But it's better than what *you* are."

I'm your God, girl, and don't you forget that.

The cramping became a wrenching pain in her stomach and intestines, and she cried out.

"Charlie?" David called, paddling toward her. "Are you okay?"

"I'm fine, please don't come over here," she managed to call back.

You'll do as I say. And today we're going to start with that little boyfucker over there.

"You haven't proved to me that he's done more than look, and even if he has, I won't let you. Not today."

She began to slit her left wrist with the razor blade. Her blood was invisible the dark water. "I'd rather die than live like this. You're not getting my permission to kill, never ever again. You asked me what I wanted, and now I want you to *go away*."

The shadow shrieked inside her head, the pain almost unbearable. A big, sandpapery shape bumped up against her body. Sharp jaws clamped down on her bleeding wrist.

It yanked her down beneath the waves and shoved her into the sandy bottom. Through the cloudy water, she could see the pearly-dead eyes of the big shark holding her down. The shark's wide, razored mouth was inches from her face.

Give. Me. The. Boy.

Charlie kicked against the shark, churning up the sand, sharp shells and rocks cutting her legs. With her free hand, she beat against the shark's snout, but the huge fish wouldn't budge. Her eyes burned, and her lungs screamed for air.

She saw movement in the corner of her eye. David was diving down toward her.

"No!" she tried to scream, but all that came out was her last bit of air in a long string of bubbles.

The shark released her and rose to meet David. She pushed off the bottom, trying to reach them, but she'd gone too long without a breath. She blacked out.

Charlie came to on a stretcher on the sand. Her left arm was splinted and wrapped in bloody gauze. Master Kim and two paramedics hovered over her. Kim's face was grave.

"Where's David?" she whispered.

"I'm right here." He pushed through the crowd and knelt beside her. There wasn't a scratch on him. "Everything's gonna be okay."

The shark's attack crushed bones in her wrist and forearm and severed a couple of tendons. She felt weaker than she ever had before. The doctors said she might never regain full use of her hand. Her shadow seemed to be gone, leaving behind a sucking vacuum of depression.

David came to visit her in the hospital the very next day. He could barely sit still, and his eyes glowed with a feverish excitement.

"It told me that I could save you, just by wanting to," he said after the nurse left.

"It?" Charlie felt a deep bone-chill.

"Yeah. It's like...it's incredible. I can kick more ass than Bruce Lee and Batman combined! I just have to be near water, and no one can stop me."

"Oh, God, David ..." Charlie trailed off as it all sank in.

Her best friend seemed not to hear her. "I'm gonna go away, maybe to New York or Los Angeles. I just thought you should know, 'cause we're buddies and all. I don't need school, I don't need Master Kim. Now I can do *anything I want.*"

"David, no, please, don't do this, listen to me–"

"Sorry, Charlie, I gotta cruise." He planted a quick, hard kiss on her forehead.

And then he was gone.

Charlie lay in bed, listening to her heart pound. Between the beats, she thought she could hear the shadow's little-girl laughter.

The Dogs of Summer

BETTY MCCOY was trying to keep her mind off her aching shoulder when she spotted a pack of dogs clustered in the kudzu at the side of the road a hundred yards ahead. Their forms were weirdly indistinct in the shimmering heat. Three big black beasts, Rottweilers or maybe Dobermans, were tearing at something, and a half-dozen smaller mutts circled skittishly, metal tags flashing in the sun. She touched the brake to get a better look as she passed.

In a flash-exposure instant, she saw the deer buried under the canine mob, eyes terrified white, foreleg thrashing. The Rottweiler worrying its neck raised a cinderblock head and barked at her, baring blood-streaked teeth. Its mad, glazed eyes seemed to meet hers, and suddenly she was back in the kitchen, Joe screaming in her face as he twisted her arm and forced her down, down to the yellow linoleum.

She made herself look away, but every bruise on her body was throbbing anew. The smells in the car, road tar and pine and Meals-on-Wheels chicken, suddenly nauseated her, so she turned up the air conditioner. The cool flute of air against her face made her feel a little better.

She picked up the clipboard and stared at the information for the next senior on her delivery route. It was a new name. Mr. Ian Dando, half a mile up on Thorny Creek Road. She read the words over and over, a mantra to dam the fear washing through her mind. Mr. Ian Dando. She hoped he'd be nice.

He probably would be; the old folks out in the country were almost always glad for company. It was the ones in town who bitched about the food and complained if you were even a few minutes late. The girl who took his call said Mr. Dando sounded pretty friendly.

She turned off the highway onto Thorny Creek. The road ramped sharply and narrowed. The pine trees were thick and tall, leaving only a narrow strip of blue sky visible. She felt as though they were closing down on her.

The road took a sharp left, and she came upon an old Airstream trailer set in a clearing. The shiny aluminum was mottled with gray corrosion and patched with flattened Coke cans in a few places. A bright little garden ran around the hulk, mums and marigolds growing between tomato stakes, melon vines and stubby red cabbages. She pulled in front of the trailer, her tires crunching on gray gravel.

The trailer's door opened and a bald old man with a cane hobbled down the wooden steps and waved at her. His arms were nearly skeletal, but his white undershirt was stretched tight over a barrel chest. He coughed into a gnarled hand, and she wondered if he might have emphysema.

When she opened her door, the air hit her like a bucket of hot water. She was drenched in sweat in the ten seconds it took her to reach the steps with the big Styrofoam clamshell of food.

"Mr. Dando? Hi, I'm Betty from Meals-On-Wheels. Got some baked chicken for you, and corn on the cob, greens, couple of rolls, and a big brownie. How's that sound?"

"Marvelous! Come in, come in, it's far too hot to be outside, eh?" He was definitely not from Clarksville – he had an odd, lilting, not-quite-British accent. "Care for some iced tea?"

She suddenly realized she was intensely thirsty. Besides, Nattie Peters was the only person left on her route, and she never minded if Betty was a little late. "Sure, that would be nice, Mr. Dando."

She followed him into the Airstream and was surprised by an absolutely frigid blast of air. When her eyes adjusted to the dimness, she saw a tidy bunk bed and chest of drawers, a big refrigerator, two red Naugahyde armchairs, and about a thousand books. Some of the books were arranged in standard bookcases, others set up on makeshift shelves of planks and bricks. Where there were no shelves, faded opera and circus posters covered the walls. A shiny new Coleman air conditioner labored in the window beside the bed. On the whole, the place was far cleaner than most old folks' trailers. She suspected he hadn't been living there for more than a year.

"Where you from?" she asked.

"Wales, originally, but I've been traveling since I was a young man, mainly in Canada. I decided it was time for a change, so I came down South. Unfortunately, the climate here doesn't suit me." He hobbled over to the air conditioner and gave it a loving pat. "So I traded my truck for this and the refrigerator. I can't bear to be hot, especially now that my body is so weak."

Betty frowned; most seniors *liked* warmth, since cold aggravated ailments like bad circulation and arthritis. Maybe living up North had turned him into a polar bear. She guessed that he must be racking up a huge electric bill. "Have you talked to the people at the power co-op to see if you can get a subsidy to help you with your utilities?"

He waved away her question and headed for the fridge. "The bills are high, but that doesn't matter. My body will be dead by the end of this month. Would you like a sprig of mint in your tea?"

"Mint? Yeah, I guess." She paused uncertainly. "What do you mean, you'll be...gone?"

Dando pulled a pitcher and a stalk of fresh mint out of the fridge. Cauliflowers of frost covered the plastic walls. "Oh, don't look at me like that! This body has lived a long time; it's time for it to die." He took two tumblers down from a cabinet. "Please, sit down, sit down."

She took the Naugahyde chair nearest the door. He finished pouring the tea and brought her a tumbler. She sipped it, found it was surprisingly sweet, flavored with peach nectar.

"Have you seen a doctor?" she asked.

He lowered himself into the opposite chair, smiling at her. For the first time she noticed his eyes, a deep, gleaming gray like polished granite. As she continued to stare at him, she realized the whites of his eyes were clear and smooth, with none of the yellow nodules and tangled bloodshot webs that marred most other seniors' eyes.

"I have no interest in doctors' opinions. It's time for my body to die, simple as that." He took a sip of his own tea. "So, what do you do when you're not bringing us old folks our supper, Betty? Are you going to school?"

"No, I got my GED after I dropped out of high school a couple of years ago, and I've been doing that housewife thing ever since." She made herself smile.

He raised an eyebrow. "No college?"

"No." She felt a lump rise in her throat. "They keep raising the tuition, and Joe just got laid off at the mill."

"But there's always loans...or perhaps someone in your family could help you?"

She shook her head. "Bein' in debt's kinda against my religion, and I haven't got any family left, none that would give me money, anyway."

Her parents had died in a car wreck when she was sixteen. She'd

L U C Y   A   S N Y D E R

escaped the fatal trip because she was sick in bed with mono. Afterward, she was too numb from shock and fever to realize that when her mother's people came, they'd find her daddy's hunting altar in the basement...

No. She couldn't waste time wishing her past had been different. She should just be glad that she was alive, that she had Joe, that he'd gotten her away from her mother's big brother. Uncle Robert had taken one look at all the candles, incense, animal skulls and rune-inscribed staghorn in the basement, and decided his dearly-departed brother-in-law was a Satanic priest. She should just be glad Joe freed her from the endless "counseling" and prayer sessions and hateful high school rumors.

She managed to blink back the tears welling in her eyes and shrugged. "Even if I had the money, it's an hour drive to the college. I wouldn't have time."

"Ah." Dando leaned forward and cocked his head to one side, peering at her. "That's quite a bruise you have."

Her hand flew to her jaw. She'd put a lot of cover stick on it that morning, but the makeup must have sweated off. "Yeah, I had an accident...I was on a stepladder in the kitchen and, um, fell."

He leaned back and gazed at her over his tumbler. "A fall is never an accident. I'd throw out such an unlucky device."

"Hey, I saw the darnedest thing on my way over here," she said, nervously picking at a hangnail. "A pack of dogs, and they'd taken down a deer. They had tags, they were somebody's *pets*, and they were acting like wolves or something, can you imagine?"

"It's probably the heat," he said. "Animals will do bloody things when the mercury rises."

"Um, yeah." She glanced down at her watch. "I've got another delivery to make...thanks a lot for the tea."

"You are most certainly welcome." After two tries, he got to his feet. "Come by anytime."

When she got to her car and looked in the rear view mirror, she saw that not even a hint of blue was showing through her makeup.

✳

When she went home, Joe was sitting in the living room watching a talk show. Four empty Miller longnecks sat in a partial pyramid on the coffee table in front of him, and the floor was littered with newspaper. The house felt stuffy, but at least it was a few degrees cooler than the swampy air outside.

"'Bout time you got back. What's for dinner?" He didn't look away from the TV.

She hurried into the kitchen, her mouth suddenly dry. "I was thinking some fish sticks, greens, maybe some mashed potatoes?"

"You feed them old folks better'n you feed me."

She paused, feeling sick to her stomach. "Is there something you'd rather have, honey?"

She heard him get off the couch, and she wished she hadn't said anything. He lurched into the kitchen, shirttail hanging out, eyes bleary, fist clenching a half-empty longneck.

"'Is there somethin' you'd rather have?'" he mimicked nastily. "You tell me. I been poundin' the pavement all day lookin' for a new job, out in all this heat, gettin' doors slammed in my face, and then this damn *poodle* bites my leg down on Main, and I come home and you want to feed me *fish sticks*? What the hell kinda dinner is that?"

"There's some chops in the freezer I can thaw out?" Betty wished she could disappear into the linoleum.

He stared at her, then looked away, cheeks flushing pink under black stubble. "Aw Jesus. I'm sorry." He wiped his brow with the beer bottle and gazed down at his boots. "I'm bein' such a jerk. My momma taught me better'n to act like this."

He set the beer on the counter and pulled her to him. He gently pushed her long red hair aside and softly kissed the nape of her neck. A shiver of pleasure ran down her spine, and she felt her fear melting away.

"I didn't mean to hit you last night." He hugged her close, rocking her back and forth like she was a little girl. "But you *know* how I feel about you working. I mean, volunteerin's fine, it's real *sweet*, you fetchin' the old folks their dinner, but supportin' us is *my* job. My momma never had to work, and neither will you."

"I know, but the bills...maybe we could find a lawyer, and try to get my folks' property back from my uncle?"

His grip tightened. "We don't need nothin' from that old preacher. I'll take care of everything."

After they dined on microwaved fish and spinach, Betty went out back to feed Rufus, Joe's schnauzer. She found the little dog gnawing the ears off a dead rabbit in the tall, dry grass by his doghouse. When she tried to refill his water dish, he stiffly straddled the bunny corpse and snarled at her as if she were a stranger.

The next day, the front page of the local paper was full of stories about sunstroke and mad dogs. Five cows had died in the fields from the heat, and two small children wound up in the hospital after their mother left them in a supermarket parking lot. A less fortunate child lost a foot to the family German shepherd, and roving dogs killed a prize sheep. The weatherman predicted a high of 100ºF, with sixty percent humidity.

The air in Mr. Dando's trailer was deliciously frigid, and she gratefully accepted a frosty glass of blackberry tea and settled into the Naugahyde chair.

"I saw that dog pack again today, less than a half a mile from here," she said.

He shrugged. His torso seemed bigger today, the white undershirt tighter, and his hands shook as he put the tea back in the fridge. "I've spent most of my life around dogs, hunted with them when I was a boy. I'd rather my body ended up part of a dog than part of a worm. To be honest, it worries me most that I've gotten so weak." He raised his knobby hands, flexed his creaking fingers in front of his face. "I thought I'd be able to take care of myself until the end."

"Is...is it cancer?" she asked.

He paused. "I have a growth, yes."

"I really think you ought to see a doctor."

"No, this must run its course. If you want to help me, honor my wishes. Don't tell anyone I'm dying."

He gazed at her thoughtfully, and it suddenly occurred to her that he must have been very handsome when he was a younger man.

"You are truly a lovely girl. Has he hit you again?"

Betty was shaken out of her reverie. "What? No. No, Joe's not like that...he's never hit me before. I mean, yeah, he's got a temper, but if he didn't, he never would have stood up to my uncle the way he did. He's been under a lot of strain since he lost his job. And he don't like hot weather, it puts him in a mood. It's...it's my fault, I haven't been a very good wife to him lately, I guess..."

Dando shook his head sadly. "It's a terrible thing when a man stops cherishing his love. You've had more than your share of bad luck, haven't you?"

He got up and opened the top drawer of his bureau. "Consider this a good luck charm." He pulled a small deerskin bag out of the drawer and held it out to her.

She took the bag and pulled open the tiny drawstrings. Inside was a ring of polished staghorn. When she held it up to the light, she saw it was decorated with an exquisitely detailed bas-relief frieze of men and dogs running through a forest. It was the kind of thing her father might have carved for her.

She felt the old, hollow ache in her chest, and before she could swallow her emotions, hot tears spilled down her cheeks.

"What's the matter?" Dando asked, eyes dark with worry.

"I'm sorry, I just cry sometimes." Embarrassed, she wiped her face with the hem of her blouse, but the tears kept coming. "It's a beautiful ring, it reminds me of my daddy. He made knives for a living, jewelry, too. Whatever he made, he always worked in a little bit of staghorn somewhere. I just never got over him and my ma dyin' like they did, and then everything that happened afterward..."

Dando passed her a box of tissues. "What happened to you?"

"It ain't so much what happened to me as what happened to my daddy," she said. "In '65, he went to Vietnam and got the last two fingers of his right hand blown off. Ma said he couldn't use it properly for a long time, couldn't do any carving or smithing, and it just drove him nuts. This was a couple of years before I was born, and I'm kinda glad, because Ma said he wasn't real pleasant to be around. She said he kept fuming about all the hippies who were running to Canada to dodge the draft, and then one day he up and hopped on a bus to Quebec. She was just frantic, 'cause she was sure he was gonna kill someone.

"But he came back two weeks later, and he was his old self again, except that deer hunting had become a religious thing for him. He made his own muzzle-loader and started casting these special slugs with runes on 'em. By the time I was born, he had this little table with candles and bones and stuff in the basement. Took me a while to figure out that everybody's dad didn't have a huntin' altar. When I asked him about it, he said that when he was up in Canada, he met a man who got him in touch with his Pagan spiritual roots."

She laughed sadly and rubbed her thumb across the edge of Dando's ring. "Too bad that Canadian didn't turn him on to praying to the Water Spirits, or maybe my daddy'd still be around. He and Ma drowned five years ago when their car got washed into a creek during a flash flood. The police contacted my uncle Robert, who's the Pentecostal minister up in Elliston. It was my fault everything hit the fan like it did; if I'd been thinkin' straight, I would've hidden my daddy's stuff, made sure my uncle didn't find a single bone in the house. But I didn't, and when Robert saw the basement, he just went ballistic. I tried to tell him it was just harmless superstition, but he was sure he'd stumbled onto a Satanic cult. Don't get me wrong, he's basically a nice guy and he means well, but the altar completely fed every paranoid religious delusion he ever had.

"He hustled me up to Elliston and put me in the private Christian high school, convinced he had to de-program me from all this horrible Satanic brainwashing. He kept trying to get me to bear witness against my father, which of course was the *last* thing I was gonna do. Jesus, he doesn't even have kids of his own; he just had no clue, you know? And then he went and told one of the teachers about my 'problem.' After that, everybody knew, and the other kids treated me like some kind of freak.

"I finally ran away, got as far as the local Denny's. I was sittin' there drinkin' a Coke and tryin' not to start cryin' when Joe came in. First time I ever saw him; he was wearin' tight black Levis and his shirt was open. The boy *really* worked out. I was sittin' there thinkin' he was probably on the football team at the public high school and probably datin' some gorgeous cheerleader, when he saw me and came over to my table! My heart 'bout stopped when he asked if he could sit with me. We started talking, and I found out he was nineteen and working at the hardware store. He was so nice, and had the sweetest smile! After a while, he offered me a ride home, and of course I accepted.

"We started seeing each other as often as I could sneak out of the house. We'd been dating a few months when my uncle caught on, and he followed us when Joe picked me up down the block from the house. We hadn't been in Joe's apartment a minute when my uncle started pounding on the front door. I thought we were dead for sure, but Joe opened the door and shouted him down, yelling 'I love Betty, and she's gonna be my wife, and I'll be damned if I'll let you keep her locked up!' When Joe was done, my uncle looked shocked and sort of shrunken, and in a way I felt sorry for the old guy, but at the same time I was just completely tickled that Joe had defended me like that. So the next day we got the rest of my stuff, and Joe and I went to the J.P. and got married. We moved down here, and I haven't seen my uncle since," she finished.

"It would seem your story would have had a 'happily every after' were it not for the current turn of events," Dando said. "Well, I hope my ring brings you better fortune."

"Yes, thanks, it really is beautiful..."

Betty felt a pang as she realized that she probably shouldn't have accepted it. The old man had so little, and as he got sicker he'd need every bit of money he could get. Oh well, she'd be back, and would be able to slip it back into his bureau. She tried the ring on the third finger of her right hand, and it went on as smoothly as if it had been made for her.

When she got home, she found Joe in his underwear, kneeling over the innards of their living room air conditioner, furiously pounding on the pieces with a hammer. A half-dozen empty beer bottles were scattered in a loose circle around him.

"This thing's a piece of crap!" he screamed, throwing the hammer across the room. It smashed into the wall above the couch, punching a hole in the plaster before it fell to the cushions. "Everything's a piece of crap! The truck's friggin' water pump blows when I'm downtown, and I don't have enough for a cab and I gotta walk home and when I get here the damn air conditioner don't work!"

He stood and savagely kicked an empty bottle in her direction, narrowly missing her shin. "I shouldn't have to walk home in this kind of heat! Why the hell weren't you here to pick me up? A man ought to be able to depend on his wife!"

She took a step back, bile rising in her throat. "You can depend on me, Joe, if I'd known you were stranded–"

"You're stayin' home from now on! No more of that Meals-on-Wheels crap!" He stared at the wreckage around him. "I need the car more than you do anyway. Damn, what a mess. Why don't you clean this place up. I'm gettin' a beer."

"Clean it up yourself," she muttered between her teeth.

"What'd you say?"

"Uh, nothing." She ran her fingers through her hair, fear squelching her spark of anger. "Nothing."

"No, I think you was sassin' me – hey, what's that on your hand?" He grabbed her wrist and stared at the horn ring. "Where'd you get this?"

"It's nothing!" She managed to pull her arm free and stumbled toward the hall. "Just something one of the seniors gave to me."

"Oh yeah? One of them old men been giving you presents, is that it?" He stepped toward her, hands balling into fists. "Or maybe he ain't so old. I'm startin' to wonder exactly how you been spendin' your time."

"No. Please, Joe, you're scaring me." She started to back away.

"I'm gonna do more than scare you if you don't tell me who you been with!"

She looked up into his eyes and saw nothing but animal rage. She bolted for the front door. Joe caught her before she got it open, grabbed her neck and jerked her off her feet.

He dragged her into the kitchen and threw her against the stove.

"Who is he?" he screamed.

Her desperate hands found the frying pan on the back burner. She swung it into his jaw.

The whack of cracking bone both sickened and satisfied her. He stumbled backward, eyes wide in shock. He fell to the floor and did not move, blood spilling from his open mouth.

"Joe?" she stammered, stepping closer to him. His broad chest still rose and fell.

She looked down at the cold black skillet, then dropped it as if it burned her. Panicked, she ran to their bedroom and threw some of her clothes into a big suitcase, then grabbed her purse and ran out to her little Ford Fiesta.

Her mind was churning as she tore out of the driveway. She realized she should have called the police. What if she'd hurt him badly? What if he died?

Before she realized what she was doing, she was on her Meals-on-Wheels route, heading down the highway to Thorny Creek. To Mr. Dando's.

Well, why not? she thought, calming down a little. No one would think to look all the way up there. The old man probably needed a little extra help anyway, and at least she'd stay cool.

She arrived at the Airstream as the sun was sinking, lighting the cloudy horizon in delicate reds and purples. She parked her car behind the trailer so nobody would see it from the road.

Dando didn't look surprised when he opened the door.

SPARKS AND SHADOWS

"Come in...what's happened?"

"Uh, well, me and Joe had a fight, and I need a place to stay for a little while."

"Certainly. You can stay as long as you like."

"Can I use your phone? I need to call Meals and tell them I won't be coming in..."

Betty was surprised by how quickly she fell into a routine there. During the day, she'd help him as he puttered in his garden, finally doing all the work herself when he became too weak. She didn't mind, though; it was a nice change to be growing food instead of simply preparing it. She liked the smells of the earth, the way the marigolds and tulips shone in the sunlight. Despite the drought, the garden produced plenty of vegetables and melons. And since Betty was able to go to the next town for supplemental groceries, Dando called Meal-on-Wheels and had them end their deliveries.

There was no running water in the trailer, so Betty spent a good bit of time hauling water from or simply swimming in a small nearby lake. It was beautiful despite the heat, a pure blue sky every day and butterflies flitting through the thistle and primrose, cardinals and sparrows twittering in the pines above. Perch nipped at her toes as she swam. She worried a little about the feral dog packs (on a grocery run she spied a paper that said the canines had taken to attacking men and cattle alike) but Dando swore up and down that the dogs never bothered him.

Two weeks into her stay, Betty brushed through poison ivy as she was carrying a bucket of water back from the lake. Her right hand, the one that bore Dando's gift, was seemingly the only exposed part of her that was unaffected by the irritating oil. The old man seemed bemused by her attempts to swab calamine on the rash around her wedding band.

"Why not take the ring off to do that?" he asked.

"Don't think it would come off right now. Finger's too swollen." She winced as she tried to move the band off a broken blister. "And I couldn't, anyway."

"Why not?" He arched an eyebrow, seeming a little displeased.

"I...I just *can't*. It wouldn't be right. My momma never took her ring off, ever, and...Joe's still my husband. Even if I'm not with him."

She paused, feeling a lump rise in her throat. She *did* miss Joe, missed his smile and the way he used to wake her up with little kisses on her neck and shoulders. She wondered if he was okay, wondered if she'd hurt him very badly.

"This'll stay right where it is until he and I and a judge say it can come off," she finished.

"Or if one of you dies, I suppose."

She looked up at him. He gazed back, his gray eyes watchful, expression inscrutable. "Yeah. I guess it could come off then, too," she agreed uncomfortably.

After that, the old man's condition grew markedly worse. His torso swelled beyond the capacity of his ribs, and occasionally she thought she could hear a faint cracking as they separated from his backbone and sternum. His breathing became more labored, and he was able to keep down less and less food.

He ran a monstrous fever, but seemed to suffer no chills, for he turned the air conditioner so high that Betty had to put on a sweater when she came in from the garden. His skin developed an unhealthy yellow pallor, and though she would not have thought it possible, his limbs lost even more flesh. Betty wanted desperately to take him to a hospital, but he insisted that he needed to die in peace.

It took her six days to realize that despite the fever and utter lack of bathing, he neither sweated nor stank. The only part of him she could smell was his breath, which carried with it a metallic sweet-sourness that reminded her of menstrual blood.

At night, she imagined that his body was a great black coal radiating heat through the trailer. She slept on a folding canvas cot he'd found in his closet, fitfully at best. Sometimes Dando would let out a moan or start murmuring in some strange language.

If the old man's noises did not wake her, nightmares did. Joe would come to her in dreams, sometimes raging, other times turning into a huge black hound that chased her through the woods.

She'd wake with a start from the nightmares, and think she heard dogs howling somewhere in the distance. She'd sit there shivering, sometimes crying, and Dando would lift his head and comfort her with soft words. In the darkness, he did not seem weak, and she could not find him grotesque.

✳

Dando collapsed one evening near the end of July. His whole body began to twitch violently, arms and legs jerking, the misshapen bulge of his torso undulating.

She was chilled to the core of her soul when she heard the dogs howling outside.

"Help me get outside. The dogs have come to end this body."

"No, wait–"

"Do it!" he gasped. "It is necessary!"

Stomach cramping with fear, she half-carried him outside into the stifling darkness. The air was thick, and smelled of ozone; a thunderstorm was on the way. She had just gotten him down the stairs when she heard a pickup truck coming up fast around the bend. Then she was blinded by the headlights, and the truck slid to a stop in the gravel in front of the trailer.

It was Joe.

She gasped in fright, clutching Dando's arm. How in the world had her husband found her?

"I called him here," the old man whispered. "Do not worry, things are in hand."

"Betty...aw, Jesus, Betty, what are you doing out here?" Joe asked as he got out of the cab. He was shirtless, and his voice was slurred. At first she thought he might be drunk, but then she realized his jaw was wired mostly shut. "I'm not mad about what happened, I mean, I was bein' a jerk, and you was scared...I promise, I won't be like that again."

"Don't listen to him," Dando coughed. "Men like him only change for the worse."

The wind started to rise, swirling dead leaves and grass around their feet. The howling dogs were getting closer, and Betty thought she heard thunder rumbling in the distance.

"Stay out of this, old man!" Joe ran his hands through his hair. "*Dammit*, it shouldn't *be* like this...look, Betty, just get in the truck, and let's go home, huh?"

"No. No, I can't–"

"Yes, you *will!*" Joe growled. "You're my wife, and you're gonna get in my truck and come home *now!*"

A brilliant arc of lightning shattered the sky, and a hideous pain tore through her body. She doubled over, muscles cramping around bones that felt as if they were twisting out of their sockets. Dando's ring glowed hot on her hand, and the pain ended as abruptly as it had begun.

Joe was screaming. He'd fallen to his hands and knees, his body shivering and twitching, face contorted in agony.

Before she could step toward him, lightning forked down from the sky with a deafening boom. The force of the near strike knocked her off her feet.

When she was able to get up, she saw Dando lying a few yards away, a smoking black gash running from his neck to his belly.

She hurried over to the old man, her husband momentarily forgotten. Dando began moaning and squirming...no, not him, but something *inside* his body.

She saw two small hands push through the wound. Before she knew what she was doing, she grasped the tiny arms and started to pull. There was a sickening shredding noise, and a gore-slick head broke through to the night air.

The boy wrestled out of the old man's body like a diver getting out of a bulky wet suit. Betty could do nothing but stare openmouthed, shocked beyond nausea and fear.

He was about the size of a three-year-old, he had the lean muscles of a young teenager. His eyes glowed with blue fire, and small horn buds poked through his wet hair. Even through the mess, he was the most beautiful thing she'd ever seen.

Lightning crashed again, and the skies opened in a torrent of rain. The horned boy lifted his head and gave a wild, high cry.

The woods exploded with dogs. They came from behind trees, from under bushes, snarling black missiles. The boy stepped aside as a dozen of the summoned canines fell on Dando's shell, ripping and devouring great hunks of flesh.

Betty made herself look away, but thought she would faint when she saw her husband. The rest of the dogs were circling Joe, snarling but not attacking. Joe's limbs and neck were stretched impossibly long. His whole skull deformed and elongated as if bone had turned to rubber. Grunting in pain, he fell forward onto his hands into the mud. In two heartbeats, fingers and toes retracted into hooves. His blue jeans split at the seams and fell away. White fur sprouted on his sweating flesh, pushing his black hair out of his scalp as horns forked out of his skull.

The white stag reared up and leaped through the canine circle.

The dogs dining on Dando's corpse had grown huge and black, eyes glowing with the boy's blue fire. The boy gave another cry and leaped onto the back of the largest hound.

S P A R K S   A N D   S H A D O W S

The hunt was on.

Howling with the wind, the dogs raced after the stag. The ring burned hot on Betty's hand, and she could not help but follow. She ran after the hounds into the black forest, branches and rain lashing her face. Her legs carried her faster and faster 'til her throat tasted like raw meat and she was sure her lungs would burst.

The dogs' madness was a live thing in the air, and every gasping breath she took infected her heart, her mind, her very bones. As the electric urge swelled in her, she ceased to feel pain, ceased to feel anything but lust for the kill.

The dogs and Betty chased the stag through miles of forest, over slick logs, through swollen creeks, until finally they cornered their prey at the edge of an abandoned quarry.

The stag lowered its magnificent horns and charged the dogs, but a St. Bernard blind-sided it and knocked it to the ground. In an instant, the stag was buried in the mob. It let out a human scream as they tore into its flesh.

Betty ached to have a piece of that flesh for herself. But she couldn't keep her balance as she joined the dogs. She fell down between their surging bodies, smothering under their weight and shaggy heat. Her world went black.

※

She came to right before sunrise. The storm and the dogs were gone. Venus shone bright in the early morning sky. She sat up, groaning as her sore muscles twinged and throbbed.

The stag's remains lay a few yards away. There wasn't much left of it, just the skull, some scattered red bones, a few rags of bloody white hide. She made herself look away, feeling sick.

"Betty."

Startled, she turned and saw the horned boy sitting astride his huge black hound. The storm had washed him clean, and his beautiful eyes and body glowed in the dim light. He had grown in the night, and looked older, stronger.

"What are you?" Betty managed.

The boy slid off his hound and approached her. "I am the master of the Hunt, and I want you to be my mistress. None of this has been coincidence, lass. Your father promised you to me long ago when I was hunting in Canada. When I found him, he was a bitter creature, full of violence. I was about to make him my stag, but when I looked into his eyes, I saw his future, saw you. So I spared him, not for who he was, but for who his daughter would become."

Betty didn't know what to think. "So...you and he just made this deal that I was going to marry you some day. When was I supposed to have a say in this?"

"Because your father died before he could prepare you for this, his promise does not bind you. And you need not decide now; the Hunt will last for seven years, and when it is over I will return here, full grown but still a young man."

He nodded toward her hands. "If you replace gold with horn, you will not grow old. And if you wear my ring still when the hunt is through, you will be my love. Think on it well. Goodbye for now."

He leaped onto his hound, and they disappeared into the forest.

Betty stood there, staring at the stag's remains and fingering the horn ring and her wedding band. A cool breeze from the East stirred the leaves at her feet.

She gazed out at the horizon lit with bright oranges and pinks by the sunrise. Seven years, and the whole world to explore. But this time, she wanted to see it all through her own prism before she gave herself away again.

She pulled off both rings, slipped them into her pocket, and began the trek back to the trailer. It was time she had a talk with her uncle.

The Jarred Heart

I wake from a dreamless sleep
into a nightmare of restless death.
I pound apart the lacquered wood,
claw through graveyard grit to an icy
night ablaze in moonlight on the snow.

My skin is cracked, glowing with fungus.
I raise my rotting paws to my face and feel
no eyes, just peeling pits in despairing bone.
And yet I see you standing over me
with my dead heart floating in your jar.

I'm cold, so cold, and I want you to love me
take me into your arms and comfort me
but your face is hard as mausoleum marble,
and your eyes glitter like Judas' silver.
I taste your poison in my throat. Remember

how you wooed me and won me,
fed me lies sweeter than the opium wine
you used to cast my boat upon the Styx;
my heart was yours long before you cut it
from my breast with your silver blade.

Did it still throb for you as you slipped it hot
into the cold enchanter's jar to trap my soul?
Your name on my lips as I slipped to the dark; now
I spit it as a curse inside my cage of bone, knowing
you free me only to complete your midnight atrocities.

I'm just your means to an end, my heart
in your hands, you'll make me warm myself
and fill the hungry void in my breast
with the blood of inconvenient innocents
who block your way to glory.

But I'm cold, so cold, my love.
I'll end my sleepwalk in a baptismal bonfire,
break the curse when my flesh is ash, and no magic
shall keep me from carrying you into my inferno
to consummate my desire in the licking flames.

The Sheets Were Clean and Dry

BREATHLESS, KATHY slipped into the fabric shop. Stavros would be furious if he discovered she'd left the house. Her blouse was sticking to the welts on her back she'd received as punishment for disappointing him. The night before, she'd mistakenly cracked open the '82 Chateau Margaux instead of the '80 as he'd ordered. An expensive mistake, and she'd paid for it in skin and blood.

Once he'd tired of exercising his belt, he curtly demanded she make a new suit for him by the next Tuesday. She hadn't any good suit fabric left in the house. But she'd known better than to tell him that. He'd beat her for not being prepared.

Kathy stared around the shop. The cabbie didn't understand English very well, and instead of taking her downtown, he'd deposited her in Chinatown. She decided to see if a nearby store – Chen's Fabric Shoppe – had something useful.

"Can I help you?" asked the stooped old woman behind the counter. Her thick white hair was pulled up in a bun secured by two lacquered chopsticks.

"Do you have any wool? Something in a gray, good for a man's suit?"

"Mmm-hm." The old woman limped through the shop to some bolts of slate-gray cloth with a fine herringbone twill. "Tibetan wool. Feel very nice on your man."

Kathy touched the fabric. It *was* quite nice, soft but substantial and had an excellent drape.

"I think he'll like it," Kathy said.

At least I hope he'll like it, she thought, biting her lip. It was becoming impossible to please Stavros. He'd been so sweet and attentive at first, but now he found fault with everything she did. She'd made the wine mistake because she'd been working 36 hours straight. She'd spent the night baking bread to replace the loaves he'd thrown out because he claimed the wheat was bitter. And then she'd spent the entire day cleaning the fifteen-room house. She'd been so tired when she'd gone down to the wine cellar, she'd barely been able to keep her eyes open.

At least he'd let her sleep after he'd whipped her.

Kathy realized she was clenching her fists, and made herself relax. She had no right to be angry with Stavros. He let her live in a mansion and had taken her on trips around the world. Without him, she'd probably still be stuck in their cramped tract house in Atlanta, picking up after her little brothers and listening to her parents scream at each other when she wasn't working nine-hour shifts at the dry cleaner's. Without him, she wouldn't even know what Chateau Margaux *was*.

She'd met him when he brought one of his suits in to be cleaned while he was on an extended business trip. The cleaners' was right by the airport. Lots of businessmen came through the place, but the moment Stavros stepped inside, Kathy knew he was different. It was in his walk, the way he held himself, the way he looked at her. Power and confidence were his pheromone, and the sound of his voice made her instantly weak in the knees. They chatted a bit as she took his suit and wrote down his information, and that might have been the last she'd seen of him if she had not slipped a note into his suit pocket.

He called her that night, and took her to Phillipe's Restaurant where they dined in candlelight and split a bottle of Dom Pérignon. The fanciest date she'd had before then was when one of her high school boyfriends took her to the Outback Steakhouse before the prom.

Their courtship lasted eight months. He treated her like a princess, and Kathy was entranced by how absolutely *cool* Stavros was. He gave her the kind of lifestyle she'd only read about in her mother's romance novels. Only after she became his wife did she finally discover that the perfect sangfroid he displayed to the world required volcanic ventings in private.

Her mother had always said a woman should count her blessings. So what if Stavros forbade her to leave the house without him? So what if she couldn't go to college, or have her own friends? He was an important man, and had worked hard for his money and position. As he always said, he *deserved* a good woman to make sure everything in his household suited him. He *needed* her. He only hit her because he loved her, and wanted her to be a better person.

Kathy realized she was digging her nails into her palms. She took a deep breath and smiled at the old woman.

"I'll take ten yards of this, thanks."

"Anything for you? You make man happy, you make something make *you* happy."

"Oh, no, I–"

The old woman produced a bolt of the black satin, so lustrous it seemed almost to glow. Kathy stroked it with her index finger; it was the smoothest, softest cloth she'd ever touched. Slightly warm, even.

"Silk?" Kathy asked.

The old woman nodded. "From spiders in the Mekong Valley. Fabric made for bed sheets. 800 thread count. Woven tight to trap dreams."

Kathy stroked the material again. Slowly. To lie naked on sheets of this satin would be absolute heaven.

She immediately tried to tamp down her desire. She couldn't think of herself; she had to consider what Stavros would want.

"No, I really shouldn't," she stammered, pulling away.

The old woman's gaze now rested on some fading yellow bruises on Kathy's wrist; they were surely from Stavros grabbing her too roughly, but she couldn't remember when it had happened. Kathy tried to pull her sleeve down to cover them, but it was too short.

"You make something make *you* happy," the old woman insisted. "Nothing make man unhappier than unhappy woman. It take a lot of strength to take care of house; you need good sleep. Silk bedsheets just the thing to keep you strong."

"Well..." Stavros seldom slept in her bed, but she could always use the satin for his suit jacket lining. Yes, he'd like that very much, she decided.

✳

Kathy worked long and hard on the suit and when she finished, it was a wonder to behold. The luster of the satin lining seemed to spread to the twill, and when Stavros put it on he glowed with power and confidence.

He posed frowning in front of his mirror, turning this way and that, searching for some small flaw. His frown deepened when he could find nothing to criticize. Finally, his face relaxed into a neutral smile.

"Fine job," he said, then gave her a quick kiss on the cheek as he headed toward the door. "I'll be back in two nights."

When he was gone, Kathy went back to her sewing room. She pulled out the rest of the satin and set to making her sheets. The fabric came together easily, almost seemed eager to join under the needle. She re-made her mattress with the new bedclothes, pulled the goose down comforter up to her chin, and fell asleep.

She woke with a cry on her lips and an orgasm in her loins. She'd dreamed that Stavros whipped her with a great cat-o'-nine-tails. Each lash brought as much pleasure as a kiss to her vulva. He beat her harder and harder 'til the walls were covered in bits of her flesh.

She rolled over and tried to go back to sleep. Her naked body was drenched in sweat, but the sheets were dry.

The next night, she dreamed it was Stavros on the rack, and she with the whip.

Silk bedsheets just the thing to keep you strong.

She beat him, again and again, flaying the flesh from his body until he came and died in the same shuddering groan. Then she fell on his body, tearing out handfuls of his sweet-salty flesh that she devoured in greedy mouthfuls. She ripped loose a bloody rib, and pleasured herself with it, driving it into her own body until at last she came.

Kathy awoke with a horrified start and stumbled into the bathroom, her belly aching. She'd started her period in the night, a whole week early, and was bleeding profusely. She swore softly; surely she'd ruined the sheets. After she put in a tampon and went back to bed, she discovered that the sheets were clean and dry.

Stavros stumbled in early the next evening, rumpled and red-eyed from his flight, still wearing the suit she'd made him. His eyes burned with the dark glow of his jacket's satin lining.

"I dreamed of you," he accused hoarsely. "On the plane, at the meeting, I could think of nothing but you. Go upstairs."

She stepped back, shaking her head, even though she was electric with sudden desire. "I'm bleeding a little–"

"Then I'll make you bleed a lot!"

She ran, and he chased her through the kitchen and up the stairs. She let herself be caught outside her bedroom. It wasn't right to have sex in her condition, but oh God, she wanted it so bad!

He dragged her to the bed, tore off her clothes, and they had savage, frenzied sex. They sweated and bled and came until they were practically empty, and throughout it all the sheets stayed perfectly dry. Stavros was still worked up into a white-eyed, mouth-frothing frenzy that neither orgasms nor ordinary pain seemed to satisfy.

"I want to fuck your heart," he said, reaching over the edge of the bed to pull something shiny out of his jacket pocket. A slim double-bladed dagger knife. "I want to feel it twitch around my cock."

Death was more than she could submit to. She grabbed Stavros's wrist and they wrestled for the dagger on the slippery bed.

Kathy fought and kicked, trying to pry the blade from his fingers. Stavros hit her across the face with his free hand–

–and she remembered her first kiss from the redheaded boy who sat beside her in her middle school English class.

He hit her again–

–and she remembered the sweet pain of losing her virginity; she could no longer remember the boy's face clearly, but she'd never forget the smell of his aftershave.

A third blow fell on her shoulder, and she felt her muscles start to tremble and weaken–

–then she remembered her childhood dreams. The dreams she had as young girl before the gauntlet of adolescence and the dulling grind of school and work made her lose herself. She had not dreamed of being Rapunzel waiting for her Prince, she had dreamed of donning armor and slaying dragons; she had not dreamed of being Lois Lane fainting for her Superman, she had dreamed of being Catwoman on the prowl.

And she certainly had not dreamed of slaving as a rich man's bitch; she had dreamed of battling pirates for their gold.

Silk bedsheets just the thing to keep you strong.

With a scream, she heaved Stavros over onto his own blade. He gasped as it plunged deep into his chest. Dark blood flowed over the bedclothes.

The sheets writhed and shimmered and drank down the gore.

Kathy watched, mesmerized, as the moisture was sucked from his body until he was a husk, then ashes, then dust, then nothing. Five minutes after she'd killed him, nothing remained on the sheets but the knife and a few gold fillings from his teeth.

The sheets rustled, the serpentine hiss of the satin whispering to her softly:

I will keep you strong if you bring me what I need...

The next evening, she put on her best cocktail dress and headed out to the downtown bars to look for a luscious young Lothario.

Maybe he'd buy her dinner first; that would be nice. She was hungry.

But more importantly, so were the sheets.

Burning Bright

NTURI HID in the darkness beneath the southern palace wall and stared up into the grey, drizzling sky. The fog-shrouded top fifteen meters above supported the antiaircraft field generators. If the information she'd paid dearly for was correct, she'd have about 40 centimeters of clearance between the top of the wall and the lower edge of the field. If not, she'd be a feast for the czar's tigers or the rats, depending on which side of the wall her charred body fell.

Am I insane? She wondered. *Is any love worth this?*

The cold air was saturated with the mingling smells of garbage, factory soot, and sweet grease from the bakeries a few blocks away. Her wrists and forearms ached from her recent surgeries. She peeled her black thinskin gloves off with her teeth and flexed the new muscles in her forearms. Artificial bone stilettos, hard and keen as steel, slid out along the edge of each hand. The ivory blades were a sharp contrast against her caramel-colored skin. Retracted, the weapons hid neatly in grooves on the surface of her ulnas, rendering them invisible to most standard bioscans. With all the tribal tattoos Nturi already sported, the centimeter-wide slits on the ridges of her wrists could be explained away as decorative scarification and might be overlooked in a strip search. The blades were meant as a last-ditch defense; though she'd planned the break-in carefully, she had to be prepared for disaster.

She slid the blades in and out, testing the new muscles. Her newly-healed flesh itched, and the slide was a good satisfying scratch. In and out, in and out…

Heat rose in her eyes and chest. Closing her eyes, she retracted the blades and ran her hands over the smooth concrete of the wall, imagining it was Alexander's muscular body. Even as an eighteen-year-old, he'd had the most wonderfully sculpted chest and abdomen. But he'd be five years older now, more fully a man.

Nturi shuddered and clenched her fists, pressing her knuckles into the stone. "God, Alex, why did they have to take you away?"

He hadn't told her how he'd come to Guevara, not right away. She'd known he was an offworlder the moment he walked into New Vanuatu village, and everyone guessed from his accent that he was Novizvezdan. He said little about his family or his history, even after they began courting. But after they'd exchanged vows at the shrine and had the shaman tattoo the Goddess' blessing over both their hearts, after they'd shared their first night in the marriage bed, he told her the truth.

She remembered how her heart beat fast when he drew out the royal signet ring with the double-headed eagle of the Romanov Empire. *I am the second son of Czar Mikhail.*

It all seemed a fairy tale: her beautiful pale offworld husband was a prince. He was born to be a duke on the empire's central world, Novizvezda Prime, but as he grew older he realized the brutality his family had wrought on the races they had conquered. He was sickened by what the Romanovs had done and by what he was surely bound to do as a nobleman. Soon after he turned fifteen, he escaped Novizvezda on an interstellar freighter and didn't stop running 'til he reached the far colonies.

They had five happy months as newlyweds before the fairy tale shattered. Nturi was helping her little brother harvest piqueberries in the misty mountains outside the village when thunder ripped the air and the summery sky suddenly turned to midnight. She remembered looking up, seeking the sun, only to see a vast round blackness framed by a corona of lightning in the fractured air. Her guts turned to ice when she realized it was a giant warship settling down to hover above her village. An instant later she realized that only the Novizvezdans had the resources to build ships of such monstrous scale. And there was only one possible reason the Novizvezdans would come to Guevara.

She abandoned her brother and raced down the mud-slick, viney footpath, ran 'til her heart pumped pure acid, ran 'til she thought her lungs would explode in her chest.

But she could not run fast enough. It was all over by the time she reached the village. The warship was spinning back up into the sky. The door to her father's house had been kicked off its hinges. Her mother wept amongst smashed furniture. Her father was dead, his chest sunken and blackened by a microwave burn.

And her husband was gone.

Her mother told her how the soldiers in their red and gold uniforms had come through the door, how her father had tried to stop them, only to be shot down like a dog. They'd torn the house apart 'til they found Alex hiding in the basement, then dragged him to the ship.

"At least they're gone now," her mother had said. "We can try to rebuild our lives."

But her mother was wrong. The Novizvezdans were back the next fall in ships bearing troops and strip-mining equipment. The small Guevaran army was defeated practically overnight, and soon the lovely skies turned a sulfurous yellow from the blasting and smelters.

Nturi could not bear to watch her family's vineyards fall beneath the grinding earth-movers, could not bear to watch her mother crumble deeper in despair. So she followed her lost husband's example and stowed away on a ship heading offworld.

She'd been determined to find Alex. She'd had so much with him, lost so much because of him... she *would* have him back by her side as her husband.

Novizvezda Prime was the richest, most advanced world in the entire quadrant – how hard could it be to reach? But it had taken her two hard years to make it to the planet, and three even harder years as a cat burglar's apprentice to gather the skills, money and information she needed to attempt the unheard of: break into the royal palace.

Nturi took a deep breath and dug her climbing gloves out of her utility vest. Five years of sweat and sacrifice and loneliness had come down to this. There was no other way for someone like her to contact her husband; he was kept secure behind layers of guards and bureaucracy. She barely even saw his image on the news. Most recently, she'd seen an article announcing his engagement to an offworld princess to seal a diplomatic bargain, and she knew she had to make her move. She would be reunited with her husband, or she would die trying.

She had a little less than ten minutes before the palace patrol would swing past again; it was time to begin. She slipped her low-profile night vision goggles into place, wriggled her fingers into the tight gloves and began to pull herself up the stone wall. She'd first learned to free-climb rocky faces as a child hunting for the tasty bracket fungi that seemed to grow only beneath the most inaccessible overhangs in the mountains outside her home village. The palace wall wasn't easy; the wet, mossy concrete was slick as sweating flesh. But her gloves worked beautifully; they'd been modeled on a gecko's atomic-bonding sticky toe pads and could support her entire weight on three fingers. She closed her eyes and focused on the odd rolling grip the gloves required, as if she were trying to knead the concrete. The burn in her shoulders and arms felt good; her body was finally being used the way it was meant to be.

Nturi crept up on fingertips and tip-toes until she finally chinned herself to the top of the wall. The force-field mere centimeters above was invisible, but she could feel an electric vibration that made her hair stand on end. Next came the tricky part: getting up onto the wall without getting fried.

She swung sideways and caught her left heel on the wall's rim, then began to carefully pull and roll her body onto the two-foot-wide ledge. It felt like her wedding night when she and Alex were trying to roll from one position to another without him slipping out of her body.

No sooner had she swung her other leg up when she heard the flat slap of boots against pavement. The patrol had arrived right on time. She flattened herself against the stone and held her breath.

The tension was delicious. She'd initially taken up burglary as a necessity; on Novizvezda, no one who wasn't a pureblood descendant of the original Russian colonists could get a decent job. Nturi's dark skin and tattoos limited her legitimate prospects to cleaning toilets or washing dishes in low-class establishments. She would never be allowed in the palace even as a scullery maid; girls of her color might be bundled in through the back door under cloak of darkness to please Czar Mikhail's exotic tastes in whores, but never as legitimate employees.

Her sex limited her illegitimate prospects to prostitution or theft. She was determined that no man would touch her but her husband, so she joined a burglary ring. It helped salve her conscience that they never robbed ordinary people; most of their jobs were for nobles stealing expensive toys from other nobles.

She quickly came to discover that sneaking into forbidden places was an incredible thrill. The greater the danger, the bigger the charge she got from it. Some jobs she'd practically come the moment she touched the prize she'd broken in to steal.

"I'm detecting heat residue," one soldier said. He sounded bored and sleepy.

"Scan it," replied the other.

Then a whine, and in her peripheral vision she saw a blue glow. "Inconclusive. There's tracks in the moss. Something might have climbed up," the first man replied. The glow went out.

The other grunted. "Probably another rat. The cats'll eat it."

Nturi waited for the patrol to move on. When she was sure they were out of earshot, she peeked into the palace compound. The bottom of the wall was bordered by dense bushes, most likely briar roses. Trees and rocks showed up as a ghostly blue in her goggles. Two large objects forty meters away glowed red: heat sources. Tigers.

The royal family had long bred Siberian tigers for size and speed. The czar's cats were unmatched killers. The average royal tiger weighed in at 320 kilograms, was over three meters long, and could sprint 60 kilometers per hour. They had fangs longer than Nturi's fingers, and claws strong enough to shred plywood.

If those two heard her hit the ground – and they almost certainly would – they'd be on her in about three seconds. Best to take care of them from aloft. She reached into her vest and pulled out her ceramic dart gun. Each dart contained enough sedative to drop a full-grown tiger for at least five hours. She had no interest in killing the beautiful beasts if she had a choice; besides, a good burglar left as few traces behind as possible, and two dead tigers would hardly go unnoticed.

She slid the miniature sight onto the barrel of the air pistol and took careful aim. The first tiger was lounging half-asleep and didn't even flinch as the dart sank into his haunch. The second tiger let out a coughing growl and worried at her flank for a moment before she tumbled onto her side. Satisfied, Nturi removed the sight and tucked the pistol back in its holster.

She rolled over the side and climbed down on her sticky fingertips. When she was near the bottom, she kicked off the wall to launch herself clear of the briar roses, twisted midair and hit the ground in a shoulder tuck and rolled to her feet.

Nturi ran over to the drugged tigers. She knelt beside the big female and pulled off her gecko gloves. The tiger's smell was powerful, wild and rank and musky, and her shallow breath stank of blood from a recent kill.

Nturi put her bare hands on her flanks and ran her fingers through her shaggy fur. Her muscles felt densely molded, like cast soft metal. The feel of the powerful beast made her shiver. A growl rumbled from deep in the tiger's chest, but she did not stir.

She could kill me in a blink, she thought. *She could kill me as easily as she turns her head.*

Nturi's heart beat fast, but she felt no fear, only the sudden swell of desire for her beloved and the thrill of her invasion.

"I'll have you soon, my love," she whispered. She planted a kiss on the top of the tiger's broad head, removed the dart and sprinted for the palace.

As she ran, she ratcheted her goggles' polarization around until the invisible net of detection lasers ahead glowed red in her lenses. In trees above the leading edge of the laser net, she could see the automated sentry weapons, set to blast anything that the lasers didn't scan as being a tiger, bird, or squirrel. When she was a few meters from the net, she got down on her hands and knees and switched on the false-field generator on her belt. It had been her most expensive purchase, mainly because of its illegality but partly because of the cold fusion cell supporting the device's immense power consumption.

The air around Nturi's body crackled and hazed blue. Her hair stood on end. The field would create the dimensions of a tiger for the detectors' benefit, but not for very long. The fusion cell would hold out for only a few minutes, and the net extended the remaining hundred yards to the edge of the palace.

Nturi began to speed-crawl through the net. Sweat ran in an itchy trickling down the groove of her back. She got through just as the field seemed to be faltering a little. She hurried into the bushes bordering the palace, pushed through to the vine-covered stone wall, and began to climb.

Soon, Nturi was clinging to the third-floor windowsill of her husband's suite as she contorted to avoid the thin laser beam of the alarm. She held on with one hand while she worked at lifting the steel bar latch through the glass with her electromagnetic multitool. The bar finally rose and fell free with a clink.

She pushed open the windows and slipped inside the room, which was dark but for a bright band of light streaming from beneath the bathroom door. The Romanovs were creatures of habit and schedule. If the details she'd bought from a recently-sacked chambermaid were correct, Alex would have just finished his fencing lesson and would be taking his evening bath. His older brother and the czar would be downstairs in the library, supposedly going over military reports, but the maid said they were just as likely to be enjoying the company of various prostitutes. Nturi was warmed by news that, as far as the maid knew, Alex had never shown any interest in the palace whores.

Nturi closed and latched the window behind her and fingertipped down the velvet-covered wall. She could hear the bath faucet running. She landed softly on the thick carpet and surveyed the room through her goggles. A leather couch and reading lamp near the middle of the room. A state-of-the-art sleeping/entertainment pod was nestled in the north corner. A richly-carved wooden writing desk and a comm station filled the opposite corner. Discarded clothes, still glowing purple from fading body heat, had been dropped in a trail leading from the hall door to the bathroom.

Nturi walked to the clothes and picked up the long-sleeved fencing shirt. The silk was damp with sweat; she sniffed it, and instantly went wet when she found the familiar scent of Alex's flesh.

She pulled off the goggles, her gloves, her vest. Letting her gear fall to the floor, she unzipped her bodysuit, peeled it away from her perspiring skin, and shucked off her tight climbing sneakers.

Her nipples went hard in the cool palace air. She ran her hands over her bare body, savoring the delicious tension. She could be found. She could be captured. She could be *killed*.

She stepped naked toward the bathroom, the hungry, burning ache for her husband intensifying with every step. When she reached the door, she held her breath, held her head close, listening.

The faucet was off. She could hear water lapping in a tub, and Alex's low voice humming. The tune was a Guevaran hunting song she'd taught him soon after they met; he'd never been able to remember all the words.

She opened the door.

The bathroom was huge, almost bigger than his room. Her husband was soaking in a big, sunken marble bathtub with golden fixtures. He practically jumped out of his skin at the sound of the opening door and dove toward what looked like a security intercom panel beside the tub–

–then stopped. He stared at her, his blue eyes wide. He'd had his blond hair trimmed short, almost buzzed to the scalp. His shoulders were broader, his chest deeper and more defined. He still bore their wedding tattoo above his heart.

"Nturi," he whispered, then continued in faltering Guevaran: "How did you...?"

"Through your window," she replied in Russian. "You look good,

Alex. The years have been kind to you."

"You look wonderful." He was staring her up and down as if she were a ghost. His shaft had gone hard, the head peeking up above the water line.

"We have a lot to talk about, but conversation can wait." She closed the door behind her, locked it, and stepped toward him, running her hands down her body. Her flesh keened for his touch. "Do you want me, husband?"

"Yes," he replied faintly. "I've missed you every day I've been in this godforsaken place."

"Then show me how much you missed me..."

Afterward, Nturi lay back in Alexander's arms as he nuzzled her neck and poured handfuls of blood-warm water over her body.

"God, I missed you so much," he whispered, his voice husky.

"I missed you, too." A lump rose in her throat, and tears welled in her eyes. Five years. Five long years; so much had happened to both of them, it seemed like virtually a lifetime had gone by. They were practically strangers to each other, now, but at the same time...he was still the Alex she remembered. The same Alex she'd loved and craved every lonely night she'd spent in cold, cramped starship air ducts or in the hot, stuffy room she'd rented above the laundry. Every night, she'd wept at the pain of missing his touch, his smile, the heat of his body, the soft kisses he'd awakened her with to make love to her in grey hours before dawn.

She took one of his broad, strong hands and kissed his palm. "I never want to be without you again."

"We'll never be separated again, I promise," he replied, gently rolling her over so she was facing him. They kissed, their hands gently roving over each other's water-slick bodies.

He took her hands in his and licked her water-wrinkled fingertips. "You're starting to prune. We better get you out of here before you melt," he smiled.

They got out of the tub and dried each other off with thick white towels, then went into his bedroom and climbed into his sleeping pod.

"Come away with me," she said as they snuggled under his blankets. "Leave this place. I can have us on a ship headed for the outer rim in three hours."

His smile faded. "I can't."

S P A R K S   A N D   S H A D O W S

"Yes, you can, you just have to trust me–"

"No, I *can't*." He took a deep breath. "And I don't want to. They'd find me, no matter where I went, and I could never forgive myself if Guevara happened all over again.

"I tried to stop my father from raping your planet, Nturi." Alex's voice cracked. "But he wouldn't listen. And I'm so sorry about your papa – your parents told me to hide, but I should have been there to protect them. I can't tell you how much I've hated myself for what I brought on your family and your people."

He cleared his throat. "Did – did your mother and little brother make it?"

She swallowed against the tide of bitter sorrow rising in her chest. "No. Kiro was killed in the fighting, and my mother...after Kiro died, she lost all hope and stopped eating. She died while they were marching us to the camps. I watched the soldiers burn her body by the side of the road. I didn't even get to say a proper prayer for her.

"Your family took everything I ever had, Alex. You were the only thing I could get back. I *need* you."

"I need you, too." He pulled her close to him. "But I also need to stay *here*. Even if we did find a place where my father wouldn't find us, what then? Billions of people suffer under my family's rule, and I could never do anything to help them if I ran away."

Nturi pulled away a little and stared at him. "What can you hope to accomplish here? Your father is–"

"–an old man who doesn't listen to anyone else, including his doctors. He's already had to have his liver replaced twice, and someday they won't be able to keep him from drinking himself to death. And he's always pissing the nobles off; a year hasn't passed when someone hasn't staged an assassination attempt. And my brother's got a taste for dueling and racing that's going to get him killed someday."

"'Someday?' How long is 'someday'?" Nturi asked, her eyes narrowing.

"Twenty years, if my father lasts as long as his father did. But then I'll be *czar*, Nturi." His eyes shone with excitement in the dim light. "I can *fix* things. I can make Guevara green again, for you and our children.

"As soon as my family fully trusts me again and lets me take on some real duties, I can start making little changes here and there. If I can help just a few people now, maybe that will start to make up for Guevara."

Nturi considered this. "So are you going to cancel the wedding I heard about?"

Alex's smile faded. "I can't. It's crucial; my father needs me to get married so he can get his hands on the platinum and uranium mines in the Taorane system. If I try to get out of it I'll have wrecked all the work I've done the past two years to get them to trust me–"

"Damn it!" Nturi exploded. "You said we'd never be separated, yet you say you're going to marry someone else?"

"You can still stay with me," he said quickly. "I *want* you to stay with me–"

"As what? Your *concubine*?" she spat. "I am your *wife*, and I will *not* be treated like a whore!"

"It wouldn't be like that," he pleaded. "Neither Princess Duria nor I expect to see much of each other. We'll just appear together to sign papers and smile at ceremonies. We'll live separate lives."

"What about the part where you're expected to produce a royal heir to really seal the bargain?" she asked, fuming.

Alex didn't say anything.

"*God!*" Nturi rolled away from him and slapped the release button on the pod door.

"Where are you going?" he asked as she rolled out.

"To the bathroom! Alone!"

She shut the door in his face and stomped across the room to the bathroom...then stopped. A thick red satin robe hung on a peg beside the door, the back emblazoned with the golden Romanov crest and the front with Alexander's initials.

I've come too far to give up now, she thought. *And I'll be damned if I'm waiting another 20 years to have my marriage back....*

Nturi glanced at the clock. It was five shy of midnight. If Czar Mikhail and his eldest son Oskar were indeed having a private party in the library, it would just be getting good.

She snatched up the robe, fluffed her short black hair, and marched for the hallway.

✳

"Am I late for de party?" Nturi asked the two guards standing at attention in front of the big double doors leading into the library. Her pidgin accent sounded painfully fake in her own ears, but she hoped the guards would buy it.

S P A R K S A N D S H A D O W S

"Where did *you* come from?" the larger of the two guards growled.

"Oh, I did need to go to de toilet on de way up from de dock–" Damn, what was the procurer's name? "–after Meester Korotkov drop me off. And when I come out, Prince Alexander is in de hallway. He tell me to go upstairs wit he. So I do. He just finish wit me."

The first guard continued to scowl at her intensely while the other dug a small bioscanner out of his belt pouch.

"You expect me to believe that Prince Alexander's been consorting with *you?*" the first asked scornfully. "He's *never* had any truck with whores!"

"Why you tink I lie?" she protested, her heart hammering in her chest. "This he robe he tell me to wear as proof for you!"

The second guard ran the scanner up and down her body while he patted her down.

"Looks like she's telling the truth," he said, switching off the device and stepping away. "She's just been laid, and the semen matches Alexander's genotype. She's clean, otherwise."

"Huh. Guess there's a first time for everything. Get in there," the first guard growled at Nturi. "And you better know how to suck, because they don't like sloppy seconds."

He gave her a shove toward the double doors. She stumbled, straightened up, and took a deep breath. Her whole body was shaking. *I could lose everything I have left in here. Don't screw this up, girl.*

She pushed into the library. The floor was littered with huge, old pornographic picture books opened to choice scenes. A handful of guards stood at discreet attention in shadowed alcoves. A dozen beautiful, naked young women were arrayed on leather couches and chairs in various poses and salacious embraces, clearly for their masters' amusement rather than their own. The eldest might have been Nturi's age; the youngest not much more than sixteen or seventeen. All were from planets recently subjugated by the Novizvezdans. None would ever have a chance at a decent life on this planet, not while the current regime was in power.

Czar Mikhail was seated in a leather easy chair in the middle of the room, his corpulent body stripped down to a pair of red velvet breeches. A girl with long, flowing black hair was sitting on the floor between his knees, sucking him.

Prince Oskar was in the middle of a richly-woven carpet a few meters to his left, pounding away at a frail-looking girl pinned beneath him.

Oskar was a man of about thirty with a shock of short red hair. He looked a little like Alexander, but he was heavier, his features coarser. He was still wearing his silk fencing shirt and trousers, the latter opened and pulled down just enough to give his equipment room to work at the unfortunate girl. She was completely naked, biting her lip as if in pain, her eyes shining with tears.

Nturi felt a terrible fire building in her chest.

"Move a little, for god's sake," Oskar snarled at the girl.

"I'll move for you, Your Highness," Nturi said loudly. "Perhaps you should try me, instead."

Oskar's head jerked up, and he arched an eyebrow when he saw Nturi. He pulled out of the girl and stood up. Nturi saw that his erection was streaked with blood. The girl lay where she was, apparently afraid to move.

"Where did you get that robe?" he asked.

"From your brother, Your Highness."

Both eyebrows rose in surprise. "Did he fuck you?"

She nodded. An unpleasant smirk spread across Oskar's face.

"Well, well, so that pale little priss decided to be a man after all. Lose the robe," he ordered.

Her heart pounding, she pulled the silken belt open and shrugged the robe off her shoulders. The garment fell in a soft heap around her ankles. She could feel a blush spreading across her skin. She swallowed down the reflexive embarrassment and fear. *Don't lose your resolve over a little exposure. You're built from steel now. Act it.*

Oskar prodded the girl with his toe. "Get out of my sight."

The girl rolled over and scuttled away behind a couch. He waggled his softening penis in his left hand and stared at Nturi. "You. On your knees before me."

Nturi did as he asked. Oskar held his blunt, bloody tool inches from her face.

"Give me your head," he ordered.

"Why would I give you my head, Your Highness," she replied, her voice dangerous and low, "when I came here for *yours?*"

She flexed the new muscles in her forearms and the bone stilettos snapped into place, sharp as tiger's claws. A split-second later, she'd leaped to her feet, skewering her left blade deep into Oskar's heart as she cut a wide smile across his throat with her right.

S P A R K S   A N D   S H A D O W S

The nearest guard gave out a shout, and the girls began to scream and scramble for the doors. In the chaos, Nturi threw Oskar's hemorrhaging corpse to the floor and vaulted over a couch toward the czar. Mikhail had been too engrossed in his blow job to realize what was happening until it was too late.

Nturi jerked his chair back, dumping him headfirst onto the floor. She landed two vicious kicks to the side of his head to stun him, grabbed him by the neck and dragged him backward to an unoccupied alcove. He was heavy, but she'd grown strong, and her rage made her stronger still.

Her back to the marble alcove wall, she pulled the czar's semiconscious form up in front of her body as a shield and pressed her right blade to his throat.

The startled guards had drawn their guns and were stumbling toward her.

"Stay back!" she shouted. "I can cut his throat before any of you can get a shot off. Bring Alexander in here! Now!"

But Alexander was already there. He pushed into the library, his face red. He'd dressed hastily, his shirt misbuttoned. He'd probably come running out of his room when he heard the girls screaming. Probably anyone within a hundred yards of the palace had heard them.

Her husband stared around and the room, his face turning pale when he saw his brother's cooling corpse and paler still when he saw Nturi with a blade to his father's throat.

"What have you done?" he whispered. His expression was an odd mix of shock, dismay, wonder and hope.

"Something that you should have done a long time ago, my love," she replied. Nturi crossed her blades beneath the czar's Adams' apple, then ripped them down and across. A jet of bright blood sprayed out in an arc from his ruined neck.

"All hail Czar Alexander!" she shouted. "Long live the new czar!"

The guards were taking aim, their guns' capacitors giving off a hard whine as the weapons powered up.

This is where I die, she thought, closing her eyes and retracting her blades.

"Stop! Lower your guns!" Alexander shouted. He pushed through the knot of men and stood before her, trembling.

"Is this what you came here to do?" he asked in Guevaran. "To take revenge on my family? A brother for a brother, a father for a father?"

"No," she replied in her native tongue. "This isn't vengeance. And it's not even close to justice. It's *necessary*. You told me yourself what you hoped to accomplish for the universe once these two were dead. Now you won't have to wait two decades to do it."

He stared at her, at the blood on her hands, considering.

"Is your wife not fit to be your queen?" she asked. "Politics and chess, my love. The queen defends the king, and after what everyone's seen here tonight, my reputation might be the best protection you could ever wish for. The nobles will think you're quite a clever boy to have masterminded a coup like this."

"Yes," he replied slowly. "Yes, I think you're right."

He took a deep breath and turned to the guards and servants. "Bring the Minister of Offworld Affairs and the Minister of the Interior to my chambers in one hour," he ordered in Russian. "I am hereby canceling the engagement my father set up for me with Princess Duria, and I will be marrying this woman, Nturi of Guevara, in a formal ceremony in one week. Until then, she is to be addressed as Czarina Nturi, and she is to be given every courtesy you would give to me. Understood?"

A chorus of stunned "yes, Your Highness," came from the assorted onlookers.

Alexander retrieved his robe and helped Nturi to her feet. "Someone bring some decent clothes for my wife," he called, wrapping the robe around her shoulders.

"And get some decent clothes and food for those girls that were in here," she added, staring pointedly at the guard who'd shoved her outside the library. "Make sure they're comfortable in the guest rooms tonight. And if I find out any of you have been molesting them, you're going to wish you'd never been born. Clear?"

"Perfectly, Your Highness," the guard replied grudgingly, then ducked out of the room.

Nturi turned to Alex and kissed his cheek. "I think this is the start of a wonderful partnership, don't you?"

He lifted her hand and kissed her bloody fingers. "Yes, my love, I do."

Roses of Gomorrah

KIRA LAY very still until she heard the brothel guard's footsteps receding down the hallway. His booted heels rang hollowly on the aluminum floor panels, the sound barely audible over the moans, thumping, and orgasmic cries coming from the Class C dormitory beside her room. The C girls were having a loud, athletic orgy. They were *always* having an orgy. Their libidos were amped up so high that they'd fuck each other until they passed out from exhaustion. They'd have to be shaken awake in the morning, but once they'd gobbled down their breakfast, they'd be horny as ever and ready for customers.

Kira rolled out of bed and stood in the darkness of her small cell. She hated hearing the Cs going at it all night, because their pleasure amplified her own loneliness. As a Class A, Kira was engineered to satisfy the refined tastes of customers who wanted conversation, dancing, or perhaps a bit of role-playing. The expensive As had both the intelligence and the self-control to find a way to escape the New Vegas space station, so the owners kept them separated and locked down.

But, at least in Kira's case, they hadn't tried hard enough.

She stood on the metal folding chair beside her costume closet and used her thumbnail to work at the screws holding the air vent cover in place. Once she'd gotten the cover off, she chinned herself up to the open vent and began to ease herself inside. Kira was a small, wiry woman, but her breasts and long black tresses inevitably got in the way, and the institutional pajamas she'd been given were too thin to keep her from getting snagged by jutting rivets and sharp metal corners. She had to be careful; cuts and bruises would be noticed and questioned during the weekly inspections. Her masters would have no qualms about chaining her to her bed at night if they thought she was getting out.

Once she was in the vent, Kira sniffed the air, trying to figure out if her beloved Seth had been able to get out of his cell. The exotic genes that made her technically nonhuman (and therefore property) had also given her a few talents that veered from the human norm. Her flesh-pretzel limberness was a planned trait, she imagined, but her rat-keen sense of smell probably wasn't.

She took a deep breath. There were tens of thousands of people on the station, the stale station air an olfactory white noise of sweat, excrement, food, oil, and hydraulic fluid. But the prostitution constructs smelled different than normal humans, sweeter and muskier. If Seth were in the ductwork...yes. He was out. His lambstew-vanilla scent slid across her olfactory nerve, and Kira felt herself getting wet.

She'd first met Seth two years before when a quartet of spacers on shore leave rented them and another pair of prostitutes for a night of group sex. The moment she'd laid eyes on Seth, she'd felt an unmistakable, undeniable attraction to him. Once the spacers had drunk themselves unconscious and the other two slaves had nodded off, she and Seth ended up making out and talking until dawn.

It smelled as if he were down a few levels. Maybe he was in the mezzanine health club? She hoped so. The gym had been shut down for a few weeks due to some sort of revenue tax problem with the station government. But the station hadn't shut off the water or electricity, and Kira loved making love with Seth in the showers and steamroom. And on the locker room benches, and on the exercise equipment, and on the wrestling mats...

Kira made her way down through the maze of metal ducts to the grate that led into the women's locker room. The grate had already been removed and was leaning against the locker room wall. She crawled through and stood up on the dry, rubbery floor. She could smell Seth clearly, and could hear the hiss of the steamroom jets.

Kira pulled off her pajamas, folded them, and laid them on one of the dressing benches. Seth's scent was deliciously strong, and she felt herself getting wetter and wetter as she crept toward the steamroom. It had been three days since she'd seen him, and it felt like three years.

When she opened the translucent glass door, the first thing she saw through the hot mist were the purple welts and bruises across her beloved's back.

"Oh no," she breathed.

He turned. There were more welts across his sculpted chest and thighs. His wrists and ankles were rope-burned. His thick blond hair had been shaved off, and his left eye was blackened and nearly swollen shut.

"Kira," he said, his voice cracking. "I've missed you so much."

She ran to him, and he grabbed her and hugged her tightly. Up close, Kira could see that the bruises on his shoulders were actually bite marks.

"What did they do to you?" she whispered.

"I haven't been able to think of anyone but you," he murmured. "I was escorting a woman two days ago, and I just...I just wasn't into it. She got mad, and complained to the owners. So I got sold for rough trade last night."

"Oh god, did they–" she began.

"Let's just say they weren't into safe, sane, and consensual," he said. "I really don't want to talk about it."

She kissed him gently, and he returned the kiss less gently, his vanilla-flavored tongue sliding into her mouth. Kira's knees went rubbery, and her loins ached with desire for him. The steam condensing on their skin ran down their flesh in warm rivulets. She felt his ridged erection harden between their bodies. He kissed her neck, licked her earlobes and traced the length of her throat with his tongue. His hands slid down her smooth back to her ass.

Kira kissed his chest and found his nipple with her lips. He sucked in his breath as she nibbled him. She slid a hand down his taut, wet belly to his erection and began to stroke him, the soft skin sliding over the thick cartilage rings around his shaft.

"I wish I could be inside you," he whispered.

"I wish that, too," she replied, caressing his balls with her other hand. "But even if you could get inside me, we'd lock up. We'd be stuck together for hours."

"If we ever get out of here," he said, "first money I make, I'm getting surgery to get these things taken off. And then I'm going to make love to you for three days straight."

"Just three days?" she teased.

"Well, after three days I'll probably be too faint from hunger to keep it up much longer."

He slid his hands around her hips to her hairless vulva. He gently spread her thighs. "And speaking of hunger, I've been dying to taste you again."

He knelt on the rubbery floor before her and spread her lips with his thumbs. "Why, hello there! Looks like someone's glad to see me."

He ran the tip of his tongue over her inflamed clitoris, and a jolt of pleasure electrified her body, dizzying her. She rocked backward, but

Seth caught her by her thighs and pulled her close to his face.

"Uh-uh," he said. "You don't get to faint until *after* I've made you come."

He began to run his tongue in slow, agonizingly wonderful circles around her swollen little bundle of nerves. He slid a finger down the slick groove of her vulva and slowly penetrated her. One ring. Two rings. Three rings. She felt him find the sweet spot between her third and fourth rings, and she felt her flesh tighten around him, her legs quivering.

"Yes, that's it," she moaned.

He stopped circling her clitoris and started giving it quick, direct licks as he pressed into the wonderful spot inside her. Kira cried out as the orgasm took her hard and fast. Her legs turned to mush, but Seth wouldn't let her fall. He drank down her nectar as her flesh spasmed sweetly against his hand and tongue.

When her climax had passed, Seth lowered her to the floor and planted a soft kiss on her lips as she lay there, stunned.

"A good one?" he asked.

She nodded. "I don't know how you do it," she whispered. "I come all the time with customers, but when I'm with you...it's like comparing static electricity to a lightning bolt."

He grinned at her. "I'm just that good, is all."

Kira got up on her knees and took hold of his erection. She leaned down and licked off the prejack beading on his glans. Vanilla cream. She started to take him into her mouth, but he stopped her.

"Do you think you could come again?" he asked.

Her flesh was still humming. "Yes. For you, I could come a thousand times and still want more."

"I want to feel that hot groove of yours. And I want to kiss you. And most of all, I want to be looking into your eyes when you come."

He helped her up, then backed her up against the warm, wet tile wall. A steam jet hissed near their heads. He kissed her deeply, passionately, and she helped him slip his erection between her legs. He began to thrust in and out, his rings bumping wonderfully against her slick flesh. She tilted her pelvis forward so her clitoris would get the best of the rub.

"More," she whispered. "Faster."

Seth was working hard, grunting as he pushed against her. She licked his neck, and tasted his sweat, salty and sweet like honey-roasted peanuts. He leaned back, staring deep into her eyes. His green eyes were dilated so wide she could barely see the irises.

"Come for me," he whispered.

Kira felt the tension rising in her loins, and she leaned into him, squeezing her thighs around his hard shaft. Each stroke brought her closer and closer to ecstasy.

"Come for me!" he shouted.

The shock of his voice brought her home. She thrust her hips against his, meeting him stroke for stroke, wishing he was inside her, aching for him to be inside her, and as her flesh pulsed she felt his body shudder and he was coming, too, howling as he greased her thighs with his sweet vanilla spunk, and this time his legs gave out, and they tumbled backward in a jumble of arms and legs and tongues and she humped against him until they were both spent.

"Ouch," he said, his body stiffening beneath her. "Please let me up."

She rolled off him. As he unsteadily got to his feet, she saw that the fall had torn open some of the scabbed welts on his back and he was bleeding. She helped him out of the steamroom, got him to sit on one of the benches, and found some peroxide and gauze in a first aid kit bolted to the wall.

He winced a little as she wiped off the blood and cleaned his wounds.

"It's not fair that we can't be together," he said, tracing a finger down her damp cleavage. "We were made to be together."

"I know," she said, blinking back tears. They'd really beat Seth up. His injuries hadn't looked nearly this bad in the dim light of the steamroom. "Dammit, why didn't the madam take you to the medic?"

"All part of the lesson," he replied bitterly. "But they'll *have* to heal all this up in the morning so I'll be a nice, clean slate for the next customer."

God, Kira thought. *What will they do to him next?*

"I can't take much more of this," he said, his jaw tightening. "I *won't* take much more of this. We've got to get out of here."

✳

The next morning, the brothel madam came into Kira's cell.

"Congratulations," the older woman said. The madam was wearing one of her many black business suits, and she'd painted her long fingernails a turquoise blue to match her short spiky hair. "You've got a date this afternoon. A real big spender, too; you'll be with him the whole night."

The madam looked Kira up and down, frowning a little. "He was very specific about how you should look. I think Tina has the sort of dress he wants you in...but we've still got to do something about your hair..."

Late that afternoon, Kira stepped into the Little Zagreb steakhouse on Level 7. Her nose and eyes still burned from the fumes of the chemicals the beautician had used to turn her straight black hair to wavy auburn. The lilac perfume they'd spritzed her with to hide the chemical odors wasn't any help to her suffering sinuses. The sequins of the green strapless cocktail dress chafed her skin, and the silver tracking bracelet was uncomfortably tight around her left ankle. The dress was a few years out of fashion, but it was what the brothel had on hand in her size. She hoped the customer wouldn't mind.

She made her way through the knot of tourists and gamblers crowding the front entrance to the maître'd's station.

"I'm supposed to meet Captain Zorleski here," she told the headwaiter.

He glanced at the reservation screen. "Yes, the Captain's already been seated in the back. Rachel will show you to your table," he said, waving a hand to summon a nearby waitress.

The waitress led Kira through the restaurant to a table occupied by a broad-chested man in the scarlet and black uniform of the Godunov royal guard.

Kira had seen a fair number of men wearing the old Godunov uniforms around the station, claiming to be veterans of the fabled war in which the bloodthirsty Romanovs wrested control of the Novizvezdan empire from the elderly, honorable Czar Petro Godunov. The vastly outnumbered Godunov guard had battled for their czar and homeland to the last man on the last ship; of 5,000 guardsmen, less than 100 were thought to have survived. The survivors were banished from the Novizvezdan territories. In the 15 years since their defeat, the Godunov guard had come to represent old-fashioned honor, determination, and unflinching courage. Of course, most if not all the men she'd seen wearing the uniform were nothing but blowhard frauds trying to impress women with tales of a war they'd only seen in videos and holos.

The Captain stood up as the women neared the table. And in that moment, Kira knew he was the real thing. He was a tall man, but even if he'd been short Kira suspected he'd still be an imposing figure. He radiated strength and calm authority. A white, netted burn scar extended over the lower half of his left face and disappeared beneath his high collar. She'd heard the Godunovs didn't believe in having battle scars removed cosmetically. His gray, wiry hair was cropped close to his scalp, and he smelled of white soap, ozone, and testosterone.

Though he smiled at her, his grey eyes remained intense and sad, and she suspected very little escaped his gaze.

He extended his right hand toward her, palm up. Each of his fingers were as wide as two of hers. "I am Nikolai Zorleski. May I have the pleasure of your company for supper?"

"Yes, of course," she replied, giving him her hand.

He planted a quick, formal kiss on the back of her hand, then moved around the table to pull her chair out for her. She sat. As he pushed her up to the table, she noticed he wore a gold wedding band on his left hand.

"What would you like to drink, miss?" the waitress asked.

"A glass of merlot, please, and an ice water," Kira replied.

"And you, sir?"

"A glass of sweet sherry to start, and a pint of ale with my meal," the Captain said. "I already know that I want the porterhouse. But the lady will need time to decide, I expect."

As the waitress left with their drink orders, the Captain evidently noticed Kira glancing again at his wedding band.

"You have questions, yes?" He raised his left hand and twisted the ring thoughtfully. "Why an honor-bound old soldier like me should be on a pleasure station like this when I have a loving wife waiting for me at home?"

Kira kept her face in a neutral smile, hoping he didn't really expect an answer. Above all, she dared not do or say anything to offend a customer, particularly a big spender like the Captain. If this man went back to the madam with complaints, she'd get rough trade or worse.

She relaxed a little when the Captain continued.

"The trouble is, my loving wife is not waiting for me at home. My home is gone. My Vanessa was murdered sixteen years ago by those scabby dogs the Romanovs dared call soldiers. I fought my way back to the homeworld to find her, and when I found her corpse...when I found her I knew that they'd done the most horrible things imaginable to her before they finally slit her throat."

The Captain took a deep breath, unclenching his fists and spreading his hands flat on the white linen tablecloth. "My wife and I had just celebrated our tenth anniversary when the war started, and we had the kind of love the angels in Heaven should have envied us for. A day doesn't pass that I don't ache to feel her beside me."

The waitress returned with their drinks. "Are you ready to order, miss?"

"Um." Kira glanced at the menu. "The cress and isopod salad, thanks."

The waitress turned to the Captain. "You wanted the porterhouse, sir? What sides would you like with that?"

"Buttered barley and the mashed turnips, please," he replied.

He took a sip of his sherry as the waitress left for the kitchen. "The last night before I joined the fleet, I took her to dinner in a restaurant much like this one. Her hair, her dress...she looked much like you do now. Your resemblance to her is...astonishing."

The Captain drained his glass and stared into the crystal facets. "I can accept that she died; we all die. But that such a sweet and loving woman should die tortured and burned and mutilated at the hands of raping beasts...no. No, no, and no. I was a madman for a long time after that, but I finally realized that no revenge upon the Romanovs could ever make up for what had been done to her. And revenge was not what she would have ever wanted.

"And then I had a dream about Vanessa. She told me, 'Do for others what you did for me. Give to other women the joy you would have given to me,'" he said.

"Today is her birthday, and to honor her memory, I will do for you whatever you desire in the time we have together," the Captain finished.

Kira paused, considering his story. "But why me?" she asked. "Why choose a whore?"

He shrugged and smiled. "Who else should I choose on this orbiting Gomorrah? The spoiled daughter of a rich businessman? A bored widow? Who else here is more in need of joy but the slave who must provide it?"

"Why haven't you gotten married again?" she asked. "It seems like dedicating yourself to a new love would be the best way of honoring your wife's memory."

"Were I a different man, remarrying would be a fine thing to do," he replied slowly. "But I'm a man of the sword, and any wife of mine would live in danger. My heart isn't strong enough to bear the death of two loves."

He smiled at her sadly. "If you can't have a real rose, a paper rose will have to do."

❋

After they finished their meal (Kira happily succumbed to the temptation of a huge slice of chocolate cake for dessert) the Captain led Kira back to his hotel suite.

He undressed her and laid her down on the satin sheets of his bed and began to give her a full-body massage. Though his hands were big, his touch was light and gentle, and when she closed her eyes and ignored her nose, it was easy to imagine that his hands were Seth's hands. It was easy to imagine that she and Seth were free and had money and could make love in their own hotel room. Yes, those were Seth's fingers caressing her sides and kneading her neck and shoulders, his palms sliding down the smooth length of her back to her thighs.

The more she thought about Seth, the wetter she got. The hands gently rolled her over onto her back. Lips – yes, she could imagine they were Seth's, though he had no stubble to scritch against her skin – planted soft kisses on her neck, her breasts, down her belly, down her thighs. She felt hot breath on her hairless vulva, and then a soft kiss on her lips. And then a deeper, longer kiss, his tongue sliding into her vagina.

"Amazing. You taste just like raspberry jelly," the Captain said.

Her fantasy of Seth deflated, and she felt her loins grow cold. "That's because I've got raspberry genes," she replied, suddenly feeling like an old woman. "The gengineers gave us plant scent-and-flavor genes so we'll always be yummy for the customers."

He slipped a finger inside, gently probing, then withdrew. "You've got rings in here?"

"Cartilage, like in your trachea," she replied. "I'm ridged for your pleasure."

"Isn't that uncomfortable?" he asked.

She shrugged. "Not really. The rings have some stretch to them. And I don't have a lot of pain receptors down there. It doesn't hurt unless the guy tries to put his fist in me. It's not like a baby's ever going to go through there. They made me seedless, too, you know."

"You seem to know a lot about your body," he said.

"One of my regulars last season was a gengineer. He designed doxies like me, and told me all about it. Seemed to enjoy his handiwork."

The Captain sighed and sat up. "It's a shame, you know. Up until I tasted you, I could almost imagine you were Vanessa."

He gave his head a little shake, as if to physically shake off his sadness, and smiled at her. "Are you enjoying this? *Really?*"

"Of course."

"Don't lie," he said gently. He touched the bracelet on her ankle. "Are you worried about this? About them listening in? Don't worry, I told them no bugs, and they knew better than to cross me. My security system would've alerted me if you'd come in here with anything but a tracking beacon.

"You can say what you like in here," he said. "Tell me what you want."

Kira got up on her knees and faced the old soldier, who was sitting crosslegged on the foot of the bed. He'd stripped down to his gray boxer shorts. The pale burn scar she'd seen on his face and neck extended down across his left shoulder. The thick hair on his chest and belly was more than half gray, but his body was still lean and corded with muscle. His erection had subsided.

"What I want most in this world," she said, "is to leave this place with my boyfriend, marry him, and live the rest of my life with him as a free woman someplace far, far away from here."

The Captain was staring at her, his expression unreadable. "Are you asking me to help you escape from this station?"

"I don't know – are you offering to help me?"

He chewed the inside of his cheek. "You're aware, I hope, that in this part of the universe, the punishment for stealing or releasing your sort is execution? I've already been banished from the Novizvezdan empire; I don't relish having to avoid the New American Confederacy worlds on top of that."

"My sort," she said. "And what am I supposed to be?"

"A thing that looks human, but isn't. A flesh machine, or so most corporate scientists say. A soulless thing created to be perfectly charming, beautiful, and an effortless liar. A lust-driven, conscienceless hedonist that can't be trusted to live free in normal human society."

"Do you really believe all that?" she asked.

"The public believes it." He bowed his head. "And I..." he trailed off.

"What?" she prompted.

"Did you know that your model is very popular?" he asked. "There's a Kira in all the best brothels and gentlemen's clubs in this quadrant. I first saw you – a Kira, rather – five years ago. I was in Nova Monaco, and had to go into a show bar to meet a client. I stepped inside the club, and suddenly I saw my dead wife dancing onstage."

He shook his head. "I was...stunned. I asked around, learned the girl's name, and found out that she was a construct, a slave of the club owner. Everywhere I've gone since then, I've seen Kiras. And all of you look *so much* like Vanessa. I feel I'm being haunted."

The Captain paused, looking uncomfortable. "You're the first Kira I've even spoken with. I tried just avoiding you, but the harder I tried, the more I seemed to see you. I thought...maybe if I bought you for an evening, I could get my heart to realize that you're nothing like Vanessa, that you're not even a real human. I could finally stop feeling this horrible longing when I see your face."

"So, your story about the birthday ritual was just a lie?" she asked.

He shook his head. "I've told you no lies. I just...didn't tell you all the truth at first." He looked ashamed. "The universe is full of freewomen who live chained by sorrow and loneliness. I'd like to think I helped ease the burden on their hearts, if only for an evening."

"What good is all this supposed to do *me*?" she asked. "You asked me what I wanted. I *need* my freedom. I *need* the chance to have what you had with Vanessa."

He smiled, staring down at his feet. "When I was a young officer, I and my shipmates smuggled a little cat onboard our warship. He would sit by the airlock and howl to be let out. I'm sure that if he'd been able to talk, he'd have told us that he needed to be outside. He'd have never understood that outside was a cold vacuum that would kill him in an instant."

Kira tried to bite back the angry frustration building inside her. "Stop patronizing me, *please*. I'm not an animal."

"No, but you've been sheltered like one. This is not such a bad place; I've seen Kiras who live far worse lives than yours. And even they live in luxury compared to many commonfolk. The universe won't be kind to someone like you."

"Do me a favor," she said, her voice low, "and please don't assume you know *anything* about my life. I have to break out of my cell at night just to spend a little time with the man I love. I spend every waking moment of every day wanting to be with Seth, and we can't even spend a single night together."

She paused to angrily wipe away the single tear that had slipped down her cheek. "Seth got depressed because he couldn't be with me, and some rich lady he was servicing decided she didn't get her money's worth and complained. Do you know what happens to us when we get customer complaints? We get put on rough trade to teach us a lesson. Right now the man I love is very likely being beaten and pissed on, and there's nothing I can do to help him. *Nothing.* And if he doesn't smile and say 'thank you, may I have some more?' and gets *more* complaints, there's a very good chance he'll get sold to a snuffer. A rich psycho will lay down his cash, and get to take him apart. Or, if the psychos aren't buying and the house feels like it's already made its target 500% profit on Seth, they'll sell him for garden fertilizer or pet food. That's what happens to us when we start to get old and sag, after all – off we go to the rendering plant.

"So don't please compare me to some pet you once owned," she finished. "I know what an airlock is. I'm living inside one."

The Captain was staring at her. "You really do love him, don't you?"

"Yes!" she exclaimed, throwing up her hands in exasperation. "*I love Seth.* Why should this seem like such a miracle to you?"

"Because true love always is a miracle," he replied.

Then the Captain was silent for what seemed an eternity.

"I want to see you two together," he finally said. "I believe that you are in love, yes, but I haven't seen this boy. If his love for you isn't real, the two of you can't survive out there. If I think that he loves you, too, that it's not just the natural lust you feel for one of your own kind – then yes. I'll help you. I've made my living fighting for other peoples' money and land – why not fight for love for a change?"

The Captain made arrangements with his ship's crew, then called the brothel to order Seth. Kira had put her cocktail dress back on and watched him from the bed.

"I don't care if he's busy," the Captain said, pacing in front of the comm terminal. He shoved his hands deep into the pockets of his burgundy robe. "I'm paying you top dollar, and I want him here on the double."

The madam frowned from the terminal screen. "He'll need to get cleaned up first–"

"Am I not speaking clearly?" the Captain asked. "I just said I want him sent here, right now. Now. Clear?"

The madam forced a plastic smile. "Perfectly. We'll deliver him in ten minutes. You'll need to pay in full when he arrives."

The madam's word was good. Captain Zorleski had barely gotten dressed in gray fatigue pants and a khaki shirt when the doorbell chimed.

"Come in," the Captain said.

The door slid wide. Outside, Seth stood between two burly brothel guards in plain brown suits. Seth wore simple, loose-fitting green cotton trousers and tunic. His feet were bare, and he was holding a bag of ice wrapped in a bloody bar towel to his nose and freshly-blackened eye. Kira saw new marks on his wrists, possibly from shackles.

"Is this the boy?" the Captain asked Kira.

"Yes," she replied.

Seth's eyes flicked from the Captain to Kira and back. He stared at the old soldier as the other men completed the transaction.

Kira saw a dark, horrible anger building behind Seth's eyes, a hateful rage she'd never thought him capable of.

"Door, close," the Captain said as the guards left with four bars of platinum. He turned to Seth. "Well, you must–"

Seth flung the bloody icepack in the Captain's face and savagely swung at the older man's jaw. The Captain neatly dodged the punch and caught Seth's wrist. He jerked Seth's arm up and down in a wide arc, throwing the young man onto his back. The Captain completed the takedown by stepping over his prone body and holding Seth's twisted arm locked against his knee.

In the next instant, Seth popped his elbow, shoulder, and wrist out of joint, his arm slithering from the Captain's grasp. The older man looked profoundly surprised as Seth lurched up underneath him, knocking him forward onto his hands and knees.

"Seth, no!" Kira yelled.

Not seeming to hear her, Seth leaped onto the Captain's back and grabbed him in a headlock. Choking, face turning purple, the Captain tried to shake Seth off. Seth pulled his arm tighter, digging his knee into the small of the Captain's back, his own contorted face turning red with anger and exertion.

"Seth, stop!" Kira shouted, jumping off the bed and hurrying toward the grappling pair. "He's trying to help us, stop!"

Her words finally seemed to clear the angry haze clouding his mind. He released the Captain's neck and sprang back a few yards, catlike. He stood in a tense half-crouch, as if waiting for the other man to retaliate.

"Captain, are you all right?" Kira asked.

Gasping, the older man nodded and sat up on his knees. He rubbed at his throat and stared back at Seth.

"That was some move you pulled," the Captain coughed. "Your joints must be half rubber."

"I wouldn't know," Seth replied belligerently. "Ask Kira; she knows that kind of stuff."

Kira went to Seth and touched his bruised face. "What's gotten into you? I've never seen you like this."

Seth's rage seemed to evaporate when Kira touched him. He smiled at her, still looking a touch unhinged, and took her hand in his and kissed her palm.

"What's gotten into me is – I'm not going back there. No. Not after today and yesterday." He swallowed nervously. "I saw this guy was alone, and had cash, and I thought we could take his money and clothes and get out of here."

"Seth, he told me he'd help us."

"Help us?" Seth laughed bitterly. "Kira, he's a *normal*. They'll never help people like us. He's just a rich guy playing with your head."

"No, it's not like that," Kira said. "I believe what he's told me."

"I told her," the Captain said, "that I'd help the two of you get off the station. *If* I think you love her."

Seth turned a cold gaze on the Captain. "The fact that you're alive right now should be proof enough. I wouldn't have stopped if I didn't love her." He hugged Kira close, wrapping his arms around her protectively. "She's the only woman I've ever loved, and right now, she's the only person I don't hate in this entire damned universe."

The Captain stared at the couple for several moments, thoughtfully chewing on his lip. "I believe you. Let me contact my crew, and you'll be off this station within the hour."

S P A R K S A N D S H A D O W S

"Wait," Seth said. "What's the catch? You *can't* be doing this out of the goodness of your heart."

"There's no catch," the Captain replied. "I'm doing this to repay a debt I owe to an old love."

"Bullsh–" Seth began.

"Seth, stop it," Kira said, gently grabbing his chin and forcing him to look down at her. "*I believe him.* If you can't trust him, then trust *me*."

"All right," Seth said, relaxing. "All right."

A young, dark-skinned woman with close-cropped green hair stepped into the Captain's hotel room carrying plain clothes for Kira and Seth. She looked at the couple doubtfully, then approached the Captain.

"Are you sure about this?" she asked.

"Yes, I'm quite sure," he replied. "Did you find the lock decoder, Loren?"

"Yeah." She pulled a small, oval device out of the front thigh pocket of her fatigues. "How long are they going to be on the ship? Are they gonna be, like, *crew*? And if they're gonna be crew, do they know how to do anything besides fuck?"

Kira felt Seth stiffen in indignation, and she put a hand on his knee to calm him. "I'm sure you'll find we have many talents that can be of use onboard a mercenary vessel. We're fast learners."

"Indeed," the Captain agreed. "A few judo lessons and this lad will be quite dangerous. Get those tracking devices off them, please. And scan them for microchips. Did you see any watchers?"

Loren nodded. "Couple of ugly guys in brown suits hanging out on a couch in the lobby."

"Then we'll be taking the maintenance corridor back to the dock..."

Kira held Seth's hand as the ship's medic, a thin redhead named Susan, ran an ultrasound wand over Seth's penis. The artificial gravity on the Captain's ship, the *Petrograd*, was only a quarter what it was on the station. Kira felt a little dizzy, and she hoped she wouldn't get spacesick.

"This feels really weird," Seth told the medic.

"I'm liquefying the cartilage," she explained. "I'll put a nerve block on you once this part's done, and then I'll extract the cartilage with a needle. And then–" she paused to lift his flaccid member and run the wand across its underside "– I'll give you a couple of seconds under the soft tissue growth stimulator, and you should be good as new. Cartilage tends not to grow back without encouragement, so we shouldn't need to do this again."

Kira watched as the rings that had kept them from truly consummating their love melted beneath Seth's skin. When the medic was finished, Kira thanked her, helped Seth get dressed, and walked with him back to their cabin.

They crawled into the big padded sleep sack on their double bunk and snuggled down for the night. Seth slipped an arm around Kira and kissed her cheek. He seemed more relaxed than she'd seen him in months, much more like his old self. He slid his other hand across her smooth belly, drawing soft tickling circles on her skin with his fingertips.

"I can't believe this has really happened," he said. "I can't believe we're free."

"Yeah," she said, snuggling closer to him and smiling into the darkness. "But I keep thinking about something...the Captain said he's met my model on a dozen stations. I wonder...I wonder if all the mes are in love with all the yous?"

"Hmm. I knew I wanted you the moment I saw you, and I can't imagine feeling any differently." Seth paused. "So, I guess if all the yous have actually met the mes, then there's a whole lot of people out there who ought to get freed from slavery, don't you think?"

His suggestion sparked her imagination. *Why stop at just our models?* she thought. *Once we've learned what the Captain Zorleski can to teach us, we could get everyone out. Station by station...*

"Viva la revolucion," she whispered. "But first, I think we out to try your new toy out. You know, just to make sure everything's working."

Seth had gone hard against her thigh. "Oh, I think it'll work just fine."

"That's good," she said. "Because I've got a couple of orgasms in me that are in serious need of liberation..."

Photograph of a Lady, Circa 1890

There she sits still, image
locked on that illusory paper,
beautiful, but a little stiff.
She was posing in a time when
photography was serious business;
you had to be a prepared centerpiece,
not a storm petrel caught mid-second
in flight over the smooth, rolling waves.

Her clothes and parasol
are the fine white of sea salt,
but her dress is soft linen armor;
that delicate skin never felt the burn
of the hot sun and she never ran through
the seaspray and the crashing waves, so cold
they seem electric in their force and shock.

No, the rough ocean was the realm of whalers
and half-naked heathen islanders, not ladies.
So she spent summertime trips to the beach
under a wide umbrella and drank mint tea,
and the vast green sea rolled on without her.

The smooth line of her jaw is fuzzy;
did the photographer's hand tremble
as he slowly exposed her image,
or was it a problem in the solution
sloshing in small waves in the pan
in his landlocked darkroom?

Her body is gone, only this
flat, crackling image remains,
but even now, still she trembles
deep in the paper, where particles
that form her likeness waltz
in quick, subatomic union.

Perhaps more of her still moves
in the scattered elements her soul shed;
she's in the ground, she's in the air,
and as her blood once thrilled
at hearing exotic tales of travel
to places that she could never see,
now she travels in a slow, millennial
circulation around the continents,
pulled by the sun and moon, and now
she knows what Ocean really means.

Flesh and Blood

MIKE INHALED sharply as the first drop of hot candle wax hit his chest. His eyes strained against the darkness imposed by Olivia's silken blindfold, arms strained against the leather thongs binding him to the bedposts. He could hear the faint hiss of the candle's flame, nearly drowned out by the rustle of Olivia slithering across the satin sheets. And by the beating of their slave's heart, so agonizingly slow now that he was sure the girl had lapsed into a coma.

If he'd undergone this delicious torture only a year earlier, he would have been sheened in sweat, shivering like a mouse. But now his skin was cool and dry as a snake's, his dead heart steady, a cold flesh clockwork.

The second candledrip seared onto his lower belly, alarmingly close to parts he *didn't* want burned, and he reflexively tried to cover himself. The leather ripped, and suddenly his hands were free.

"Oops. Sorry," he mumbled.

Olivia sighed. "Michael, will you *never* learn to be still?"

He pulled off the blindfold and blinked at her in the candlelight. "We could try regular handcuffs next time."

"And have you ruin the finish? I think not."

She caressed the dark bedpost. Mike remembered her telling him that she'd had the bed since 1850. It had been part of the dowry she'd brought with her from England, and it was only piece of furniture she'd been able to rescue from her then-husband's estate before Sherman's troops burned Atlanta. He wondered how many thousands of lovers she'd entertained on it since.

"You're so strong, Michael, even for one of us." She lay down beside him, her long white hair tickling his shoulder, and ran her hand across his broad chest. "Are you like Samson? If I cut off those lovely dark locks of yours, will you be weak for me?"

He smiled grimly. "I don't think my hair has much to do with it."

He'd known real weakness: multiple sclerosis. It first struck him when he was twenty. He was at the gym, on the bench press doing an easy warm-up set of a hundred pounds, when suddenly his arms went weak and numb and the bar crashed to his chest. The spotter who heaved the bar off him to help him up had to call a cab because Mike's hands were too numb to pick up his car keys.

He had a cousin in Toronto who had MS; she'd been wheelchair-bound since she was thirty-five. She couldn't even pee without help. The doctors insisted that Mike's illness wasn't likely to get that bad, since he almost fully recovered from the first episode less than a month after it happened. But the specter of living his life in a chair drove him wild. He started spending all his money on women, parties and trips, trying to cram as much living into his existence as possible while he searched for something, *anything*, that would cure him.

Two years later, he'd blundered into the Outland in a drunken haze, and woke up the next morning in Olivia's bed, a pint lighter. While he never told her of his disease, she could apparently smell his desperation in his sweat. Her offer of eternal life had been tempting, but it was the implication of eternal *strength* that had swayed him.

"Barbarian. You have no sense of the romantic." Olivia sat up, and picked up the scarred arm of their unconscious slave. "Care for another drink?"

Mike looked at the teenager, who went by the name Onyx; he thought her real name was Betty Lou or something. She was one of the dozens of little girls who hung out at the Outland, hoping to get the attention of one of the members of Olivia's circle. Most of them were underage, getting into the club by way of fake IDs or blow jobs for the bouncers. The unlucky ones simply clustered near the front door, trading stories and clove cigarettes until the cops busted them for breaking curfew.

Onyx had been plump and comparatively healthy-looking only a few months before when Olivia had picked her up, but now her ribs stood out in plain relief, her skin so thin and pale her whole body was traced in a webwork of blue veins. Her small breasts rose and fell with every shallow breath, silver barbells glinting in her pink nipples. Her neck and wrists were crusted with dried blood.

He shook his head. "I don't think we should take any more from her tonight."

Olivia laughed. "What does it matter? There are dozens of these little tarts for us. This one's a runaway; nobody will miss her."

"*I'd* miss her. She's a good little dancer."

"Hmph. I see you haven't got any sense of value, either." Still, she put down the girl's arm.

He made a mental note to take the girl out for a decent meal once Olivia was occupied with somebody else.

Suddenly, there was a rap on the door.

"Phone call for Michael," Adrian announced.

"I told you not to bother us. Whoever it is, send them away," Olivia replied, frowning in irritation.

"I tried, but she keeps calling back. Some girl named Julie. Says it's an emergency."

Olivia fixed Mike with a cold purple stare, her enormous pupils contracting to pinpoints. "A mundane girl? Calling *here?*"

"Look, I don't know how she got this number; *I* sure didn't give it to her." He rolled off the bed and dug his jeans out of the pile of discarded clothing on the floor. "She's just a girl I went out with for a while last year before you initiated me. Whatever this is about, I'll take care of it."

"Make sure she never calls back."

He dressed and went up through the maze of concrete corridors and steel stairs that led up to the Outland's business office. The building dated from the early 1900's, beginning its existence as a bank. During Prohibition, the Mob took it over, converting the underground vaults into secret accounting offices and storerooms for liquor. Now, the subterranean complex served well as dark apartments for the thirteen members of Olivia's circle.

Mike climbed up through the trap door in the coat closet and stepped out into the smoky club manager's office. The fluorescent light momentarily made his eyes hurt, and he had to stare at an old dark Bauhaus poster for a few seconds to ease the pain.

Adrian took a drag off his cigarette and held out the phone. "She's all yours, man."

"Thanks." Mike lifted the receiver to his ear. "Hello?"

"Mikey, is that you?" Julie sounded as if she had been crying.

"Yeah, how did you—"

"Oh, thank God I've found you! Look, I know it's been a long time, but I've *got* to talk to you...this is my last quarter, can you meet me at the coffeehouse on the corner of Ninth and Wilshire?"

"Wait, I—"

"Please, Mikey, it's a real genuine emergency! I'm here at the cafe now, promise you'll come? Please? You're the only one left." Her voice was shaking, strained to the point of cracking.

With Julie, *everything* was an emergency; her life was one self-inflicted crisis after another. But he'd never heard her sound quite so upset before. "Oh, hell, okay, I'll be there in a while."

"Olivia's gonna be pissed," Adrian commented as Mike hung up and passed the phone back to him. No doubt he'd overheard the entire exchange. "I'd tell you to just blow this girl off, but I got the feeling she'll keep calling back if you don't show. She musta called a dozen times before I came to get you."

"Yeah, she's persistent, that's for sure," Mike sighed. "And I need to find out how she tracked me down, so I can make sure none of my family finds out where I am. Hey, is it still light out?"

"Yeah...here, take my shades and my trench." He pulled a floor-length gunmetal gray suede coat off the wall hook and dug a pair of Gargoyles out of the inside pocket. "It's too warm out for a coat, but people are gonna think you're a freak anyway."

A half-hour later, he was hurrying down the sidewalk toward the coffee shop. He kept his head down, hands jammed deep into the coat's pockets, collar turned up high to protect at least some of his face from the rays filtering through the overcast sky. It was an utter myth that his kind would burst into flames if they were exposed to the light of day, but the sun was definitely not their friend. Soon after he'd been converted, he'd made the mistake of staying out past dawn in a T-shirt. In ten minutes, he'd ended up with a blistering burn on his face and arms that left him shivering and sick for days. All part of the cost of changing from mortal to immortal.

Changes. His gums itched around his loose canines; Olivia said his new fangs would push through in another month or two, and the rest of his teeth would be replaced during the coming decade. Happily, he hadn't lost his superficial sexual ability, though he no longer produced semen. He'd look less and less human as the years passed, become more like Olivia in every way except his size and gender. She was a beautiful creature, to be sure, but couldn't be mistaken for anything but what she was. All her teeth were as sharp as a serpent's. The flesh beneath her skin had turned from red to purplish-blue, her gums and tongue sometimes almost black if she hadn't fed in a while. Her irises had grown huge, her pupils the size of dimes. She could only safely expose herself in the freakshow atmosphere of the club, though she was so light-sensitive she'd banned strobes and blacklights. Still, she sometimes went out into the city to hunt, cruising the dark streets in her big black Lincoln. He suspected she did it as much for the thrill of the risk of exposure as for the bloody satisfaction of taking unwilling prey.

Like the other young ones, Mike was merely pale, his lips slightly bluish, though he was far too muscular to be taken as anemic. He didn't sweat and had lost all body odor, and he'd noticed that alone was enough to alert some people's instincts and make them recoil. It almost seemed part of the grand design that they could pass for human their first twenty years, since that was often the span it took them to completely break their ties to family and unconverted friends.

He'd thought his relationship with Julie had been too slight to ever need re-breaking.

He pushed through the front doors of the coffeehouse, thankful that the place was dimly lit, grateful to be smelling coffee, chocolate and cinnamon instead of the oppressive diesel-and-garbage stink of the subway and city streets.

The pay phone was a few feet from the door, and Julie was leaning against it, chewing her thumbnail and sniffling. Her left eye was badly bruised, nearly swollen shut, and she had finger-shaped bruises on her left forearm. Her strawberry blond hair was uncombed, and she was wearing a ratty Kurt Cobain tee and torn jeans, the kind of clothes she'd wear around the house but would never willingly go outside in.

Her eyes widened when she got a good look at him, and she took a step back.

"Mikey, is that you?" she asked uncertainly.

He took off the Gargoyles and squinted at her. "Yeah, it's me. What's happened to you?" On second appraisal, he realized she'd gained about twenty pounds since the last time he'd seen her.

"Um, well, it's sort of a long story...maybe you just need to see her."

Mike followed her back to her booth. A few-months-old baby girl lay asleep in a yellow plastic carrier on the seat. She wore pink polkadot footed pajamas, and loosely clutched a white blanket.

Dear God, this woman couldn't keep a cactus alive, and now she'd had a *baby*?

"This is Rebecca; I named her after Tank Girl. I guess I named her after my aunt, too, but she killed herself and I heard it's bad luck to name a baby after suicides."

"Cute kid," he said aloud as they sat down, she by the baby and he across from them. "Who's the lucky father?"

"You. I think. Which is why I had to talk to you," she stammered.

His? She expected him to think that this child was his? After she'd openly cheated on him? He felt as though his heart should be pounding, but it stuck to its dull, slow funeral beat.

He stared at her, and she flinched and averted her gaze. "You said you were on the Pill," he said.

"Well, I was...sort of. I guess I missed a couple of days."

He shook his head. Those that didn't want, got, and those that wanted had to go without. His sister Nina, an architect with a dull but utterly reliable husband, had been trying for years to get pregnant. They had a beautiful house out in the country, the perfect place to raise kids. They'd recently tried to adopt the child of a teenaged girl in their town. Nina had shown him snapshots of the baby: she'd had skin the rich color of milk chocolate and a cap of black curls framing her sweet little face. But, in the end, the girl's family insisted she keep the baby. Afraid of having her hopes raised and dashed again, Nina had not tried for another adoption.

"What makes you so sure she's mine?" he asked. "I seem to recall I wasn't the only guy you were fucking last year."

Julie looked as if he'd slapped her, and her lips twitched for a moment before she could get any words out. "Jamar is Black, so she can't be his. I thought she might be Tony's, he's the guy I'm living with now, the one you, um, found me with–"

"Is he the one who gave you that black eye?" Tony was a wiry coke freak who worked as an auto mechanic, though his temper made it hard for him to hold down steady jobs. He had aspirations to be a professional kickboxer, and played guitar in some kind of garage band. Girls found him handsome and charming. Mike had disliked him on sight, hated him bitterly when he found the guy going down on Julie in the back room of a friend's house during a party.

"Yes." She started crying again. "Becky doesn't look anything like Tony, and he knows it. She looks like you," she added defensively. "If you don't believe me, we can get a blood test–"

"Don't worry about it." He wasn't sure he even *had* a blood type any more; a paternity test would only prove he was no longer human. "So let's say, hypothetically, that she *is* mine. What now? I wasn't cut out to be a father before, and I'm certainly not the daddy type now that I'm... dying."

She gave a start. "Dying? I – I thought you looked kind of...ill, but... it's not AIDS, is it?"

"Leukemia."

"Oh." She was silent for a moment. "I'm so sorry–"

"Don't be. It's no great loss." He rubbed his eyes; dim as it was, the overhead lights still bothered him. At least the sun was finally going down. "So what did you want from me? I don't see how I can help you. You and Becky should go to the women's shelter."

"I know," she sniffled. "And I *want* to, but...I got so scared this morning when he started to hit me, I just grabbed Becky and ran. I don't have my credit cards, clothes, or anything. I had to buy diapers and formula at the drugstore, and I have two dollars left. I can't go to the shelter without my stuff, but I'm scared to go back to get it alone. So I called you...I figured, you'd maybe...want to help, on account of Becky and all."

She looked up at him, her eyes pleading. "I mean, you're so big, Tony would never mess with you."

Big. Clearly, he'd missed his true calling as a knight in shining armor. He sighed, wondering how many other ex-boyfriends she'd fruitlessly called for help that day.

"Okay," he finally said. "I'll go with you back to Tony's apartment, we'll get your stuff and go to the shelter. And then," he leaned over the table 'til his face was inches from hers, "you will never, ever call me again, and let me die in peace."

✳

On the subway ride to Tony's apartment, Julie told Mike that she'd found out where he was from one of her girlfriends, who frequented the Outland on techno nights. Mike normally eschewed makeup and outrageous outfits, but realized now that perhaps he should put on vampire drag, blacken his lips and eyes and tease his hair into a scary mess every day, just to keep from being recognized again.

Becky was fretful during the trip, and worked up to a genuine squalling fit halfway through. Mike offered to hold her, and managed to unobtrusively hypnotize her and put her back to sleep. It was one of the first tricks Olivia had taught him; he never thought he'd use it on a baby.

As Becky slept, he realized he'd never held a baby before. She was so small, and fragile. And awfully cute. He gently traced the curve of her face with his index finger. Would her nose be his, or Julie's? She had his jawline, he was sure of it. He tried to imagine what she would look like when she grew up. A heartbreaker, he decided. No doubt, she'd drive the boys wild. Then he frowned as he began to think of all the grubby, horny boys who'd be after his little girl.

His frown deepened as he thought of Olivia. He'd been away from the Outland too long, but perhaps she hadn't noticed his absence yet. She'd be absolutely furious if she found out what he'd been up to.

Tony's place was, unsurprisingly, in an utterly appalling part of the city. The hallways of the apartment building reeked of mold and spoiled food and urine, but at least it was dark.

They got no answer when they rapped on the apartment door. Tony was probably off at one of the neighborhood bars. Julie silently unlocked the door and let them inside.

The apartment smelled even worse than the hallway. The stove top was crusted with burnt macaroni and cheese; papers, dirty clothes and candy wrappers littered the floor and furniture. The TV was on, showing an ad in which a smiling suburban housewife mopped her kitchen so her toddler could crawl on a shiny, germ-free floor.

"Let's get this done quickly," he said as he shut the door. "I'd just as soon not have to deal with your boyfriend tonight."

"Okay." Julie cleared off a section of the couch and set down the still-sleeping baby.

He watched her slip into the bedroom, presumably to pack some clothes. She'd seemed increasingly afraid of him on the subway ride. Realistically, there wasn't much he could do to keep from being frightening, but he did feel bad about having to be so harsh with her. Better for her to be frightened than for her to call the club again and attract Olivia's tender attention.

He heard the elevator door open at the end of the hall. Booted feet began to clomp toward the apartment. Tony, or just a neighbor?

He got his answer as a key scrabbled into the lock and the door swung open. Tony jumped in surprise when he saw Mike, and clumsily pulled a Glock-10 semiautomatic out of the pocket of his motorcycle jacket.

S P A R K S   A N D   S H A D O W S

"'The fuck you doing here?" he demanded, pointing the pistol at Mike's head. Tony stank of whisky, and Mike thought he detected the acrid tang of crack smoke.

Great. Julie never mentioned the guy carried a piece. Of course, given the neighborhood, nobody but an idiot would go out alone without protection.

"Calm down, Tony, I'm just here to help the lady get her things. Another minute or two, we'll be gone, out of your hair, you'll have the whole place to yourself." He stepped forward, staring into Tony's bloodshot eyes. He'd never tried mesmerizing a druggie before. Olivia had told him drunks and stoners were trivially easy, but crackheads and speed freaks were liable to spook, snap awake as if from a nightmare and lash out at anything that moved. He couldn't tell what chemical ruled Tony's brain. "Just be calm, and put down the gun."

Tony's eyes glazed, and the nose of the pistol dipped.

"Ohmygod, Tony, put that down!" Julie shrieked, running out of the bedroom.

Tony's eyes snapped wide in disoriented terror, the spell shattered. His finger reflexively jerked on the trigger. Two rounds slammed into Mike's belly. Mike's vision clouded in the bright vortex of pain.

Mike stumbled backward against the wall, numbly staring at the purple blood spilling down his shirt and pants. Would he bleed to death? No, the wounds were already starting to heal.

But he'd lost precious blood. His veins burned with a horrible thirst.

Tony was still firing wildly around the apartment, hollering incoherently. Mike shook off his momentary shock and sprang forward, batting the gun out of Tony's hand. He grabbed Tony by the hair and threw him to the scarred wooden floor.

Tony shrieked and thrashed wildly as Mike's blunt teeth clamped around his throat. But Mike could not be thrown off. In seconds he'd crushed the man's trachea, gnawed open his carotid. The blood came out in a bubbling fountain, and Mike drank 'til he could hold no more.

As he came up for air, he saw himself reflected in Tony's dead eyes. Cold horror extinguished his predatory fury. Sweet Jesus, what had he just done? Behind him, the baby was screaming. He couldn't hear Julie; the girl was probably petrified with terror at what she'd just witnessed.

He fairly sprang away from the corpse, and turned, trying to think of something he could say to her –

Julie was on the floor, dark blood spreading beneath her. He knelt beside her and gently lifted her head. A stray bullet had hit her in the temple. She was dead.

The baby abruptly fell silent, and he felt the hairs on the back of his neck rise.

"Well, you've made a mess of things, haven't you?"

He slowly looked up, his whole body electrified with dread. Olivia was standing in the doorway of the bedroom, a vision in a black lace dress. She'd apparently climbed the fire escape and slipped in through the window. Just to drive home the point that she was far better at this than he, no doubt.

He stood and stepped away from Julie's body, nervously wiping the blood off his face. "How did you find me so quickly?"

"I *made* you, Michael. I could hear the beat of your heart halfway around the world." Smiling sardonically, she glided into the room, delicately lifting her skirts to keep them out of the blood and debris. "In my day, this would be considered the result of blind stupidity, but we live in more enlightened times, don't we? Now this sort of thing is called a 'learning experience.'" She stared at him. "So tell me, Michael, what have you learned tonight?"

"That what you told me was true," he stammered obediently. "That if they're not fit to be converts, mortals are playthings or food. Nothing more."

His stomach churned as he spoke, curdled blood rising in his throat. He didn't believe a word of it, but he dared not anger her further. Though she'd always cooed over his strength, they both knew she was more than a match for him. She was fiendishly fast, and had a century of experience as a murderess; he'd watched her single-handedly disarm (and then eviscerate) a pair from a rival circle who'd broken into the club basement.

"Don't feel too bad, Michael, for I also had a learning experience tonight. I should've heeded your advice to leave little Onyx alone. No great tragedy, true, but I had not intended for her to die so soon. A mistake is a mistake."

Becky gave a low, frightened whimper.

"Ah, but the night's not a total loss," Olivia said, fixing her gaze on the baby. "I do so love little children. Is she yours?"

He paused. "Yes."

"Not any more." She stared at him, her eyes daring him to challenge her.

He could not. She would destroy him, as easily as he'd destroyed Tony. Maybe easier.

But if he let this happen, let her kill a baby who might be his only child, what was the point of his existence? *Fun? Pleasure?* He'd never asked himself those questions before. He'd known the price of joining Olivia was losing his soul. But to let her kill Becky...that would cost him his heart. Mike bowed his head, wondering how many hundreds of children she'd murdered to satisfy her palate.

Out of the corner of his eye, he spotted the pistol lying on the floor. He remembered the shock of the bullets slamming into his own flesh. Maybe there was still a chance.

"I don't care," Mike lied. "Take her."

She smiled and gave a satisfied nod, then turned to the couch to take Becky.

Mike dived sideways, praying the magazine had not been spent, and scooped up the pistol. Olivia turned on him with alarming speed, shrieking in rage. He pointed the Glock at her midsection and furiously pumped the trigger.

Two firecracker pops, then impotent clicking. But he'd hit her. She stepped backward, staring in mute surprise at the ichor-spilling holes below her breasts.

That hesitation was all he needed. He threw the pistol aside and leaped into her, ramming his left hand into her razored jaws as he dug the fingers of his right into her solar plexus.

He'd thought the impact would knock her down, but she stood fast, snarling and slashing his face with her sharp claws. He had to shut his eyes to keep from being blinded. Dear God, she was strong! He shoved his fist deeper into her mouth, and she savagely worried his hand. His fingers broke with an audible popping.

Ignoring the pain, he managed to hook a leg around and kick her feet out from under her. They fell in a heap beside Julie's corpse. The momentum of the fall helped him pierce the skin beneath her breastbone with his fingers. She bucked and thrashed, hammering his head and shoulders with bone-cracking blows as he worked his hand deeper and deeper into her slick, cold flesh. She got her claws around his neck, ready to tear out his throat. His fingers closed around her coarse, pulsing cardiac muscle. He yanked it free.

Her heart came out in a great gout of ichor. Olivia's body convulsed, and then was still. As Mike watched, her dead flesh deliquesced, skin and muscle melting into grayish goo over crumbling black bone. Her heart turned to foul jelly and slipped through his fingers. The stench of rot greased the air.

He stood up, feeling nauseated as the ragged edges of broken bones in his skull and arms scraped against each other. He gingerly explored the lacerations on his face and scalp, thankful he'd been able to kill her before she'd done much more damage. The blood loss made him desperately hungry, but he could endure it until he found a dog or rat. He couldn't bear to dine on the cooling blood in Julie's corpse.

Becky was wailing. What was he going to do with her now? The answer came to him instantly: if his sister had been desperate to take some poor stranger's child, she'd certainly take custody of her only niece.

He wiped the rest of Olivia off on his jeans, then hurried over to the infant.

"Hush," he said, mesmerizing her with his black eyes. "It's okay, I'll take you someplace nice. It's got trees, and a barn, and when you're a little older you can have a puppy, I bet."

Wrinkling his nose in distaste, he poked through Olivia's sodden dress until he found her car keys. The Lincoln was likely parked no more than a few blocks away; Olivia had always hated walking. He shook the keys free and stood up, breathing deeply.

People were making noise out in the hallway. It was only a matter of time before the police arrived. He'd have to sneak out by way of the fire escape, go up and over the building if a crowd had gathered on the street below.

His sister's house was an hour away from the city. He wasn't sure what he'd tell her; the truth would probably work, or most of it. He'd make sure to leave a note granting his sister guardianship. With luck, Becky's first few months in chaos and single evening in Hell wouldn't leave lasting scars. She could grow up with parents who would love her, and she would be free to make her own dreams. He hoped that she'd do better than her biological parents, but if she didn't, well, at least the mistakes would be hers to make.

He washed the gore off his face, hands and arms in the kitchen, then gathered up Becky. His body itched; his flesh and bones were starting to knit. He had strength, he had freedom. And he might just have eternity.

And wherever he ended up, he would make sure his existence *meant* something.

Soul Searching

THE BOOKSHOP'S screen door slammed, jarring Henry Schleicher awake from a sweet dream of the heroes' party he and the other boys from his division got in Honolulu the day the Japs surrendered.

Heart pounding from the shock of waking, cheeks warm from sleep and embarrassment and dream champagne, he rose from his old chair behind the cash register and fumbled for his trifocals.

"What can I do for you..." He trailed off.

The girl stood at the sci-fi shelf, and God Almighty, she was a *looker*. She wore tight, worn-out cutoffs that barely covered up enough to keep her from getting arrested, and she was barefoot. The first three buttons of her black silk blouse were open, and he could see her breasts swaying free under the fabric. Thick hair, as shiny and black as her blouse, hung nearly to her waist. Henry wondered if her hair would feel like silk.

She pulled a paperback off the shelf and held it out accusingly. "What's this doing here?"

She had an accent. Korean? Japanese? He couldn't tell.

"I – I don't know, missy...what is it?"

"*Forbidden Passion*. This is *not* science fiction."

The girl walked up to the cash register, and he caught a whiff of her perfume, a dark musky-rosey scent that made his whole body tingle. She had deep green eyes, like jade, but prettier. The color reminded him of a silk nightie he'd bought his wife when they had honeymooned in San Francisco after the War. She was as tall as he was, and he'd been a big man, six foot three, before old age had shrunk his spine. And the girl didn't look quite as young as he'd first thought. Sure, she still looked like a kid, but hell, everyone under thirty looked like a kid to Henry.

She tossed the book onto the counter. "You ought to put this where it belongs, like in the trash."

He blinked in mute surprise. The girl breezed away to explore other parts of the shop. Her bare feet left prints in the fine dust like smudges of grease on dry wood.

He heard the stairs creak as his wife, Violet, came down the stairs from their bedroom above the shop. When they had married in 1946, Violet had been just nineteen. She had been like a china doll to Henry, a small, delicate treasure of a girl. But Violet had kept adding little layers of fat, year after year, just like a tree adding rings. Now, she was as round and soft as the doughnuts she made for his favorite breakfast.

"Who's that?" Violet stopped at his elbow.

"Just some girl." He winced, knowing what his wife would do next.

Violet walked down the aisle to see for herself. She came back a few seconds later, whispering, "I don't like the looks of that one, Henry. Moment you turn your back, she'll be out of here with as many comics as she can grab."

Henry sighed. "Oh, give it a rest, Violet, she's just looking at books."

"She's dressed like a two-bit whore, and she ain't even wearing shoes," she whispered back, her voice sharp with jealous indignation. "Look at her, her feet are just *filthy*! 'No shoes, no service.' Tell her that, Henry. Get rid of her."

Arguing with Violet about the girl would be a monumental waste of time. Violet's great-grandfather fought the Mexican Army alongside Sam Houston in the Texas Revolution, and her granddaddy rode a thousand miles on a mule to serve under Lee in the Civil War. Her family had always hated foreigners, from Republican carpetbaggers to Cantonese immigrants, and Violet wasn't the kind of woman to break with family tradition.

His wife's prejudices had only cost him sales twice that he could think of: one was a cookbook he would have sold to a black professor from the local college, and the other was a French dictionary he would have sold to a little Filipino girl. He was never sure whether they'd heard Violet's whispers or if they'd simply been driven off by her icy stares. Either way, two books didn't amount to much. He was about to go out into the stacks and start pestering the girl for a sale when she rounded a corner with a volume entitled *War in the Pacific*.

"You gonna buy that?"

"Oh, I guess so. Nothing else in here is very interesting, is it?"

Henry heard Violet mutter something under her breath, but he chose to ignore both females. "That'll be fifteen even."

The girl managed to get two fingers into her pocket and pulled out a crumpled five and ten. She picked up the book, gave Violet a Cheshire cat grin, and left.

"Good riddance!" his wife proclaimed when the front door closed.

But Henry couldn't get the girl off his mind, her perfume, the way she'd looked. He'd always thought Oriental girls were some of the prettiest women in the world. Not that he'd ever told Violet that, of course. But Orientals did tend toward being a little flat-chested, and they were almost always short. Henry had never thought he'd ever see a woman like that girl in the silk blouse. There sure hadn't been any girls like her around in his day.

When they got into bed that night, his good-night kiss was more than his usual cursory peck.

"Well, what's gotten into you?" Violet asked.

"I – I don't know...I just thought, maybe we could..."

"You haven't wanted to do *that* for three years," she sounded suspicious.

"I know, but I'd really like to..." Damn it, why did he always have to beg his own wife to have sex with him?

She'd never seemed to like it much, no matter what he did. There was a lot she'd never let him try. And when she was finally pregnant at thirty-two, the labor was hard and long and their little girl was born dead. After that, she'd often turn him down flat, saying she was tired or had a headache. And after she went through menopause, once a year was about all he could get out of her; it was like trying to negotiate an arms treaty with the Russians.

"Oh, all right," she sighed.

He started to kiss her neck, nibble her earlobes. Violet just lay there, like she always did.

Goddamn it, do something! he wanted to yell at her, but he didn't. He couldn't. After all, he was sixty-seven years old, and his wife was the only woman on the face of the planet who would have an old man like him.

So Henry just closed his eyes as he carefully climbed on top of her and entered her. He tried to pretend that the soft, sagging body beneath him was firm young flesh. He tried to pretend that the thin gray hair he caressed was a long, silken cascade. And as always, his imagination worked, at least as long as his eyes were shut.

Henry was kneeling beside an 18-year-old soldier with a chest full of shrapnel, and he couldn't stop the bleeding. He could hear the Zero making another pass over the island. The kid was dying, no matter what Henry did. The plane was zooming closer, and Henry knew he had to get to cover.

He tried to pull away, but his hands were stuck. Henry looked down at the soldier. The kid had turned into a rotting corpse. Henry was being sucked inside.

He couldn't get free. No matter how he struggled to get away from the horror, it just pulled more of his arms inside, first up to the elbows, then up to his shoulders. Henry had to fight to keep his head out of the nauseating mess. The Jap started firing. The sand exploded in lines heading straight for Henry...

He sat bolt upright in bed, breathing hard. Violet moved sleepily beside him.

"What's the matter, Henry?" she mumbled.

"The Zero...and the kid," he replied, his voice shaking.

Violet rolled over, her back to him. "I thought you stopped having those dreams."

"So did I." His voice nearly broke. Why was it back after forty years? Hadn't seven straight years of the nightmares been enough?

"Prob'ly just a fluke." She was already dozing off again. "Go back to sleep, Henry..."

He lay down, and soon Violet was snoring softly. But he couldn't even close his eyes. The dream had left him with the vague sense that he was about to remember something awful, but every time he tried to probe his memory, he came up against a cold blank wall.

✳

The girl was back the next morning. She was wearing black jeans and a short white T-shirt that showed just a tantalizing hint of her taut belly. Violet was about to go out to her bridge club meeting, but stopped when she saw who had come in.

"Henry, it's *her* again," Violet whispered as the girl began to browse through a set of shelves by the window.

He just wasn't in the mood for this. "Violet, she's just looking at books! Go to your club meeting, and quit being silly!" he whispered back.

"But Henry–"

Whump!

The pair jumped in surprise as the girl dropped a thick textbook on cardiovascular disease onto the counter beside the register.

The girl stared at them, her expression inscrutable behind purple-lensed sunglasses. "Ring me up, would you?"

That night, his dreams carried him to a frozen garden, everything iced solid and white. The pond was a rippled sheet; he could see harlequin goldfish frozen a few inches below the surface. The glorious blooms of bushes and trees were entombed in clear, delicate crystals. He drifted soundlessly over the paths, feeling no chill, just the unnatural stillness.

A savage, gleeful laugh tore the silence, making a chandeliered willow tremble in anticipation. Henry turned to listen.

"Henry..."

The laugh came again.

"Henry, help me..." Violet was calling to him, but her voice sounded far away.

He ran toward the voices and came out of the garden at the edge of an immense lake. A woman in a flowered dress was lying face-down on the ice about a hundred yards from shore. He recognized the dress; it was the one Violet used to wear every Easter.

He ran out across the ice to his wife. When he reached her, he knelt and carefully rolled her over. Violet opened her eyes and smiled at him. He blinked. Violet was young again, as young and pretty as the day they'd married.

"Henry, help me!" Violet suddenly cried, grabbing his arms.

Before his eyes, Violet's face began to bloat, fatten, sag into wrinkles, her blond hair turning dull and gray. The ice began to crack beneath her.

"Help me!" she gasped, grimacing in pain. The grimace froze, and her skin went a grayish white. Her flesh began to wither and blacken and slough away from her bones.

He screamed and pulled away.

The skeleton grabbed his arms again and gave out an angry, piercing shriek.

The ice shattered all around them. Henry was swept down into the black water, down through nets of clinging weeds. The weeds wrapped around him, strangling him, dragging him deeper and deeper into the cold, dark mud...

Henry awoke with a start, fighting the bedclothes that had somehow gotten bunched up around his neck. He threw off the twisted sheets. Shivering, he rolled over to feel the familiar warmth of his wife's body. She wasn't in the bed.

He sat up and looked around. Violet was lying face-up in front of the open window, her body bathed in a pool of moonlight. Dream-lake chill washed over him when he realized that she wasn't breathing.

✳

They buried Violet three days later on the 6th of August. Violet's relatives drove down from Dallas for the funeral. Before the church service, they all stood out in the foyer, comforting Henry.

"At least the heart attack took her right away," said Rudy, Violet's nephew.

"Yes," agreed Judith, Rudy's wife. "Thank the Lord Violet didn't have to suffer. Her cousin Rose spent her last fifteen years in the nursing home after her stroke." She shook her head. "Bad circulation. Runs in the family."

Their little girl, Vicki, began to cry and pull at the pink bow in her white-blond hair.

"Judy, give the kid a lollipop and see if that doesn't quiet her down," Rudy said, frowning absently.

She rummaged through her purse and came up with a lemon sucker of the variety given out at banks. The crying ended as quickly as it had begun.

"She's a little cranky from the car trip," Judith said apologetically, glancing at her husband.

"You still running that book shop out of the first floor of your house?" Rudy asked.

"Yeah, I guess I'm gonna run it 'til the day I die," Henry replied numbly. "My daddy would have wanted it that way. Sorta makes up for me disappointing him by not going to college like he wanted, I guess."

He'd planned to go to college and become an engineer after he got out of the Army, but the War changed everything, made all his ambitions seem small and pointless. He'd been able to keep himself together long enough to marry Violet, have a nice honeymoon and get settled in a job at a hardware store, but nine months after the war ended his nightmares began. He lost his job, and for the next seven years the dreams left him a numb husk of a man, useless for anything but sweeping out his father's bookshop. Violet suffered him more or less silently, but his parents were genuinely patient with their only child and supported him and Violet until he got healthy. After all that, he felt obligated to take over the shop when his father died, even though he really had little interest in books.

He sighed. "You know, I never thought anything like this would happen. I always thought she was gonna outlive me."

He shivered, recalling Violet's transformation in his nightmare. He felt the horrible almost-memory gnawing at the back of his brain. He didn't *want* to remember any more, but somehow knew he had to get past that cold obsidian barrier in his head. But what in God's name was his mind going to churn out when the wall came down?

In the silence, little Vicki decided that she was tired of her lollipop. She pulled it out of her mouth and threw it at Henry. The sucker stuck to the cuff of his black slacks.

"Vicki!" Judith exclaimed, her cheeks flushing pink.

"Aw, it's okay. Little kids do stuff like that." He bent down and peeled the lollipop off his cuff. Judith took it from him, wrapped it in a Kleenex, and stuck it back into her purse.

Vicki was staring up at Henry with big blue eyes, wiping her sticky fingers on the front of her pink jumper. Henry had always imagined that his own little girl had pretty blue eyes like that, but the doctor hadn't let him see her. It was a damned strange world back then; he'd lived through a war where he'd seen men get blown to hamburger, and some country doctor decides he couldn't take the sight of his stillborn baby girl.

Then again, maybe the guy had been right.

❄

After he'd seen everybody off in Rudy's Dodge Caravan, Henry drove home alone in his old Buick. The day almost seemed like fall rather than summer; the sky was a deeper blue than usual and the smell of burning mesquite chips from someone's barbecue was faint in the air.

When he reached the house, he found the girl leaning against the shop door.

His heart started to beat a little faster. "The shop's not open today, missy."

"I read about your wife in the paper today," she replied. "I'm sorry."

"Yeah," Henry mumbled, running his hands over his thinning gray hair.

S P A R K S   A N D   S H A D O W S

She was still standing there, looking at him like she wanted something. Maybe he should politely ask her to leave, so he could mourn for Violet by himself like he was supposed to.

Problem was, he didn't *want* the girl to leave. Just the smell of her perfume made him as warm and dizzy as if he'd downed a triple bourbon. As he unlocked the door, he wondered if one night of sex with the girl would make up for forty-five years of disappointment.

"My mother died on this day," the girl announced as she followed him inside.

"Uh, yeah? What, uh, what happened to her?"

"My brother. She died while she was trying to give birth to him." The girl stared at Henry, then went over to the child care shelf and pulled out a book of baby names. "Of course, she's got plenty of company; today's the day you guys nuked Hiroshima. Hell must have an incredible maternity ward."

You guys. Henry felt his cheeks grow hot. "Look here, Missy, I don't like the sound of what you just said. I fought in that war, I watched my buddies die in the mud, and as far as I'm concerned, the A-bombs they dropped on Japan were gifts from *Heaven*," he told her harshly. "They *ended* it. The Japs weren't going to stop. If it hadn't been for the Bomb, millions of soldiers, ours *and* theirs, would have been killed."

"As opposed to the hundred thousand helpless women and children who were burned alive."

"Jesus Christ, don't come in here spouting all that revisionist crap at me! Your people started the whole friggin' mess at Pearl Harbor, and I don't see any liberal hearts bleeding over the innocent boys who died in that cheap shot of a sneak attack!"

"Innocent?" She gave him a cold glare. "They were soldiers, and soldiers are *never* innocent. And there's no real proof it stopped the war. The rice crop sucked that year, and you guys had already torched most of the other cities. Hirohito wanted to end it. There was no good reason to release Fat Man and Little Boy."

"You weren't there, you don't know what you're talking about!" He shook his head in exasperation. "Jesus, and you keep saying 'you guys' like I was personally involved. You may as well blame me for the bombing of Dresden. Hell, while you're at it, blame me for the concentration camps! My granddaddy was German, I'm sure I'm responsible for it all *somehow*!"

The girl's eyes were filled with bleak anger and sadness. "If they'd simply needed to deal out another atrocity, they could have slaughtered everyone just as thoroughly with normal bombs, like they did with Tokyo. But they wanted to see how their evil new toy would work, and it's Pandora's Box all over again. And you *are* a part of it, whether you wanted to be or not."

She looked down at the book of baby names in her hand. "236,962 souls burned away. Did you know that all the babies that were stillborn after the bombings are still around, in buckets of formaldehyde in a lab someplace? I saw a picture of one in a magazine once; a scientist was holding it, gently, almost like you would a live baby, only it was this gray, shriveled-up thing. Could you imagine that, having to exist for eternity in a bucket of formaldehyde?"

Henry felt sick. "Get outta here."

She held up the book. "I need to buy this."

"Then give me ten bucks and get out, and don't come back!"

That night, sleep took Henry to the hospital corridor beside the delivery room where Violet had been in labor for sixteen hours. Henry heard her cry out, and then he heard a baby start squalling. The doctor pushed through the white door, pulling his cloth mask down around his neck. His white scrubs were spattered with blood. Henry stood up, waiting to hear the news.

"I'm sorry, Mr. Schleicher," the doctor said evenly. "The baby is dead."

Henry could still hear his daughter wailing in the delivery room. "What are you trying to pull?" he demanded. "The hell she's dead, I can hear her crying. Let me see her."

He tried to go to the delivery room door, but the doctor blocked his way. "Your daughter is dead, Mr. Schleicher. It would be better if you just stayed in here."

He shoved the doctor away and pushed into the delivery room, calling to his wife.

The world exploded in a blossoming chrysanthemum of boiling smoke and flame. Blinded by the heat, Henry fell to his knees as a fiery wind roared in his ears.

The fire abruptly evaporated. He found himself lying on a vast plain of wreckage. He got to his feet and looked around. Steel girders fused by terrible heat rose up around him. White ash covered everything and floated in the sky like snow. There was no sound except the hollow whistling of the wind going past a jutting metal edge.

"What are you doing here, Yankee?"

He turned. A Japanese woman stood a few yards away from him. She was burned all over, face a mess of char and blisters, clothes in carbon tatters, fingers blackened stumps.

"I – I was looking for my wife, and my baby girl..."

"All the women and children here are dead."

He was suddenly aware that he could hear an infant whimpering somewhere nearby. "But that crying, I think that's my little girl...I've got to find her."

"You seek your daughter? Why should you find her here, when the fire you brought has taken my own child from my body?" He saw that she held a tiny, charred body in her ruined hands.

"But I didn't *do* this." The wailing was getting stronger. "Look, I've got to find her," He insisted, fear pulling at his throat. "She's the only child I'll ever have."

"And this was my only daughter!" the woman shouted, holding up the little corpse. "Look around, Yankee, this is the only legacy you will leave!"

The hidden baby began to scream, louder and louder, suffocating his mind with noise. The screeching went up, up, held one long note until –

Henry popped wide awake as his hand went down on his buzzing alarm clock. The room was warm from the morning sun, but Henry couldn't stop shivering.

✳

The girl came in around noon the next day, barefoot, dressed in her cutoffs and a tissue-thin white tee that clung damply to her breasts. Her face and arms were sheened with sweat, staining the canvas book bag slung under her left arm.

He stood up, ready to order her out. But the look on her face killed the words in his throat, made him shiver to the core of his soul.

She had the spooky, unnatural grin he'd seen on the faces of shell-shocked soldiers who'd cracked to the point of endlessly giggling at the horrors they'd seen. Her eyes were glassy, and he wondered if she were sick, or on drugs.

"I came to apologize, Henry." Her words came out in a breathless rush as she stepped toward the cash register. "I was a bitch, wasn't I? Shouldn't be bitchy to a nice old man like you. So very nice."

The scent of her rose perfume was thick in the air, but under it was the faint stink of sulfur and scorched metal.

"I mean, I can't be *mad* about what happened, can I?" she asked. "You guys fixed Japan up so nice afterward, and put in bases to protect us...my own father was a G.I., and if not for the Bomb...I wouldn't even be here, and I should be *glad* to be alive, huh, Henry?"

He was sure the girl was utterly out of her mind. "What do you want from me?" he stammered, starting to inch toward the telephone mounted a few yards away on the wall. For the first time in forty years, he wished he owned a gun; after the War, he'd given his deer rifles to his cousin and had not touched a firearm since.

"I want what everybody wants...that special someone who'll make me...*complete*. I feel so alone, and I think you do, too. Are you the man I'm looking for? I said yesterday that you're a part of things, but I've got to make sure..."

She lunged forward and pinned him to the wall. He struggled and hollered for help, but her arms were iron. She pressed her body against his. He couldn't help but thrill at the feel of her silky hair tickling his neck, her hard nipples brushing his chest.

"Shh, I'm not going to hurt you. Just relax."

She started to kiss his neck, and her right hand slid down his body to rest over his fly. He squeezed his eyes shut. Trapped between terror and lust, he could do nothing but moan as she unzipped his pants and pulled him free.

When she went down on him, a blue shower of sparks exploded behind his eyes. Oh, dear God in Heaven, Violet had *never* done this, never would have done it if he'd begged and pleaded, oh dear *God!*

"Who...who *are* you?" he gasped raggedly.

He felt the buzz of the girl's muffled laugh, and she bobbed faster and faster against him to match the slamming of his heart, and suddenly a part of him was afraid he'd have a coronary then and there, but the rest told him this was not a bad way to go –

He came, a hot, sweet explosion that rocked his whole body, buckled his knees and turned his mind to stunned mush.

He felt the girl pull away, and he slid down the wall to lie in a sweaty

S P A R K S   A N D   S H A D O W S

heap. When he finally realized he hadn't, in fact, had a stroke or heart attack, he opened his eyes and fumbled his pants back on.

The girl was gone, but a book entitled *The Myths of Japan* lay on the floor a few yards away. She'd taped a note to the front cover: "Can you guess my name?"

Trembling, he crawled to the book and opened it at the page she'd marked. He began to read about Izanami, mother of the gods, who became ruler of the underworld after she'd burned to death giving birth to Kagu-tsuchi, the god of fire.

When he finally stopped reading, his whole body was filled with cold dread. He climbed to his feet, joints creaking like rusty gates, got his checkbook and car keys and drove out to the local gun shop. A few hours later, he returned home with a shiny new Smith & Wesson pistol and a box of 9 mm hollow-point bullets. As he loaded the gun and set it on his bedside table, he sorely hoped he wouldn't have to use it.

✳

His best friend's chest exploded in a crimson spray. The young soldier fell twitching in the sandy mud. Henry helplessly tried to do something, *anything*, for him with the pathetic canvas medical kit. His buddy's eyes rolled up into his head as he let out an awful wet noise. Then he was dead.

Henry dropped the kit and stared over their sheltering coconut log at the Japanese machine gun nest. The Japs were still firing, black smoke snaking from the slits in the bone-pale concrete bunker. He looked down at the sticky blood on his hands, at the black flies that were already crawling over his buddy's wounds.

His field of vision started to twitch in time with his pounding heart, and bile rose hot in his throat. Those filthy yellow cockroaches were gonna pay for this. He grabbed his M1 rifle and a grenade and vaulted over the log. Screaming at the top of his lungs, he pounded across the clearing. He felt lances of fire slash his shoulder, his thigh, as he pulled the grenade pin and hurled it into one of the black slits.

The percussive gust nearly knocked him down, but as soon as the orange bloom of fire died he kicked open the door and fired a half-dozen rounds into the bunker. When no one returned fire, he jumped down inside.

A half-dozen Japs lay sprawled on the concrete floor, faces and bodies torn apart from shrapnel. Then he heard a ragged moan and saw one of them start rolling around. The Jap was maybe sixteen or seventeen, his face a blood-speckled mask of shock. His close-cut hair looked like the down of a black duckling.

In two strides Henry was on the Jap and bashed his face in with the butt of his rifle.

"Ah, truly the deed of a *mighty* warrior!" came a laugh behind him.

Henry whirled around, but found his arms were paralyzed, his rifle useless.

One of the corpses rose, and in the dimness he initially thought it was a man dressed all in black. But when it stepped into a shaft of sunlight, he saw it was a naked woman, her whole body charred almost beyond recognition, cooked flesh peeling from the bones of her face and hands. Her eyes were bright amber, live coals glowing in the ruin of her face.

She raised a hand, and his dog tags slithered up his chest. The chain jerked tight, then broke, leaving a stinging track on his neck. The tags flew into her open palm.

"Henry Schleicher, a corporal," she read aloud. "You please me. You've sent many souls to my realm today. Now you'll drop your weapon and please me *more*."

Henry's hands released the rifle and he staggered backward to fall against a pile of bodies in the corner. To his utter horror, he realized he had an erection, and the woman was coming for him, her grin baring rows of gray shark's teeth...

Henry woke with a moan, then had to lurch out of bed to be sick in the bathroom. As he washed his face, parts of the dream replayed themselves in his head. *That* was what he had been blocking so long, the mother of all his nightmares.

He realized he'd had it once before, when he was recovering in the hospital in Honolulu. His buddies had carried him out of the bunker; he'd escaped his crazed charge with a bad case of shock and a few superficial gunshot wounds. They all said God must have been looking out for him. He got a Purple Heart and a Silver Star, but nobody ever found his dog tags.

"Can you guess my name?"

His heart froze. The girl stood beside his bed. Her slim body was shoehorned into torn, faded jeans, a black tee shirt, and tall boots. She'd cut off all her hair, buzz-cut it nearly to the bone.

"How'd you get in here?" he stammered, blushing at the hard-on

S P A R K S   A N D   S H A D O W S

straining against the elastic waistband of his pajamas. He crossed his hands in front of his fly.

"What, you won't even *guess*? You're no fun," she pouted. "Anyhow, I'm Miko, and I'll be your demon for the evening."

"How'd you get in here?" he repeated.

She nodded toward the open window. "Climbed your ivy. Same as when I came for your wife."

It took a moment for the implication of her words to sink in. His guts turned to ice. "You...you killed Violet."

Another nod. "She was distracting. Not very satisfying, though; I had to kill an old man in a nursing home today, just to make sure I'd be halfway sane when I came here tonight."

He couldn't keep from staring at the gun on the table. There was no way he could get to it before Miko did.

She followed his gaze. "Is that for me, Henry? You can't kill me, you know...thanks to dear ol' mom, I have no soul. What'd my mother look like when she raped you, Henry? Burned or wormy or what?"

"Your moth– oh dear God." The room started swimming before his eyes.

"She looks like a big smoke cloud now. She and my brother were fighting over the souls in the War, and Kagu-tsuchi tricked her into being at Hiroshima when Little Boy blew," the girl continued. "Did you know that the mother's responsible for giving her child a soul? Kind of an automatic thing, usually, but since mine's the Queen of the Dead, she gave me a jones for murder, instead. Mother likes 'em young, and so she made sure I'd send plenty of kids her way."

She sat down on the edge of his bed and gave him a grim smile. "I guess you could say my soul is on layaway; I get it as soon as I've made up for what my brother took from my mother. Kagu-tsuchi gets the souls of people who burn to death, and at Hiroshima and Nagasaki that was pretty much everyone. Mother was really angry about losing the souls, not to mention being vaporized, so I have to match the A-bomb body count: 236,962 people. And since I can't use fire, bombs and guns are out, so I pretty much have to take lives one by one. So far I've only managed to send off 538. At this rate, I won't be done for another twenty thousand years."

She rubbed her face. "I wish you guys had just nuked *one* city, a much *smaller* city. I'd be lying if I told you killing wasn't a kick, but I'm ready to do something else for a change, you know?"

"Why...why are you telling me this?" he asked.

"Because you can get me out of this. You're my father, and if you willingly give me your soul, I'm freed from my birth curse."

She seemed absolutely, horrifyingly sincere, but Henry reminded himself she *had* to be insane, or some sicko getting her kicks at his expense.

"Why should I believe this crazy story of yours?" he demanded nervously. "All that was just a dream I had, and you're just playing with my head. I...I can't *possibly* be your father."

She dug into her pocket, pulled out a silver chain and flipped it through the air. "Catch."

He caught the chain. Two dog tags lay in his palm, gleaming like razor blades. They bore his name, rank and number. The metal was flecked with brownish gunk that might have been blood or rust or both. He turned the tags over and saw the crude American eagle he'd etched with his pocket knife in a fit of barracks boredom. His heart dropped to the soles of his feet.

"Where did you get this?"

"Mother likes to play games. She gave me a box full of hundreds of dog tags a few decades ago, and told me one of them belonged to my father. I've blown a lot of old men, Henry, and you're the only one who tasted of my mother's poison."

Her mother's poison.

Miko met his mortified stare. "I'd always expected my father would be a man who was responsible in some concrete way, maybe Oppenheimer or the pilot of the *Enola Gay* or *somebody*, but it was just you," she said quietly. "You didn't ask for this, but neither did *I*. And if you don't give me your soul, nearly a quarter of a million people are going to get something they didn't ask for, either."

She stood up and went to the window.

"Do I have a choice?" he stammered.

"You have all the choice in the world. Your soul's no good to me if I have to take it by force. If you want to give me and everybody else a chance at a normal life, you'll meet me tomorrow at midnight on top of Mount Nebo. Otherwise, you can just stay here, and I won't bother you again. By the taste of you, I'd say you'll live to a ripe old age, maybe even see one hundred."

S P A R K S A N D S H A D O W S

She swung a leg over the window sill. "I guess it all depends on whether you're still willing to die for your country or not."

And then she was gone.

＊

At dawn, Henry was still awake, staring down at the gun and the dog tags that lay in his lap. Miko *had* to be crazy. The nightmare about the bunker was just that – a nightmare. And Violet died of a heart attack. Perfectly natural causes.

There was no way the girl could be his daughter. He already *had* a daughter, and if she'd survived she'd be living in one of one of the tidy houses down the street, married to a banker or maybe a doctor, and she'd be a teacher at the local elementary school. And she'd have given him two or three grandkids, towheaded little sprites who'd come over for stories and milk and cookies and comic books, and the house would be filled with their laughter instead of this awful empty silence –

Henry's eyes were burning. No frigging way Miko was *his* daughter.

Problem was, he couldn't deny that the dog tags were his. He stared down at the chain draped across his knee. How had the girl gotten hold of them?

Maybe she wasn't crazy. Maybe one of the Nips had survived and taken his tags back to Japan, where he passed them to one of the dead soldiers' families as a revenge heirloom. That *had* to be it; she'd cooked up this wild story to get him to go out to the boonies so she could nail him for killing her grandfather or uncle or whoever.

He should call the police, let them deal with her.

But when he got up to call them on the phone, he started thinking about the time he and Violet had been robbed downtown. They'd been coming out of the bank when some kid grabbed her purse and took off through the city park. A dull-eyed deputy came and took a few lazy notes as Henry and Violet described the thief. The deputy told them he'd "get right on it," but no arrest was ever made.

If the local sheriff's department couldn't handle a straightforward purse-snatching, how could they possibly take care of slippery Miko? Hell, the cops might not even believe his story; they might think *he* was the crazy one.

Maybe he should just ignore it all and stay at his house that night. But what if she got mad, and came for him again? Worse yet, what if she'd seen his in-laws come to the house, and decided to go after Rudy and Judith and little Vicki?

What was he going to do?

He took a shower, dressed and went downstairs to make coffee and microwave his breakfast. For the past few days, he'd been living on the baked chicken and casseroles Judith brought him before the funeral. He knew how to barbecue and mix drinks, but beyond that he was lost in the kitchen. He'd tried to fry an egg once, but he'd burned it to a black mess that he'd had to chisel out of the skillet with a steak knife.

When his drumstick and corn casserole was warm, he poured himself a mug of instant coffee and sat down at the kitchen table to eat. He stared into his mug, the coffee shining black like Miko's hair, and suddenly he could almost feel her lips on him, the heat of her body...

He tried to put her out of his mind as he ate. His efforts failed miserably, and between Miko and his lack of sleep he was supremely distracted as he opened up the shop.

When a local schoolteacher came in to buy a gift certificate, he botched three of them before he finally wrote everything down right. Later, a woman came in to buy an armload of romances, and he gave her a dollar too much change. A couple of construction workers came in shortly before noon to look over the pornography Henry kept in a back room. After they left, he realized one of them had shoplifted a deck of girlie cards right under his nose.

This just wouldn't do. Henry put up the "Closed" sign, locked his doors and went upstairs to take a quick nap. Maybe a little more sleep would clear his head.

The bunker nightmare came to him almost instantly. Instead of mercifully ending before the burned goddess took him, it played through to the horrible end.

He woke with a scream. He lurched to the bathroom to lose his breakfast, then tore off his clothes and got in the shower. He scrubbed his body red, his skin crawling at the memory of those skeletal hands, those vile, cracked lips, the breath hot and stinking of a thousand corpses.

When he finally ran out of hot water, he stepped from the shower and shambled into the bedroom to get dressed. He saw himself in the bureau mirror, his face a bad grey, eyes red and glassy. How could something that felt so real be just a dream?

He opened the top drawer of the bureau, took out the tray that held all his old medals and ribbons and stared down at them. The tray told him he'd been a hero, once, and like his daddy always told him, heroes took care of business, never shied away from what had to be done.

He felt cold deep in his bones. If Miko had been telling him the truth, he had to deal with her, had to stop her from killing anyone else. But how could he stop a demon?

He went downstairs and re-read the Japanese mythology book, pored over the entries on Izanami's other deadly child, the god of fire. If the gods truly feuded as Miko claimed they did, then Kagu-tsuchi wouldn't want his little sister to complete her task. If all this was real, then he ought to be able to contact the god of fire, somehow.

After much pondering, Henry went to his bedroom and arranged his medals in a big glass ashtray. He carried it down to the kitchen, set it on the counter, cracked open a bottle of brandy he'd been saving for company and sloshed the liquor over the decorations. Part of his brain hollered at him for wasting good booze and ruining family heirlooms, but the rest reminded him that he had no real blood relatives left to inherit his treasures...except Miko, if she was telling the truth. And if she was, then contacting the god was a hell of a lot more important than a few medals.

"Okay, Kagu-tsuchi, if you're out there, tell me what to do," he muttered, then lit a match and threw it in the ashtray.

It blazed bright, and he stared into the flames. The Silver Star began to blacken, and the ribbons crackled as they caught fire. The crackling got louder, and suddenly he heard a hissing voice inside his head:

"While the mother survived, the daughter shall die."

The fire grew hotter, brighter, and suddenly the ashtray exploded. Henry stumbled back, momentarily blinded, eyebrows singed.

When the gray afterimage finally faded, he saw that the ashtray and medals were scorched slag, a black, bubbled mess melting into his counter top.

At eleven-thirty that night, he stood before the mirror again, now dressed in his old Army uniform. The seat of his pants sagged and his belly bulged around the waistband, but the fit wasn't that bad, considering.

He slipped the shiny Smith & Wesson and a road flare into the left pocket of his jacket. Then he carefully slid a mason jar filled with homebrew napalm into his right pocket. He'd made the jellied gasoline that afternoon by soaking packing peanuts in gas; he hoped he'd made enough, hoped the jar wouldn't leak.

He headed downstairs to his old Buick. It was a hot night, so he turned the AC up high as he drove. Mount Nebo was fifteen minutes outside town, hardly a mountain but certainly largest bump in the flatland for miles. A local rancher had lived on Mount Nebo for a few decades, but five years ago his house had been hit by lightning during a drought and burned down, killing him and his family. Somebody back East had inherited the land, but nobody ever came out to do anything with it.

As he turned up the farm road toward Nebo, he saw the ruined chimney and walls silhouetted against the full moon. Below, he saw a flickering light, maybe a campfire? He parked the car off the road, clicked on his flashlight and began to hike up the hill.

He had to pause midway to massage the rusty ache in his knees, and was wheezing badly by the time he reached the top. His shirt was sodden with sweat. When the blood stopped roaring in his ears, he realized he could hear Miko singing nearby, too softly for him to make out any words, but the sound sent an electric buzz through his chest and loins.

No. She was his enemy, and he had to stop her. He pulled out the Mason jar and unscrewed the lid with shaking hands, then hobbled around the weathered hunks of burnt wood and cinder blocks to find Miko.

He turned a corner into what might have been a bedroom, and his breath caught in his throat. Miko was dancing naked on a red blanket surrounded by dozens of candles, from tiny white votives to slim tapers to enormous three-wick cylinders. The thin flames curled and flickered in the hot night breeze, and Miko's dance mimicked them, her body twisting and rippling, the light gleaming on her hair, her breasts, her taut arms and legs. Maybe she had more muscles than he'd been brought up to think a woman ought to have, but she was the most beautiful thing he'd ever seen. The words to her serpentine melody were Japanese, but he understood the message: *Come to me, my love.*

He wanted more than anything to go to her, to touch that wonderful body, but he knew what he had to do. She was the enemy. Swallowing nervously, he pulled out the road flare and sparked it against a piece of cinderblock.

Miko stopped singing and turned to him, eyes wide.

"No! Put that stuff down, you don't know what—" she began, rushing toward him.

S P A R K S   A N D   S H A D O W S

Heart hammering, he slung the Mason jar at her. She knocked it away, but jellied gasoline splattered on her arm, her breasts, her face. She started screaming even before he threw the flare.

She virtually exploded. Her flesh seemed eager to burn. Henry watched, transfixed in horror, as her hair ignited like flash paper, her skin crisping and peeling, fat and muscle sizzling and popping under the burning napalm. Howling, she frantically beat at the flames spreading across her body. She stumbled backward into the candles and collapsed.

The air was thick with the smoke from her burning flesh. Bile rose in Henry's throat as he watched her thrashing, scattering her candles, fighting the flames that had already destroyed her lovely eyes, her skin, her fingers. He wanted to turn away, but found he could not even shut his eyes.

Finally, her howling fell to a whimper, and then the whimper faded into the crackling of the dying flames. Henry realized he was crying, realized he could move again. He turned and staggered away, wishing he'd brought a handkerchief to cover his mouth and nose, wondering if he'd be able to keep from blowing out his brains when he got back to his empty house.

"Father, please don't leave me like this..."

Oh dear God.

He turned, and saw Miko's corpse stir in the ashes and congealing candle wax. Her face was that of Death, eyes and nose black holes, charred scalp peeling away from red bone. He wondered how she could still speak, how she could still be alive.

"Where are you?" She tried to raise herself up on an elbow, but couldn't. "Please, not like this...Kagu-tsuchi won't take me. Neither will my mother. No one will come for me. When my bones rot away I will still be trapped here."

She made a choking noise, and her whole body started to spasm. It took him a moment to realize she was sobbing.

Dear God, what had he done? Not even Satan himself deserved what he'd done to Miko. To his own daughter. Heroes didn't burn beautiful women alive, didn't damn them to an eternity of agony in a wasteland. He squeezed his eyes shut against the hot tears streaming down his face.

"Father, please..."

Heart hammering madly, he turned and made his way through the wreckage to Miko.

L U C Y   A   S N Y D E R

"What can I do?" he stammered.

"Take me in your arms."

Swallowing against a wave of nausea, knees creaking, he got down on the ground and lay down beside her. She slid a hand across his chest and wriggled close to him, her skin crackling with every movement.

He stared at the full moon overhead, his vision twitching with every beat of his heart.

She kissed his cheek, her lips dry and hard. A cold thrill coursed through his body. He felt his heart stutter, then cramp down. The pain was exquisite.

Miko pulled him tight, her breath hot and ragged in his ear. As he gasped for air, he felt a strange tugging in his chest, his crotch, his mind. Something deep inside started to peel free.

"Oh yes, please, yes..." she whispered.

His soul tore free. Her body convulsed against his, and she let out a hoarse, animal groan of delight.

As his vision began to fade, he turned his head and saw fresh skin spreading across her face and body, new eyes blooming open in her sockets.

Before the cold blackness engulfed him, he felt her gently kiss his forehead. Her lips were soft as funeral roses.

"Thank you," was all she said.

Forgetting

THREE DAYS after Elissa buried her daughter's pet Labrador, Corky, she awoke to find the dog on the foot of her bed. Blood-muddy dirt clods matted his fur, and several broken ribs protruded from his skin where the UPS truck's front tire had slammed into his body. Soil was impacted in the broken ends of the bones. Elissa screamed and scrambled out of bed.

The dog jerked awake, woofing in fright. Then he spotted Elissa and jumped off the bed to cower against her knees as he always did when he was scared.

Oh sweet Jesus, did I bury the poor thing alive? she wondered, then reached down tentatively to stroke the dog's head. He nuzzled her hand, licked her fingers. His tongue and gums were a greenish-gray, and his breath stank of dirt and rot.

Elissa's entire body broke out in a rash of chill, and it was all she could do to keep from keeling over in a dead faint.

"C-corky, stay. Stay in here," she stammered, inching toward the door. There were muddy paw prints on her cream-colored carpet. "Stay. That's a good dog."

She slammed the door shut behind her and ran down the hall toward her daughter's bedroom. Elissa's only thought was that they had to get out of the house, fast. She burst into the room only to discover that her daughter Melanie's bed was empty, the teddy bear bed sheets a rumpled ball at the foot of the bed. She realized she could hear her daughter laughing in the kitchen.

Elissa was trying to remember where she'd put her car keys as she pelted down the hall into the kitchen...and slid to a dead stop.

Her daughter was still in her pink footed pajamas, sitting on a stool at the breakfast table, giggling. The frozen chicken Elissa had been thawing in the fridge was *dancing* on the Saturday morning paper in front of the little girl. The headless, gutless, clammy-pale chicken was hopping and cavorting on its stumps of legs. The paper was soaked through with water and blood from the thawed bird. It did a clumsy, teetering pirouette, and the little girl clapped her hands with glee.

"Melanie, honey, come over here," Elissa said weakly, her voice shaking so hard she could barely speak. "Get – get away from that thing and come here."

Melanie looked over at her mother, her smile fading as she saw the terror on her mother's face.

"Mommy, it's okay. This is my new pet. I'm gonna call him Stumpy. After I fixed Corky this morning, I realized Stumpy was looking so sad and cold in the fridge. I wanted to fix him, too. Can I keep him for a pet, Mommy, please?" Melanie wheedled.

"Oh God...no." Elissa took a few steps backward, bumping into the fridge. She felt sick and lightheaded and didn't know whether to faint or vomit.

"But he won't eat much. He hasn't got a head," the little girl pointed out.

This has to be a bad dream, Elissa thought, screwing her eyes shut and pinching herself and taking deep breaths. *Gotta wake up.* She took another deep breath, and realized she could smell blood from the chicken and dirt from the dog. She never smelled things in her dreams.

Shit, this is real. Got to get a grip, Elissa told herself.

"Melanie, honey, what do you mean you 'fixed' Corky?"

The little girl gazed up at her mother, her big blue eyes round and worried. "Well, you were really sad when that man didn't watch where he was going and ran over Corky. I was really sad, and even the man was really sad. And I know Corky was sad to hurt so bad like that. So when I woke up this morning, I thought I could make things better. You've been so sad, Mommy, ever since Daddy went away. I didn't want you to be sad anymore. I know Corky looks kinda ooky right now, but he'll get better. We can give him a bath. And you can put a patch on the spots where he's torn, like you did with my rag doll after Corky chewed her up. Maybe you can use that pink cloth you used before. That way Corky and the doll will match, and everyone will be happy!"

Melanie started chanting "Happy, happy, happy." She grabbed the chicken and started hopping around the room with it.

"Melanie, stop it!" Elissa screamed.

The little girl stopped and dropped the chicken, her mouth a small "O" of worry. The chicken hit the floor with a damp slap and hobbled away on its stumps to hide under the breakfast table.

"These animals are dead, honey," Elissa said, trying to keep her voice steady. "How can you make them move like this?"

"Did I do something wrong, Mommy?"

"How did you do this?" her mother demanded.

"Well, they told us all about souls in Sunday school, and it just sort of made sense. When the body gets hurt too bad, the soul doesn't want to stay. So I figured if I loved Corky enough, as much as I love you, maybe he'd forget about all the hurt and his soul would come back. So I went out and dug him up, and thought about how much I loved him and wanted him to forget the hurt. And he came back. So then I wondered if I could do it again, and I saw Stumpy in the fridge..."

Melanie trailed off, staring at her mother uncertainly. "Did I do something bad?"

"Yes. Yes, this is *very* bad, Melanie. You mustn't ever do it again, do you understand?" her mother said.

"But Mommy...remember what the doctor said about Daddy's heart being bad? He might get a heart 'tack. And then I could go visit him at the cemetery, and love him, and make him forget all about the bad in his heart and forget about wanting to be with that lady he went away with."

She stared down at her feet. "I – I know it's my fault he went away. I wasn't good enough. If I'd been good, he wouldn't have wanted to go away. But if I love him enough when they've put him in the ground, he'll forget everything but us and come back and we can be happy."

The little girl's eyes were pleading. Despite the abject horror that sat in the pit of her stomach like a cinderblock, Elissa thought her heart was going to break. She took Melanie's chicken-sticky hand, drew her close and gave her a hug.

"Honey, I know you were just trying to help. I know you just wanted to make everyone happy. But this – this isn't right. It goes against what God tells us. God didn't mean for things to live on after they've died. He meant for their souls to go to Heaven. We all have to try to do what God wants, Melanie."

She gently kissed her daughter's forehead. "Honey, can you put them back like they were?"

"I think so, but–"

"No 'buts', Honey, dead things have to stay dead. It's God's will."

Tears spilled down the little girl's cheeks. "All right, Mommy. I can make everyone remember the hurt. Their souls will go away again."

Melanie closed her eyes.

And Elissa remembered her hurt.

Her mind was suddenly flooded with the memory of her last conversation with her husband. She'd called him right after his lawyer had served her the divorce papers; it would be three more weeks before Corky got run over.

"Why are you doing this to me?" she'd asked him, her tone pleading, accusing.

"The marriage was a mistake, and you know it." Ed's tone was cold, so unlike the voice of the man she'd fallen in love with. The man she'd thought she'd married. "I never wanted a kid. Hell, she doesn't even look like me."

"What are you saying?" Her voice flared bright with anger. "You got a lot of nerve suggesting that, after going off with that little bitch of yours. I've always been faithful to you, and Melanie is very much your daughter." She stopped, trying to sound less angry, less accusing. "She's your daughter, and she loves you. She needs you. Don't do this to her."

"I'll send the child support checks. Don't expect anything else. And stop phoning me. If you want to tell me something, talk to my lawyer."

The line went dead. Elissa sat there clutching the phone to her breast, tears stinging in her eyes. Her body ached to feel Ed's caress, to feel his body breathing next to hers, the rise and fall of his chest like the gentle swell of the ocean waves.

But Elissa was just so much unwanted furniture to him, an expense to be paid off and forgotten like a parking ticket. He didn't even want his own daughter. And yet she couldn't stop loving him, couldn't stop wanting him, would crawl naked over broken glass if only he'd just come back and love her, just a little.

She was overcome by a horrible emptiness, a lonely, cancerous ache in her chest and bones. The sorrow boiled out of her in hard, wracking sobs. If she couldn't have him, then she wanted to forget. All she wanted was to forget.

She found her bottle of Valium in the bedside table, and went into the kitchen to unlock the liquor cabinet. Of all the men in her life, Jack Daniels was the only one who'd never let her down...

Elissa came out of the memory to realize that her throat and lungs were on fire and her mouth was filled with the bitter acid taste of vomit and whiskey. She tried to take a breath, but couldn't. Her tortured lungs were filled with the stuff. She fell to her knees on the kitchen floor as her world started to go black.

"You drank too much, Mommy," Melanie said, crying. "I woke up in the morning and found you on your bed. You were all blue and cold. You'd gotten sick in the night and couldn't breathe. I didn't want you to be dead. I hugged you and thought about how much I loved you, and you came back. I'm sorry I kept you from Heaven, Mommy, but I didn't want you to go."

Elissa tried to reply, but couldn't. She fell face-first onto the white linoleum and died for the second time that July.

Elissa woke up three days later, feeling groggy. What was she doing on the kitchen floor? She glanced at her wristwatch. 1 p.m. She realized that her arm looked awfully blue. Shouldn't it be pink? She couldn't remember. It probably didn't matter.

Corky came padding up to her and nuzzled her face with his wet nose.

"Ugh, Corky, knock it off," she groaned, her voice rough and hoarse. Her mouth tasted like her tongue had died.

The dog barked at her and chased his tail a few times, wanting to play. She squinted at him. Should his ribs be sticking out like that? She couldn't remember.

"Hi, Mommy." Melanie was standing over her. "I'm sorry, but I missed you too much. After I let you remember, I didn't know what to do. I ran out of cereal and milk and soup, and there was nobody to take me to the pool, and all my clothes were dirty, and I was lonely. I need you, Mommy. I can't let God have you, not yet."

Elissa got to her feet, her head pounding. God, she had a hell of a hangover. How much had she drunk? She needed coffee, ASAP.

Melanie followed her to the counter as she started to fumble with the coffee maker.

"I'm really hungry, Mommy. Can you fix me lunch?"

"Sure," Elissa replied numbly. This coffee-making business was hard; she had to read the can to remember how much she was supposed to put in the filter.

Melanie was staring at her intently. "Would you make me *pie* for lunch? And can I have ice cream with it?"

"Sure, anything you want, sweetie."

Melanie's gaze didn't waver. "I don't want to go to school. Will you take me to the amusement park?"

"Sure."

The little girl's voice lowered to a whisper, her eyes shining with excitement. "And then can we go to Daddy's house?"

"Sure, sweetie. That sounds like a good idea."

Glowfish

they say that fancy angelfish
glow brightest right before
they die. I never had an angel
just a mother
and she glowed so bright
the sun fled my sky

hired guns in white coats
can't slay the knight
on his ivory horse
but they'll boast
they know the cold odds
and bet you a warm future

tepid nurses
hang futile silver bags
while the crab devours my mother
I hold her close
and memorize the lines
in her palms

the Moirae weave
a tricky double-helix
genes don't lie
but they can hide
more spiders
than Arachne's closet

in my empty home I scrub
her blood from my clothes
when the sun finally comes
I find her ghost
in every photograph
and mirror

But. I know I must
look to my own hand
to unravel the strands

dwelling in the webs
inside your own head
makes for a crabbed life
better to be a fish and swim
as hard as you can to the sun
and glow

The Dolls' Hearts

I HAVE never liked china dolls. They look too human, too alive. Their eyes give me the creeps. I'd rather have a teddy bear, something soft and furry.

My mother thinks I like china dolls. Or rather, I think *she* likes them, and she's never cared for bears. Just like she's never cared to make a scene. When I was little, she never tried to stop my father from yelling, or hitting, but she'd be there to dry the tears afterward. And then she'd promise to get me something nice to make up for my father's rage and her silence.

If he left a bad bruise or bloody nose, the something nice was always a new china doll.

Now I've got sixteen china dolls, all lined up on my bookshelf. An enviable collection, I'm told. Their faces are fine porcelain with glass eyes, their dresses lace, satin, and velvet. Delicate and perfect and scary as hell. I wanted to leave them behind at the house when I went away to college, but my mother insisted I take them with me. I left without them anyway. Two days later they all arrived at my student apartment in a huge UPS box.

I hate the way they seem to stare at you like you've done something wrong, like you've been a huge disappointment to them.

When I was little, I'd have nightmares. One was about a baby doll that cried and cried until my father hit it so hard that its head broke wide open, releasing a flood of darkness that drowned the whole world. And sometimes I'd dream that I was watching myself be born – my mother would be lying on her big brass bed, moaning and gasping like she was going to die, and suddenly the baby would push through in a big gout of blood and mucus. My father would be smiling and laughing in the dream, because I had come out a boy. Seeing him happy was almost worse than seeing him mad. His happiness never lasted. He was only going to get that much angrier when something inevitably happened to spoil his mood.

After I had a nightmare, I'd wake up to see the dolls' eyes glittering down at me in the moonlight filtering through my window. That'd scare me worse than the dreams, so I'd turn them all so they faced the wall. My mother would always turn them back around so they faced the bed whenever she came in to change my linens.

I can't throw them out or give them away – they're too expensive. My parents would kill me if they found out I'd wasted that kind of an investment. I've tried to sell them, but no one who wants them can afford them.

I haven't got the closet space to store them, so I leave them on the bookshelf. I've put strips of masking tape across their eyes. I can study much better this way. My father wants me to become a doctor, like him, and my mother wants me to make him happy. I'm majoring in biology, but I would've done it anyway. Maybe I can make everybody happy by becoming a veterinarian. I'll take animals over people, any day.

Whoever designed the zoology lab hadn't had aesthetics in mind. The lab tables, big black rectangles of stone on plain wooden cabinets, are gracelessly utilitarian. The sinks between the tables are stained gray from the hard water and lab chemicals. The drains stink from the residue of all creatures, great and small and dead.

I sit down on the hard wooden stool at my table and wait for the professor to arrive. The only color in the room comes from the anatomy charts on the walls and from the plastic models in the glass cases along the walls. Mounted skeletons of small animals sit atop the cabinets.

I spot the skeleton of a small dog wired to a plank, its tail up and jaws open as if it is barking at something. I think it might have been a terrier, and I think of the little terrier/chihuahua mix my mother had briefly when I was a child. She would take him with us when we went to the supermarket because he liked car rides. She made me wait in the car with the dog. "Scruffy's small, and somebody might steal him and sell him to a lab," she'd say. Since then, I've found out that Scruffy, who had bad knees and worse eyes, was in little danger of being dognapped. Beagles are the preferred laboratory dog because they have roughly the same lung capacity as humans and are usually easy to handle. My father couldn't handle Scruffy's yapping, and he made my mother give the dog away after a few months.

The professor and his graduate assistant come in lugging big white plastic buckets. I think of the huge lard buckets that warehouse groceries sell. The professor pries open one bucket with a screwdriver and reminds us that today is the dogfish dissection day.

I have never liked any dissections, but the dogfish sounds better than some of the alternatives. The anatomy students next door are dissecting cats.

I saw the specimens out in the hall yesterday. The cats were rowed like sardines inside huge transparent plastic bags. I noticed one, a skinny mackerel tabby whose fur pattern reminded me of my cat Teddy. I stood there for a moment, looking at the tabby's chemical-clouded eyes and matted, slimy fur and couldn't help but wonder where it had come from. Had it been a stray, rescued from a slow death of disease and starvation by a quick death at the hands of Carolina Biological? Or had it been a child's pet that had wandered away and been trapped by Animal Control? I stared at the pitiful corpses in the bags, remembering Teddy patting my leg with his paw, green eyes bright, mewing softly as he begged for a dish of milk. I remembered him curled up in my lap, his fur smelling of dust and leaves, his purr loud and warm. I had to turn away and hurry to the ladies' room when I realized I was going to cry.

The professor tells us to bring our dissecting trays up to the front table so that we can get a dogfish. I get my battered aluminum tray out of a drawer and stand in line. The tray is just like a small baking pan, except that the bottom is lined with black wax so that pins will stick.

The TA pulls a dogfish out of the bucket with a pair of barbecue tongs and lays it across my tray. The ugly little shark's snout and the tip of its tail stick out over the ends of the tray. The shark is a uniform, unnatural gray and it stinks of plastic.

The professor tells us that the school is no longer purchasing formalin-preserved specimens because formaldehyde is a carcinogen. I don't know what this new preservative is, but it is a welcome change. The dead-fish smell of formaldehyde always sickened me more than the actual dissection.

I take the dogfish back to the table and get out my lab manual and dissecting kit. I stare down at the shark, briefly imagining it swimming through seaweed in a warm ocean, a cold-blooded predator, yes, but still alive and therefore beautiful. I think that this is the irony of the laboratory; I am studying to become a biologist because I love living creatures, so I end up spending most of my time with the dead and dismembered.

I pull out my scalpel and a probe. The lab manual says I'm supposed to cut open the belly and locate the spiral valve of the stomach, then expose the heart. Sharks do not inspire the same feelings in me as cats, but still, I hesitate, feeling uncomfortable. I know that I'm being silly; millions of creatures die every day in ways that are much less pleasant than those of dissection specimens. Violent death is a rule of nature.

I roll the dogfish onto its back. It is as stiff as if it really was made of plastic, and the plastic smell makes my eyes water. Its color is so unlike a living thing that I can believe that it is not real, that it is just another plastic model made by Carolina Biological.

The shark is a doll, a plastic doll. That's what I keep telling myself as I cut into the gray flesh.

Winter's here, and I've gotten much better at dissections. The smell hardly bothers me at all anymore, and I'm learning to not feel anything when I cut up animals. The dolls are getting to me, though, even with their eyes taped shut. I'm having my old nightmares about the birth and the baby doll again, and I'm not getting more than three hours of sleep a night.

I've gone beyond tired; in the morning, my whole body vibrates in the corona of eclipsed pain.

Early in the morning when I'm walking to class, sometimes I look at passersby and they've got the wide, staring eyes of lab dissections: milky-filmed and dead-fish gray. I blink, and usually they go back to looking like people again. Usually.

At mid-terms, I stayed awake for almost forty-eight hours cramming for my tests. When I stepped outside my apartment, the six inches of snow had turned to a blanket of pink plastic baby dolls. I tried to ignore them, and took a few steps into the yard. The dolls broke open under my feet with a wet crunch. They had real guts. Blood and bits of flesh stuck to my boots.

I ran back inside and, once I'd stopped shaking, made myself go back to bed. I slept over sixteen hours, and I missed three exams. I felt terrible about it, but it couldn't be helped. I hope my parents will understand.

For better or worse, the semester is over, and tomorrow I'm driving back home for Christmas break. I've loaded all the dolls into the trunk of my car. I'm giving them back to my mother, and I'm going to tell her that if she ships them out again, I'm giving the box to the Salvation Army. She won't like the idea of poor people having her fine dolls. I hope she sells them; my parents might need some extra money.

Last night, my mother called to tell me that my father's resigned from his job. This sounded odd to me; he's been head of neurosurgery at the metro hospital for years and has never said a bad word about the job.

They've always spent most everything he brings in. My father won't settle for anything but the newest computer, the best wine. It won't take long before they're deeply into debt.

I pressed her for details, but she wouldn't tell me anything. Her silence makes me think that perhaps he was forced to resign, that perhaps he lost his temper and beat up someone at the hospital.

My father is a very good neurosurgeon. He perfected several medical innovations, such as a technique for using miniature ligatures made from collagen to reattach the nerves of patients who've had a limb severed.

My parents got married soon after he got his joint MD/PhD from Yale. Right after she got pregnant, he got a special offer to do a postdoc at UCLA. So he left my mother behind, and went off to California. He came back briefly to attend my birth, but I was nearly two years old when he came back for good.

I wish they'd tried for another child. But they probably just decided I was enough trouble as it was, and another kid would be too much. I'd have liked to have a little brother. I know he might've been a brat, since no doubt my father would have spoiled a son silly. But at least there would've been someone around I could talk to.

I pull into my parents' driveway. My mother has put strings of little twinkly white lights in our bushes, and there's a huge red-bowed wreath on the front door. No doubt she's Christmased the rest of the house within an inch of its life. She's been in the Daughters of the American Revolution for a long time now, and all the DAR ladies take home decoration as a deadly serious business. She has her image as the perfect doctor's wife to uphold.

My mother opens the door before I can ring the bell. Her hair is sprayed into a tidy bouffant, and she's wearing her Christmas ball earrings and matching apron and sweater. She probably hasn't gone outside today, but she's wearing mascara and rouge. When the holidays hit, it's like my mother is transported back in time to some alternate 1950's universe where the Holy Trinity is composed of Emily Post, Betty Crocker, and June Cleaver.

"Oh honey, you're home early! Did you have a good drive? I just put some cookies in the oven, and I have a batch of cheese straws cooling on the counter. Are you hungry? You look awfully thin. Have you been eating okay?"

She keeps talking, never allowing me the chance to respond, as she ushers me inside, helps me shuck off my coat and snow-wet boots, and hands me a cup of hot chocolate. Frank Sinatra's singing Christmas carols on the stereo. Everything is spotlessly clean, perfectly matched and decorated. I feel like I've walked onto the set of some Hallmark Christmas Special.

There's a soft bump against my leg and a meow. I look down, and Teddy is winding his way around my ankles.

"Hey, Tedster." I kneel and pick him up. He's much thinner than he was before I left, and his fur is tatty; my parents leave him outside when I'm not around because they don't like dealing with his shedding. I think they forget to feed him after they've put him out.

Teddy settles happily in my arms, purring as I carry him into the huge kitchen.

"Where's Dad?" I ask.

My mother's smile freezes into a panicked grimace for a fraction of a second. "Oh, he's down in the basement. Tinkering with the snowblower, I think. It wouldn't start this morning. He's in a bit of a mood today."

I realize that there's a faint outline of a black eye under her makeup.

I stare down at Teddy, who gazes back at me with his big green eyes. *Felis familiaris.* Happy familiar. He's never had the knowing, self-satisfied smile most cats possess. He's always looked a bit mournful, and although he's still purring, his ears are cocked, alert to danger.

I look back up at my mother, and give a start. She's got the huge dead-fish eyes I see on early morning strangers. I blink, but she doesn't change back to normal.

"Are you okay, honey?" she asks.

I don't answer, because there are heavy steps on the stairs coming up from the basement, and Teddy is struggling in my arms. I release him, and he lands with a soft thump and dashes away to hide in the hall closet.

My father emerges from the stairwell. He's a cadaver. His blue jogging suit is soaked through with formaldehyde, his salt-and-pepper hair sticking up in slimy peaks. His eyes are gray jelly. I can smell the formaldehyde, even from across the room, and I have to swallow against a wave of nausea.

"H-hi, Dad," I stammer.

He scowls at me, and pulls a sodden paper out of his pocket. It's my grade report.

"What the hell is this?" he rumbles. Foul green fluid spills from his mouth.

Mother is standing back against the fridge, dead eyes wide. Her mouth is sewn shut with coarse black thread. Her left hand clutches the needle and spool.

"Um, my grades? I had a bit of trouble at midterms, but I can ex–"

"A 'C' in Spanish and physics? And a 'D' in chemistry? What the hell am I paying your tuition for?"

"I got 'As' in English and biology–"

"Goddamn it, a freaking *monkey* could get an 'A' in freshman English! You'll never become a doctor with grades like these. Goddamn. It's not as if Wisconsin is a difficult school. You couldn't freaking get into Yale or MIT. Freaking retards get into Wisconsin, and you can't even pass your first semester. Goddamn. I should've sent you to hairdresser's school. Any idiot can cut hair."

He's shouting in my face now, and I am bent backwards against the stove to get away from the stench of him. His breath is an unspeakable mix of dead fish and rotten meat. Cadaverine and putrescine, those are the chemicals that make up the stench. I learned all about them in chemistry. I would've made an 'A' in the class if I'd been allowed to make up the mid-term.

"Look, if it's the money, I can pay you back. I can get a job–"

"Damn right, you'll pay me back!" he roars in my face.

The stench is rolling off him in sickening waves, and I am sure I'm going to vomit any second now.

"Please get out of my face," I whisper.

"How dare you tell me what to do, you worthless little shit!" He raises his arm, hand balled into a fist.

I don't think, just react. My right hand finds a cold cast iron pan on the burner behind me, and I swing it into his temple, hard. He tumbles backward and crumples on the floor. Black, clotted liquid spills from the gash in his head.

I hear a gasp from my mother. I look at her, and see she's completely cadaverized now, too. Her apron is stained and soaked with embalming fluid, and her earrings have turned to eyeballs impaled on fish hooks. She's got the strong plastic stink of the dogfish. My eyes and nose start running.

She starts shrieking, tearing her lips loose from the stitches. "Oh my God, what have you done, what have you done, we've got to call 911, oh my God–"

Her hysteria's the whistle of a tea kettle that needs to be taken off the burner. To quiet her, I step forward and give her the pan. She falls and is silent.

The way her head is crushed reminds me of the baby doll in my nightmare. In the dream, the doll is in the basement, in a corner that's now covered by my father's workbench. I wonder what happened to the doll after my father broke its head.

I go downstairs to my father's workbench and start pulling the tools off. When it's unloaded, I use a crowbar to pry it from its wall bolts and pull it out of the corner. There's a square, shoebox-sized section of the wood floor that seems to have been sawn out and then replaced.

I find a buckled edge and pry the floorboard up. There, nestled between two sewer pipes on the concrete subfloor, is a mummified infant. A boy child. He's naked, his flesh a dusty brownish-gray, and his skull is deeply sunken and gashed.

I feel tears spill down my cheeks, but my heart feels dead and empty. Why did this have to happen? My father always wanted a boy, and so what if he'd cried too much? They could have given him away. They gave the dog away. Why'd they have to put my little brother down here with the spiders and silverfish?

I wonder if my parents have hearts at all.

I go back upstairs, and discover that my parents have turned into giant dolls, plastic on the outside, dead flesh on the inside. I take a good, sharp fillet knife from the block on the counter, and start the dissection.

It is six hours later, and I'm sitting with Teddy and my little brother in the living room. We're watching "Frosty the Snowman". Teddy was really scared at first, but I coaxed him out of the closet with a dish of milk and some canned salmon. Now he's settled down and is purring like a motorbike. I put my little brother's chair close to the TV so he can see everything. He's such a quiet, good little kid. I think he really likes cartoons, but Teddy likes the nature shows best. We'll have to flip a coin to see what we watch next.

I never could find the dolls' hearts. I cut and I dug and I probed. I took everything out and coded each organ with colored pins and bits of ribbon I found in my mother's sewing box. I found gallbladders and livers and spleens, but no hearts. I probably just overlooked them; I'll check tomorrow morning after I've had some sleep.

The doll-bits were making the kitchen slippery, so I stacked the pieces in my parents' whirlpool tub. I'll have to go to the store and get some pickle buckets to put them in soon, or they'll start to smell up the house. I won't mind so much, but the neighbors might be bothered. I should clean the kitchen, too, in case the DAR ladies come by.

Tomorrow I'm going to use my father's circular saw and crowbar to take up more boards in the basement. I think my mother's china dolls will fit nicely down there between the pipes. And the pickle buckets can stay under my father's workbench.

Maybe I'll take my little brother with me when I go shopping. He's such a good kid. I bet he'd like a toy or two for Christmas.

So Lonely As The Grave

DIANE HILLSON pulled her Saturn into the gravel parking lot in front of the old stone church, tears clouding her eyes. She parked and lifted the square, black ceramic urn from the passenger seat. It contained the ashes of her parents, who'd been crushed when their little Toyota was rammed by a tractor trailer whose driver had fallen asleep at the wheel at 90 miles per hour on the interstate.

The ashes meant she was completely alone, now. In her thirty-four years on the planet, she'd lived in twelve states and three countries seeking her place in the world, and still it all came down to this: the old family plot deep in the heart of rural South Carolina. All her kin were here, and one of the only people she'd truly counted as a friend.

A single tear splashed down onto the urn's shiny flat top. Diane wiped it away with her thumb and rubbed the rest from her eyes with the back of her hand.

"Mom, Dad, let's get y'all settled," she said hoarsely. "And then we'll see about getting *me* settled."

Hugging the urn to her chest, she stepped out onto the gravel. The hot, oppressively humid air smelled of pine and honeysuckle, and the buzz of the cicadas was a high-fever tinnitus.

Diane could hear the bottle of pills rattling in her purse as she walked to the limestone church. She went up the steps and banged the round cast-iron door knocker on the white oak front door. Waited. Then banged it again. No sound but the aural haze of the cicadas. Her bra and white cotton blouse felt like they were completely soaked in sweat, and the late afternoon sun stung the bare skin of her arms and face. She wished she'd thought to wear a hat.

Shit. The groundskeeper said he'd be here.

She went around to the side of the church and peeked in the windows. All dark. She dug her cell phone out of her purse and redialed the number she'd been given to arrange the burial. After three rings, the answering machine clicked on.

"You've reached the Honea Path Funeral Home." The recorded voice was that of an old man she'd never heard before. "Your call is important to us. Please leave a message–"

Diane clicked off her cell phone.

"Well, looks like I'll be doing this alone," she told her parents' ashes.

She went back to her car and popped the trunk. Her parents' simple marble memorial plaque lay on spread newspapers:

Bud Hillson   Angela Harris Hillson
1940 - 2002   1946 - 2002

We cast aside these mortal coils
to be reborn in the love of God.

Beside the marker was an old canvas duffel bag that contained her emergency roadside supplies: a blanket, flares, jumper cables, a bottle of tire fix-it, leather work gloves, a liter bottle of water, a couple of spare engine belts, and a folding Army surplus shovel. She dug out the shovel, gloves and water bottle and walked out toward her parents' final resting place.

The first part of the cemetery was the oldest, some graves dating to the early 1800s. Diane walked among the mottled, decaying marble stones, some so worn that she could barely make out that there had ever been inscriptions on them. The ground was a patchwork of velvety dark moss, gravel-embedded soil, and short green grass. She ran her hands over the tops of the markers as she walked, the worn stone rough and gritty. Some of these people were born before the nation had its independence; all had died before it was torn by the Civil War.

Old stones gave way to newer markers and crypts. The inscriptions became recognizable, and so were the family names. Harris. Keller. Smith. Calhoun. She walked among the long-buried bones of the families that had given rise to nothing but her. She was the only-surviving child of two generations of only-surviving children. Before the turn of the century, her family had been strong, thriving. But two World Wars and Korea killed off most of the men in the prime of their lives, and accidents, illness, and alcohol took the rest.

She came to the Hillson plot, where her father's parents lay beside the tiny graves of his twin sisters, killed as toddlers by an outbreak of the flu, and his older brother, slain on the sands of Iwo Jima. At the foot of these older graves lay two newer graves. To the left was the grave of Diane's little brother Bob, who died at age nine during a Little League game when a fastball struck him in the chest and stopped his heart. He'd have been 32 the next October. To the right was the grave of her little sister Susan, who as a ten-year-old got sucked down by an undertow when they went to Folly Beach. Susan had loved horses and dogs and wanted to be a veterinarian. She would have turned 29 just the previous month.

"Hi, kids," Diane said, swallowing against the lump rising in her throat. "Mom and Dad are here to keep y'all company now."

There was a place between her sibling's graves that would be just big enough for her parent's marker. She pulled on her gloves, unfolded the shovel, and began to dig into the rust-red Carolina clay.

Two hours later, the sun was setting and Diane knelt exhausted and drenched in sweat in front of her parents' grave. Her canvas sneakers, jeans and white shirt were smeared with red mud. Her palms were red and blistered. Her arms quivered and her back ached from the effort of lugging the 50-pound marker across the graveyard and shoving it into place above her parent's ashes.

But the weight of the stone was nothing compared to the hopelessness and failure and loneliness she felt. After her brother and sister died, her parents had retreated into themselves. Their house grew quiet as any crypt. Diane had spent her whole life wanting her family back, wanting laughter and love and the sounds of a happy household. She'd dreamed of finding a soul-mate, a best friend she could raise children with and grow old with. But what she'd ended up with was a string of broken affairs, a dead-end job as a telephone computer support technician and a one-bedroom apartment in Portland, Maine.

"I tried," she told her family in their graves. "I did the best I could to make my own family so we could carry on. So we'd be remembered. But it ain't gonna happen, I see that now."

She laughed, but her smile turned into a grimace. "I really did try. Did the college thing, did the bar scene, joined clubs, answered singles ads, all that and a side of fries. I think I must be invisible."

She pulled off her gloves and touched her parent's marker. "Remember those boys I loved in college? Joe and Chris and Mark? Remember how they said they didn't want a commitment? They're all married now. Got kids, too. So commitment wasn't ever really the problem; it was *me*."

Five days before her parents were killed, Diane had broken up with her most recent boyfriend, an older man named Jack. They'd been dating for two years, and he was separated from his wife. He was only the second man who had claimed to love her with any conviction. He'd pursued her like a Sherman tank. Flowers, love poems, you name it; no man since her first boyfriend Jeremy back in high school had ever given Diane that kind of attention.

"Elizabeth and I are *over*," he'd told her. "The divorce is just a formality." He'd hugged her tight, gently rocking her back and forth as if she were a little girl. "You're the lovely lady I want to spend the rest of my life with. Marry me, Di. Let's move to Nashua. We can get a nice house there, and a yard big enough for our kids to play in."

Moving day arrived, and Diane had all her things boxed up. She waited for Jack to arrive with the truck. And waited. And waited.

Her calls to his cell phone went unanswered, and his land line had been disconnected. Anxiety and dread felt like the twin jaws of a vise closing down on her heart. She played DOOM on her laptop all evening to distract herself.

Late that night, she got an email from Jack explaining that his wife had fallen ill, and he felt he had to go to California to be with her. Her frantic reply to him bounced; the account had been shut down.

And that was the last she'd heard from him.

"I'm just *done*," she told her parents. "I don't want to live alone anymore, and it looks like God has been telling me *alone* is the only way I get to live."

She opened her purse and pulled out the bottle of pills, a mix of over-the-counter sleeping pills, motion sickness medication and some prescription painkillers she'd saved. She'd found the recipe on someone's suicide website.

"I'm gonna go away for a little bit, because I can't do this in front of y'all," she told her family. "But I'll be back with you real soon."

Diane got to her feet, brushed some of the dirt from her blouse and jeans, and carried her pills and water bottle to a nearby plot for the McMullen family. She found the grave of Jeremy McMullen, who had been her first boyfriend and first love in high school. He'd been a fine defensive lineman for their football team and was all set to go to Georgia Tech on a full athletic scholarship. But his back snapped in a bad tackle in one of the last games his senior season. Faced with a wheelchair-bound life in a small town, he'd killed himself with one of his father's pistols the following summer.

Diane sat down on his grave and traced the letters on his headstone with her fingertips. "Hi, Jer. How's it been? It was a heckuva drive getting down here. The AC started giving out on me just past Richmond. It was worse than that trip we took down to Key West in your dad's old Buick.

"Do you still remember the first time we made love?" Her voice was a whisper. "I do. I remember how nervous you were, how worried you were that you were gonna hurt me. But it didn't hurt a bit. I still dream of you at night, sometimes. But sometimes I have to look at your yearbook picture to remember your face."

Diane hugged her knees to her chest. "I should have followed you out here that last summer. It would have saved a lot of time, and we could've spent the last seventeen years together."

She opened up the pill bottle and started swallowing the pills along with sips of water. When both bottles were empty, she leaned back against his headstone, the marble still hot against her skin, the earth of his grave warm against her hands and legs. The reddened sun had disappeared beyond the horizon, and Venus was high in the darkening sky.

"I'm not the girl you knew – I'm what's left of her. I hope you'll still like me."

She was starting to feel a little nauseated and very drowsy. "Do you remember the junior prom? When we snuck up onto the roof of the gym and kissed in the moonlight? That was like magic. You were so strong and handsome in that tux, and I felt like I'd never be alone in the world again..."

✳

Diane snapped awake at the sudden icepick of pain in her stomach. She rolled over and vomited up a bitter stew of bile and pills. Trembling, she sat up. Darkness had completely fallen, but the graveyard was lit by the cold rays of the nearly-full moon. The world looked shiny, as if it had been carved in silver.

"Why are you doing this, Di?"

She looked up. Jeremy was standing beside her, dressed in his usual fall outfit of his red-and-white letter jacket, Van Halen tee shirt, blue jeans and high-topped leather sneakers. God, he looked so *young*. As she stared at him, she realized he was translucent, and a faint bluish aura surrounded him.

"I don't want to go on feeling this alone," she replied, staring up at the boy she still loved after all these years.

"There's nothing so lonely as the grave," Jeremy said. "The worms don't make very good company."

"Honey, don't do this," she heard her mother say.

Diane turned. Her parents were standing there. Behind them her brother Bob and her sister Susan were holding hands, children forever. And behind them were the aunts and uncle she'd never known, the girls in matching Easter dresses and the young man in his Marine uniform. Beside them were her grandparents in their church clothes, her grandfather looking younger even than her own father but her grandmother a wizened woman of 70.

"You're the last of us," her grandmother said. "Don't waste your life like this."

"But my life *is* a waste," she replied, standing up. "I'm thirty-four years old, and I've done nothing of any consequence. I'm adrift. I'm a nonentity. All my life, I've wanted a best friend, a lover, a life companion. I know it's a tall order. But it's what I *need*. I need it like I need air and water, and I can't get it. I'm a failure, and I'm sorry about that. But I don't belong out in the world; the world doesn't want me. All the people I love are here, so *here* is where I belong."

Her little sister stomped her foot. "I never got to go to any proms! I never got to go to college! I never even got to have my own horse, or kiss a boy!"

Her little brother was furious, too. "I could have been a big-league ball player! You got to have a life, and now you're just throwing it away! You stink!"

"You can't give up," her father said. "We only ever wanted you to be happy."

"Happiness is all I ever wanted, too," she said. "I am not happy alone, and I never will be. I feel empty, and I can't go on like this."

"You don't know what it's like here," said Jeremy. "I would give anything to have my old life back, even the one in the wheelchair. I could still eat ice cream. I could still feel the sun on my face. I could still listen to music. And I could've still touched you, even if I couldn't make love to you."

She stepped toward her family, then looked back at Jeremy.

"If you covet my life, you can have it," she said. "Don't make me live my life alone."

They looked at each other, shimmering uncertainly.

She spread her arms wide toward her family. "Don't you understand? I'm *hollow*. Tell me you love me, and fill me up."

Jeremy stepped toward her.

"I love you, Di," he said.

Then he stepped into her. She felt something akin to an electric shock as his consciousness merged with hers. The rush of his memories and dreams nearly made her faint. She was breaking through a wall of grunting flesh and bone and sacking the quarterback under the bright Friday night lights. She was pinning a corsage to the front of a pretty girl's silk prom dress – *her* dress. She'd never realized how beautiful she'd been in his eyes. She was waking up in the hospital to the sight of his mother's tears and a tingling dead weight below her waist. She was sitting by his bedroom window in a wheelchair, staring down at a gun gleaming in his lap.

Her little brother and sister ran to her, into her, and after them came the others. The flood of memories and sensations and emotions was overwhelming. The joyous agony of childbirth. The wet shock of a Japanese bullet finding its mark in her chest. The exhilaration of riding a galloping horse so fast she thought she was flying. The sweet crack of ash connecting with horsehide, and seeing that baseball going, going, gone over the fence as the crowd went wild.

She was not alone.

She was not *alone*.

Her breath caught in her throat, and she stumbled backward and collapsed across Jeremy's grave.

Diane jerked awake as the first wave of bitter vomit spilled from her lips. She was on Jeremy's grave. There were no ghosts surrounding her.

Just a fucking dream, she thought as she retched again. *Just another one of my stupid delusions. I'm alone, just like I've always been.*

It was hard to move; her head was spinning from the drug cocktail, and her arms and legs felt numb. She lay back against the headstone and stared up at the night sky. The stars were distant, cold specks, lonely as the souls of stillborn children in Limbo.

Another wave of nausea was coming on hard and fast. She knew she should turn her head and roll over, but she couldn't find the strength.

The bile welled up in her throat and she was choking, the acid burning her lungs. She gagged, coughed, tried to take a breath, but the air just wouldn't come.

And then the pain was gone.

Diane was standing by Jeremy's grave in the moonlight. Disoriented, she looked down, and saw herself sprawled there in the final twitching throes of death.

"We told you not to waste your life," came a voice behind her.

She turned. It was Jeremy and her family, their faces hard and cold as cast iron.

"We offered you our *love*, we offered you our *company*, and you *rejected* us," Jeremy said through gritted teeth. "You were just *so* in love with dying, weren't you?"

"You were our last chance at getting to finally live," her little sister said. "And *you ruined everything*!"

"Wait, I–" Diane began.

"We would have stayed with you forever," her father said. "We would have helped you find someone better than that sonofabitch Jack. How could you have fallen for that bullshit he fed you? I thought I raised a *smart* girl."

"You had your chance," said her mother quietly. "And now we've nothing more to say. You wouldn't listen anyway."

Her family walked away, fading into the darkness. Diane knew they wouldn't return. She was alone.

Forever.

A ghost among ghosts.

...Next On Channel 77

TOM WILSON woke in the gray early-morning light to the smell of coffee percolating and the sound of dishes rattling. A moment later, he realized that his girlfriend Myrna was still sleeping beside him and his heart jumped like a rabbit: *Ohshit there's a burglar in the apartment—*

—and then he heard a woman's voice humming "Strangers in the Night."

Aunt Fran? No. It wasn't possible. She was back in Barlow Gap, Montana. No way she'd suddenly show up in downtown Chicago at this hour.

"Thomas! Coffee's ready!" Fran called.

I'm still asleep, he thought. *This is a dream.*

He slipped out of bed and found his jeans. Myrna mumbled a sleepy protest, then rolled over and started snoring softly. Tom pulled on his pants and crept toward the living room.

His 80-year-old grand-aunt Francine was standing in the tiny kitchen that adjoined the living room. She was wearing her favorite Sunday-go-to-church outfit: her lilac dress, white pearl-buttoned gloves, and white straw hat. She was carefully pouring coffee from his stained pot into a pair of her best antique china teacups on her silver serving tray.

"Aunt Fran?" He slowly stepped toward her. She looked the same as when he'd said goodbye to her at the bus station in Barlow Gap nine years before. She'd been the only member of his family to see him off. "What – what are you doing here?"

"Good morning, Thomas! Do you still take cream and sugar in your coffee?"

"Uh, yes, ma'am...but what are you doing here in Chicago?"

Her blue eyes twinkled mischievously. "What makes you think we're in Chicago?"

The room rippled, changed. Cracked beige paint became crisp striped wallpaper, dingy hardwood turned to tidy cream-colored carpet.

They were in Fran's living room.

"What the—" Tom began.

"Come, your coffee's getting cold." Fran was sitting on her couch, the china tea service sitting on the coffee table in front of her. A black plastic RCA TV remote lay beside the tray. She poured a splash of cream into one of the cups, then smiled at him and patted the cushion beside her. "Sit down, sit down! I'm not going to bite."

Dazed, Tom sat beside her. She passed him his cup, a silver spoon, and a tiny plate stacked high with sugar cubes. He hadn't seen anyone use sugar cubes in years.

He stirred two cubes into his coffee and took a tentative sip. Yep, it was real joe. If all this was a dream, it was far more realistic than anything his mind had churned out in a while.

"Let me see your hand," she said.

"My hand?" *What the heck does she want to see my hand for?*

"Yes, your right hand."

He held it out. She put on her spectacles and peered down at his index finger. She lifted it and waggled it back and forth. "Well, your dialing finger isn't broken. How come you never call me, boy? The comic book shop's doing pretty well these days; you can afford a few calls back home."

Tom blushed deeply. "I— I'm sorry, Fran, I just — you know, got busy, but I think about you lots and I meant to call—" he stammered, then stopped. "Hey, wait a minute, how did you know about the comic shop?"

Tom had helped Myrna open her comics shop, the *25th Century Five and Dime,* on North Halsted a little over two years ago. It was finally seeing a profit, partly due to the coffee bar they'd added. Until recently, Myrna had been financing the shop with money she'd inherited from her grandfather.

"You'd be surprised what you learn once you're dead," Fran replied primly, sipping her coffee. "The future and the past both become clear."

"D-dead?"

"Well, not *dead* dead...my heart's still ticking away, but my brain checked out last night after the stroke. So my body's still warm and breathing in the hospital, but I'm not in it anymore. My heart's going to go soon, though, and then they can put me in the ground."

She paused. "Dying's not so bad. The hard part is having to leave so many things undone. There's so *much* I wanted to do that I just never had time for. Never *made* time for. And then there's some things I dreamed of doing that I simply never *could* do, just because of the time and place and family I was born into.

"Did you know that, ever since we got our first TV back in 1960, I wished I could be a TV news reporter? No, of course you didn't, because I never told anyone. It was impossible; women didn't become TV reporters back then, especially not 40-year-old housewives. I might as well have dreamed of becoming an astronaut or a fairy princess."

She picked up the TV remote and clicked the power button. The big console TV in the corner came on, the screen fuzzing bright blue before the image resolved.

Fran was on TV. She wore a smart green suit and held a microphone with a round "77" logo on the front. In the background, Tom could see the Barlow Gap Community Hospital.

"Luckily for our ALTV-77 viewers," said smiling newscaster Fran, "many dreams *can* come true in the afterlife. But will *all* my dreams come true? Will my favorite nephew attend my funeral? As my body lingers inside this hospital, young Mr. Thomas Wilson must decide to telephone his estranged family to make arrangements to pay his last respects to his loving aunt."

Fran clicked off the television. "It's very important that you be at my funeral. I *need* you to be there. I expect it'll be next Tuesday. Call your mother; she'll be awake soon."

God.

Tom hadn't talked to his mother since the day he left home. She'd been stoned on tranquilizers that day, as usual, and acted as if he were just going down to the store or something.

Acted as if he weren't really leaving home for good.

As if she didn't care about him.

Which she likely didn't. She hadn't seemed to care all that much for him once he was too old to be a cute attention-getter down at the grocery store. And when he left, she had his two little sisters to keep her occupied. With a seven-year-old in pigtails and frilly skirts and a cute-as-a-button babe in arms around the house, Tom was the unsightly teenage stain of the family. No one besides Fran seemed to want him around, and even she agreed it was best he leave for the big city.

The first few years after he'd left, Tom sent his mother Christmas cards, a few letters, Mother's Day cards and such, but he never got a reply, so he stopped sending them. Ever since, he'd been so angry at her for so long, he didn't know what to say to her – or if he *had* anything to say to her.

"But–" Tom began.

"I know it's going to be hard. But please promise me you'll come?"

"Okay...okay, I'll come."

She patted his knee. "You always were a good boy..."

Fran and her living room faded into the gray dimness of his and Myrna's apartment. Tom found himself sitting alone on their old tweed sofa. He still held Fran's teacup, the coffee inside it hot and steaming slightly in the cool apartment air.

He drained the cup in one gulp and held it in both hands. The eggshell china was a delicate rose pattern of pale pinks and greens and a little interwoven gold-leaf filigree that had rubbed off in a few places. The lip of the cup had a small chip, and age had spiderwebbed the glaze. The cup had to be at least as old as Fran...was.

He glanced at the clock in the wall. It would be just past 6 in Montana. And his mother always awoke at 5:30, no matter how many pills or glasses of wine she'd had the night before. Growing up on a farm made her an incurable early riser.

He stared at the phone and felt dread building in the pit of his stomach. After nine years, what was he supposed to say? *Hi, Mom, still hooked on Valium? Dad still an unbearable jerk?* Sheesh. Why had he agreed to go back? He'd washed his hands of his parents, and apparently they had done the same of him.

At least it would be nice to see his sisters, Lisa and Joanie. He hoped they remembered him. He hoped they'd had a better time of it than him. His father always went out of his way to belittle him; Tom chalked his behavior up to some weird Freudian competitiveness. Probably his siblings' being female would take the edge off his father's temper.

He stared at the phone.

The phone stared back: *Well, ya big wuss, you gonna call your mother or not?*

"Crap," he sighed, then picked up the receiver and punched in the number.

After a few rings, his mother answered. "Hello?"

"Hello, Mom?"

"I think you have the wrong number."

Click.

Tom stared down at the receiver. *Oh,* this *is going well. Once more, with feeling...*

He punched in the number again, and when his mother answered, he quickly said, "Wait! Don't hang up! This is Tom, your son. Remember me? I was just calling to see how you all are doing."

"Oh. *Tom,*" she said, sounding supremely surprised. "Hello. Well, uh, we're fine. Me and your father and your sisters, we're all...fine."

"How's Aunt Fran doing?"

"Well, she ain't doing too well, actually. She had a stroke, and...well, she don't have much time left. A day or two at most."

"I'd like to come to the funeral," he said, "but it's going to take me a few days to get out there. The bus ride'll take about a day and a half."

"Well...it surely would be great to see you again. You, uh, you can stay here at the house if you want. I turned your old room into a sewing room, but you're welcome to one of the couches."

"That'd be great, Mom. Thanks. I'll call you when I find out when I'll be getting there, okay?"

"That'll be fine."

"Good. Talk to you soon. 'Bye."

Tom hung up the phone and leaned back on the sofa, idly playing with Fran's empty teacup. *I can't believe I'm actually going back there...*

Myrna shuffled out of their bedroom, cinching her blue satin bathrobe around her narrow waist. "Who was that?" she asked.

"You want the single, or the dance mix?"

"Gimme the single. It's too early for dancing."

"That was my mother. My Aunt Fran's dying. I need to go to Montana for her funeral."

"Wait, wait, I gotta sit down for this." She plopped down beside him and pushed her dark red hair out of her eyes so she could stare at him. "Lemme get this straight. You hear *nothing* from your family for close to a decade, and now you're gonna drop everything and spend beaucoup bucks on a plane ticket to go home for a funeral? What, exactly, have they done to deserve you spending *any* amount of time and money on them?"

"Two things: first, I'll take the bus, so the bucks won't be beaucoup. Second, I'm not doing this for them, I'm doing it for *Fran.* You know how much she helped me out when I first came here. I'd never have made it without that two grand she gave me. At the very least, I owe her the courtesy of showing my respects at her funeral."

"I understand wanting to do it for Fran...but it's not like she's really going to know you're there."

"She'll know," Tom replied, staring down at the teacup. "Trust me on this one."

Myrna sighed. "I suppose I can cover most of your shifts myself. I can probably sweet-talk Ralph into working the coffee bar."

Tom set the teacup down on their paper-strewn coffee table and pulled her close. "Tell you what...when I get back, I'll work the shop for a few days. You can watch movies, catch up on your reading, take bubble baths. And then we'll both take a day off, go out for breakfast at the Melrose, catch a matinee, and then do whatever we want. Sound good?"

She giggled. "Sounds good. Just be careful in Montana...I wouldn't want you getting hurt in a freak cow-tipping accident."

※

Three days later, Tom stepped off the Greyhound as the sun was setting behind the mountains. It was a gorgeous sunset, all pinks and oranges and purples, and the sun was a gigantic ruby. He'd forgotten how pretty it was out there.

He shouldered his duffel and garment bag and went into the station to look for his mother. He scanned the people in the narrow yellow plastic chairs; none looked familiar. He walked toward the pay phone to call for a cab.

"Tom?"

He turned. Two girls, one close to ten and the other about sixteen, stood by the snack machine staring at him uncertainly. The younger girl had short blond hair and wore overalls and a blue corduroy 4-H jacket. The older girl had long, straight honey-blond hair, green eyes, a smattering of freckles, a long, graceful neck, and a great figure that she was apparently trying to hide under a floppy sweatshirt and loose jeans. Her eyes were rimmed red, as if she'd been crying for a long time. Something about her stance reminded him of his mother.

"Lisa? Joanie?" he asked.

The younger girl broke into a wide smile. "See, Lisa, I *told* you it was him! He's just like in the picture, only he's bigger!"

He stepped toward his sisters. "Wow, you two look *great*. You girls really got pretty while I was gone."

He leaned down and gave each of them a quick, awkward hug. "Where's Mom?"

"Uh, she wasn't feeling well," Lisa replied, looking embarrassed. "So she sent us to pick you up."

"You've got your driver's license now? Oh, man, I *have* been away a long time."

The girls led him out to Lisa's little Dodge Neon.

"The funeral's tomorrow morning," Lisa said as they loaded his bags into the trunk. "It's supposed to storm, so we might not be able to do the graveside service."

Her lip began to tremble, and a tear slipped down her cheek. She pulled a wad of Kleenex out of her jeans pocket and turned away from him. "Sorry. Just give me a minute."

Deciding it was best to give her space, Tom climbed into the back seat. Joanie crawled onto the seat beside him and started telling him all about 4-H (which she'd apparently just joined) and about the lamb she was raising as her first project. The girl's words tumbled over each other like eager puppies. But one look at her eyes told him she was just as sad about Fran's death as Lisa was, but she clung to her pretense of cheer as though everyone depended on her to be the Designated Happy Child.

Lisa finally got into the driver's seat and took off without another word, content to let her little sister's chatter camouflage the heartbreak that hung between them all.

It took them half an hour to get to the family ranch. According to Joanie, their father had sold off their cattle and most of their grazing land to a neighbor. They still had the good hunting land around the creek and a few wooded acres in the foothills that Joanie liked to ride her horse in.

Lisa parked the car in front of their old two-story house and they all piled out.

The teen was the first one through the front door. "I made some fruit salad and ham sandwiches; they're in the fridge. We left you a pillow and a blanket on the couch in the rec room." She was blinking fast, as if she were about to burst into tears. "I, uh, I gotta go."

With that, Lisa bolted up the stairs like a scared cat.

Joanie tugged at his sleeve. "I gotta go feed Bo. Wanna come out and see him?"

"In a minute. I better say hi to Mom and Dad first."

"'Kay." She ducked back outside, the screen door slamming loosely behind her.

Tom stood alone in the foyer. Dueling TVs blared from the kitchen and the darkened living room. Yep, home was just the way he remembered it: TVs on in practically every room, conveniently removing the need for conversation and real human interaction.

Tom heard his father's cough and the creak of him getting up from his recliner. The elder Mr. Wilson shambled out of the living room like a groggy bear. He wore a pair of old denim overalls and a white T-shirt. His face was puffy, and he'd gained about forty pounds. His hair had gone almost entirely gray. He loosely clutched a longneck in his left hand; the old man had probably already killed three or four of its brothers that evening.

"Hi, Dad," Tom said.

"Well. You're back." His father looked him up and down, then shifted from foot to foot.

"Yep. I'm back," Tom agreed. "For a few days."

"You look good, son. Real good. Got tall. Still got that faggy earring, though."

"Yeah." He touched the silver ring in his left ear. "My girlfriend really digs it."

His father grunted and gestured toward the living room with the longneck. "Ya wanna grab a beer and come watch the ball game with me?"

This, Tom knew, was as close to a warm welcome as he was likely to get. "I'm kinda stiff from the bus ride, so I'd like to walk around outside first, if that's okay?"

"Uh-huh," his father grunted, then turned and shuffled back into the living room. "Got ham sandwiches if you're hungry."

Tom went down into the basement rec room. Even the TV down here was on; he turned it off and surveyed his quarters. The air was musty, and smelled like old sneakers. The pool table was stacked high with old board games and paper bags of magazines. He wondered if anyone used the room for anything but TV these days. The old red sofa had been cleared off and supplied with a pillow and a neatly-folded blue blanket. Tom set his bags on the sofa and headed upstairs to the kitchen.

His mother was sitting in a faded pink housecoat at the kitchen table.

The old portable black-and-white TV on the counter was deafeningly loud; some kind of medical drama was playing. His mother's eyes were glazed, staring unblinking at the flickering screen. A half-empty bottle of red wine and a Looney Tunes juice glass sat on the table beside her left hand. A forgotten cigarette was burning down to a gray tube of ash in her right hand. She'd only recently turned forty-three, but she could've easily passed for sixty.

"Mom?" Tom called. "Mom!"

No response. She didn't even move.

He went to the TV and turned it down a few notches. She gave a little start, then blinked.

"Oh...*Tom*," she slurred, then smiled wanly. "You're...how was your trip?"

"It was fine. A little long." He leaned over the table and gave her a quick kiss on her forehead. The smell of alcohol clouded around her like cheap perfume.

"I'm sorry I couldn't meet you at the bus station. I wasn't...feeling well." Her eyes focused on him, then unfocused as they suddenly brimmed with tears. "You've gotten so big. My little boy's gone. All gone."

"Shh, it's okay, Mom," he said, trying to comfort her. She seldom got maudlin when she was drunk, but this was a welcome change from her usual zombielike stupor.

She wept into his shoulder. "I'm so s-sorry, Tommy. I wasn't...I'm not...much of a mother."

You're a fine mother, he willed himself to say, but the lie stuck in his throat and refused to come out.So he just held her.

"I wanted you to stay," she sobbed, "but I didn't know how to ask. I didn't know what to say."

"I couldn't stay and watch you kill yourself. God, Mom, why do you *do* this to yourself? Why do you do this to *us*?"

He knew the answer; he'd known it in his heart for a long time. She'd married too young and had a child too early by a man who didn't know how to give her the love and attention she needed. And so she crawled into the nearest bottle to escape the stress and loneliness she didn't know how else to cope with.

Her grip on his arm was starting to loosen, her eyelids fluttering. "I...didn't know..."

She slumped back in the chair, snoring softly.

S P A R K S   A N D   S H A D O W S

Just like ol' times, Mom, he thought, shaking his head.

He knew from experience that she'd wake up in an hour or so and put herself to bed. He quietly took the bottle off the table and poured the rest of the wine down the sink. Then he went to the fridge and found a plate of plastic-wrapped sandwiches on the bottom shelf. He took one and a can of ginger ale and went outside to find Joanie.

The cool country air was a welcome relief from the stuffiness of the house. He took a deep breath. It was oddly comforting to smell hay and manure instead of car exhaust and garbage. No matter how much he loved Chicago, Montana still felt like home.

He popped open the soda and munched on his sandwich as he walked around the house to the barn. Two half-grown kittens were stalking something in a loose pile of hay by the door. Inside, he could see the soft yellow glow from an electric lantern.

Tom stepped inside the barn, straw crackling beneath his feet. Two horses in stalls to his left chuffed and peered at him curiously. A few yards away, Joanie was sitting on a milking stool in the middle of a chickenwire pen. She was bottle-feeding a sturdy-looking lamb and brushing his wooly coat with a curry comb.

"Hi Joanie," he called.

"Hi! Come meet Bo!" the girl called back.

Tom walked to the pair and stepped over the yard-high pen wall. "That's some lamb you've got," he said, his eyes watering from the smell. He'd forgotten how powerfully sheep stank, even clean ones.

"Isn't he great? He's just a few months old; he was born premature and his momma died. They didn't think he would live, but I fed him and kept him warm and now look at him! If he gets big enough, I'm gonna show him at the next county fair. He gets awful dirty, though, even when he's just here in the pen. You know what I use to wash him?"

"No, what?"

"Woolite!" She laughed, but her smile didn't make it as far as her eyes.

They were both quiet for a moment.

"I'm really sorry about Aunt Fran," he said gently. "She meant a lot to me, so I know she must've meant a lot to you and Lisa. And...I'm sorry I left you girls. I hoped things would be better for you two than they were for me...but I guess they haven't been. Anyway...I'm sorry. Things got so bad between me and Dad, I just didn't know what else to do but go away."

"S'okay," Joanie replied, her eyes downcast. "I think Lisa was mad at you for a long time, but I wasn't. It would've been cool to have a big brother and all...but I want to leave, too, sometimes. Mom and Dad... they're here, but they're someplace else most of the time, you know? It was Aunt Fran who took care of me when I was little. Her and Lisa."

A tear trickled down her cheek. She wiped it away and forced another one of her patented cheery smiles. "I just don't know what's going to happen now. It feels like everything's broken, and if I let myself get sad, it'll all just fall apart."

Slate-black storm clouds steadily built on the horizon during the graveside service the next morning. The preacher had to raise his voice to be heard over the rising wind. As they lowered the brass-handled casket into the ground, the first cold raindrops splattered down on Tom and his family.

As soon as the service was completed, everyone hurried back to their cars. The rain was pounding down by the time they got back to the house. Once they were inside, the Wilson family silently scattered to their various havens: his mother and Lisa to their rooms, his father to his beer and TV in the living room, and Joanie to her lamb in the barn.

Tom was left alone in the kitchen. The table was crowded with casseroles and pies the ladies from the Presbyterian church had brought by that morning before the funeral. Most of the church ladies adored Fran, but none cared to stay very long at the Wilson house.

Well, now what? Tom thought as he sat down at the table. Fran had been adamant about him coming all this way, but to do what? She hadn't made an appearance at the funeral. *Why am I here?*

Tom jumped as the kitchen TV switched on. As if possessed, the TV's dial ratcheted around until it landed on Channel 77.

"Welcome back to ALTV-77, your channel for the Guardian Angel Network's news from the afterlife." Fran was wearing a beige pantsuit and a Jackie Kennedy-style pillbox hat with a black veil. She looked a solid twenty years younger than when she'd visited him in his apartment. "Many viewers still don't realize that suicide is a leading cause of death of North American teenagers. Teens are particularly at risk after the death of a loved one.”

Tom felt his blood run cold.

“You need to talk to your sister, Thomas, and do it *now*.”

The TV switched off.

Tom pushed away from the table and hurried to the stairs. When he got to Lisa's room, he put his ear to the door to listen. She was sobbing. He rapped on the wood.

“Lisa, can I talk to you?” he called.

“Go away.”

“No, I won't go away...I really need to talk to you.”

Panic scrabbled at the back of his throat when she didn't answer. He tried the knob. It was locked.

“Look, if I have to kick the door open, I will!”

He heard the floor creak as she moved toward the door, then the click of her unlocking it. The door swung in. He stepped inside.

“What do you want?” Her tone was nervous and surly. She was holding something behind her back.

“What have you got there?”

“Nothing.” She backed up, but he grabbed her arm. “Let go! It's none of your business–”

She had a bottle clenched in her fist. He pried her fingers open, and a bottle of pills fell to the floor.

Their mother's tranquilizers.

He released her arm and picked up the bottle. It was only half full.

“Ohgod. Please tell me you didn't–” he began.

“No. I didn't.” She sank to her knees on the bare floor. “I was *about* to...I'd been psyching myself up to do it for the past half-hour.”

“But *why*?” he asked, kneeling beside her. “You've got your whole life ahead of you–”

“That's bullshit and you know it!” she flared, then started crying anew. “*What* life is it that I'm supposed to have ahead of me, huh? I got no friends at school; everyone thinks I'm some kind of freak loser on account that everyone knows my parents are a couple of drunks. School's boring, and my grades suck because the work just makes me want to scream, it's all so stupid. And the other kids – *god!* They're either cowboy jerkoffs or they're running around in baggy jeans listening to rap and pretending to be these little white gangstas. Gangstas! Here in Montana! What a freakin' joke! This whole place is a joke. And I'm the biggest joke of all, 'cause I don't fit in and nobody but Aunt Fran cares whether I live or die. And now she's gone. So I might as well die and save everyone the trouble."

"*I* care, Lisa."

"You do *not*," she snapped. "Tomorrow you're going back to Chicago, and you'll forget all about me like you did before."

"I'm sorry I let you down, Lisa. The last thing I wanted to do was hurt you – I just wanted to get away from here."

"Yeah? Like I *don't*? All I think about is being someplace besides here...but I'm too scared to leave. I can't go off by myself like you did. God. I am *such* a *loser!*"

"You are *not* a loser. Number one, you are a very pretty girl – now, don't give me that look, you *are* very pretty; you'd have to beat the boys off with a stick in Chicago. If the yokels around here are too dumb to see what a beautiful person you are, that's their loss.

"Number two, you are a smart girl, *too* smart to throw it all away like this. Number three, think of how bad you felt when I went away – now how do you think Joanie would feel if you went and killed yourself, huh?

"And number four, I felt just like you do now when I was your age, and I can tell you that *it does get better*. There's so much more to life than high school. Everyone's got this idea that high school is some kind of carefree golden age of youth, but the truth is that for most of us, it's a hell you just have to endure to get that diploma. And, speaking as a guy who dropped out, *not* having that little scrap of paper is a major pain.

"You've stuck it out for sixteen years; what's two more?"

She sniffled and wiped her eyes. "But...what then?"

"Okay," he said slowly, "how 'bout this for a plan: you apply to colleges in the Chicago area, then come to live with me and Myrna while you go to class. Or, if you don't want to do the college thing right away, you can come out to Chicago, stay with us, and we can show you around. I know the big city can seem kinda scary – but man, it can be *so* much fun, you wouldn't believe it! We'll help you find your own way. How's that sound?"

She smiled; it was like seeing the sun come out from behind the clouds. "You promise?"

He crossed his heart with his index finger. "I won't let you down again."

S P A R K S   A N D   S H A D O W S

He helped her to her feet. "Why don't we go downstairs, and I'll fix you some iced tea. Then maybe we can find Joanie and go out for ice cream or something?"

"Okay."

The headed down to the kitchen. Rain pelted the windows, and the wind was lashing the branches of the big trees in the front yard.

The kitchen TV clicked on.

"Welcome back to ALTV-77," said Aunt Fran.

Lisa's eyes went wide. "Ohmigod, that's–"

"Shh!" he said, putting his hand on her arm.

"We have a special weather report for our viewers in the Wilson Farm area. A funnel cloud has been sighted near Thorny Creek; it's going to become an F2 tornado in the next half hour. Bo got loose, and Joanie's looking for him by the creek. She'll be in the tornado's path when it touches down."

"*Shit!*" exclaimed Tom. "Let's go!"

"But that can't...no way..." Lisa looked completely stunned as she gaped at Fran's fading image on the TV.

"We've got to *go!*" Tom pushed her toward the door.

The pair raced out of the house and across the field toward the tree-lined creek. Tom could see the funnel cloud dipping down from the huge black wall cloud not two miles away from them. The violently shifting wind threatened to knock them off their feet, but Tom ran on, pulling Lisa along with him, willing his legs to move faster.

After five minutes of running down the nearly-dry creekbed screaming the girl's name into the rising gale, they found Joanie and Bo in a small stand of alpine spruce on a rocky rise. The girl had tied a rope leash around the lamb's neck, and was fruitlessly trying to pull the terrified, bleating little beast along with her.

"Joanie!" Tom shouted. "What the heck are you doing out here?"

"Bo got loose while we were gone," she yelled back, looking like she was starting to panic. "The thunder scared him and he ran off."

Tom and Lisa hurried to her.

"We've got to get to lower ground!" Lisa's face was white with fear.

"He won't move!" Joanie dug in her heels and pulled. "He's too heavy–!"

The wind rose to a freight-train roar. The hairs rose on the back of Tom's arms and neck as he heard the rumble of the newborn tornado.

Touchdown.

"I can carry him." Tom grabbed the leash and scooped up Bo. The wriggling lamb was surprisingly heavy, but once Tom had him firmly in his arms he quit struggling. "Come on!"

The trio pelted down the hill, their sneakers kicking up gravel. They jumped down into the narrow cleft of the creekbed and threw themselves flat in the muddy sand.

Tom could hear nothing but the roar of the twister. He squeezed his eyes shut, covered his head with one arm while he gripped the lamb's rope with the other. *Please sweet Jesus, don't let us die out here...*

And then it was over. As quickly as it had come, the tornado sucked back up into the sky. Tom lifted his head and peered up at the clouds. The black clouds were already starting to break up.

Tom rolled over and got to his feet on rubbery knees. "That was *way* too close for comfort."

Joanie burst into tears, letting out all her pent-up and long-denied sadness in huge, wracking sobs.

"Hey, kiddo, shh," Lisa said, crawling over to her little sister. "We're safe now."

"Let her cry," Tom said. "We all need a good cry sometimes."

So they held their little sister, rocking her back and forth until, at last, her tears seemed spent.

"J-jeez," she hiccupped, "We're *filthy*. Mom's gonna kill us."

Tom looked down at himself. The front of his shirt and jeans were completely covered in mud. And he smelled very strongly of Bo.

"She won't kill us if we take care of the laundry ourselves," he replied. "But next time Bo runs off in the middle of a thunderstorm, *tell someone*, okay?"

She sniffled, her lower lip quivering. "But he's my responsibility–"

"And you're *our* responsibility. You could've gotten killed up there!" He stopped himself, tried not to sound angry. "We need to *talk* to each other when bad stuff happens. We'll do a whole lot better trying to work out our problems together than by trying to go it alone."

He helped his sisters to their feet and handed Bo's leash back to Joanie. The lamb was nibbling at a dandelion growing in the sand, the terror of the storm already forgotten.

"Think you can take him from here?" Tom asked.

She nodded, smiling.

S P A R K S   A N D   S H A D O W S

"Good," he said, a mischievous smile spreading across his face, "because first one back to the house has dibs on the shower!"

And the race was on.

✳

A few hours later, the freshly-showered trio sat around the kitchen table, eating Neapolitan ice cream and giggling. The washing machine and dryer were a comforting hum in the background.

Tom wasn't surprised when the TV clicked itself on.

"This is a special report for our viewers at the Wilson Farm," Fran said from the screen. She was standing just outside their kitchen window. Over her shoulder, Tom could see himself sitting at the table.

Joanie's eyes went round as saucers, and she nearly dropped her spoon. "Whoa. That's *Aunt Fran!*"

"You did good today, kids. I love you, and don't you ever forget that. I can't be with you, but I'll always be watching over you. Be good to each other."

She straightened her shoulders. "This is newswoman Francine Wilson signing off for now. But I'll be back when you need me on ALTV-77, your channel for the Guardian Angel Network's news from the afterlife."

The screen went dark.

"How did she *do* that?" Joanie whispered.

"She's always been an angel," Tom said. "I guess God decided the job suited her pretty well."

Lisa reached over and touched his hand. "Are we going to be good to each other?"

"I'll call you, every Sunday night. And you can call me anytime you want to talk. And I'll come back for Thanksgiving. And the Chicago offer still stands." He paused. "Sounds good?"

She grinned. "Sounds good."

Tom heard floorboards squeak. He turned, and saw their parents standing in the doorway. Mr. and Mrs. Wilson peered around the kitchen as if they'd never seen their children before.

"What're you kids doing?" his father asked.

"Eatin' ice cream," Joanie said. She pushed the carton toward them. "Want some?"

"Think I might," his father said.

Tom passed his parents spoons and bowls. "We were thinking of going to a movie later...would you two like to come along?"

"Well. That'd be fine," his mother said.
And then she smiled.
It reached all the way to her eyes.

Darwin's Children

I CAREFULLY raised the lid on the styrofoam cooler. The water snake lay inside, quiet at last, coils relaxed into a damp double S. His only movement was the lazy flicker of his black tongue. I reached down and grasped him behind the head. Immediately, he flipped around in my hand and made a series of whipping strikes before he fastened onto my thumb.

"Damn!" I jumped back, cracking my head on a low wooden support beam. I pried his jaws off my thumb with my free hand and then grabbed him behind the neck again. I held him clamped in my fist and glared at him as he tried to thrash free.

"Rotten snake," I muttered. He only glared back with those angry, rusty eyes and hissed. "Pull that again, and I'm gonna make you into a wallet. Comprendo?"

Of course he didn't. You couldn't fill a thimble with his brain. I'd been feeding him and cleaning his cage for a year, and he hadn't learned to recognize me. Probably, he never would.

"Damn snake." I pried up the lid of his clean aquarium and dropped him inside. I quickly clamped the lid down and then heaved the tank into its slot in the display wall. After everything was situated, I looked down at my hand. Four rows of perfectly spaced pinpricks were welling up blood, and the skin on my thumb was torn as though I'd been slashed with a tiny hacksaw.

I stomped out from behind the exhibit and into the main room. Carlie was cleaning the front of the 500-gallon fish tank. "What were you yelling about?" She spritzed the aquarium with Windex. A striped bass snapped at her hand as she wiped the glass.

"Snake bit me," I grumbled.

"Oooh, is it bad?" Carlie stopped wiping and trotted to intercept me as I walked towards the laboratory. She shoved her glasses up the bridge of her nose and squinted down at my injuries. "Oooh, he really got ya, huh? When's the last time ya had a tetanus shot?"

She was still following me as I got to the basin and began to vigorously soap my hand.

"I bet you'll need a tetanus shot."

"It's just superficial."

"Yeah, but the snake's been in that scuzzy water, and he's probably got—"

"*I don't need a tetanus shot!*"

I wished Carlie would lose her morbid obsession with the diseases we could contract from the animals. When we had an opossum, she was on a rabies kick. When we got our snapping turtle, it was salmonella. So far, nothing had made me sick but Carlie.

"Hello, ladies, how are you doing today?" George Bloom, our curator, stepped into the laboratory. He was cheerful and tidy as always, dressed in tan slacks and a striped shirt. His gray hair was still damp from his morning shower.

Three years before, he'd retired from teaching at a university in Arizona and had moved to Edgewater. His wife, Edna, had family in Edgewater, and George liked the area's lakes and small mountains. I met George soon after they moved to town. The nature center was just getting started, and George and I were both hired in the same month. At first, I pretty much dismissed George as just another old guy who liked animals.

My opinion of him changed drastically after I joined the local Natural Adventure Club and went on one of their rock climbing trips. As we were getting our gear out of the jeeps, George slipped out of his sweatshirt to change into a T-shirt. He was fifty, but from the neck down he didn't look any older than thirty-five. Every muscle on his torso and arms was defined in hard, tanned flesh. I was impressed. And I was even more impressed when we hit the rocks – George could climb like a gecko.

The final stage of my attitude readjustment came when I was going across a rock ledge. Stupid me, I was checking out the buzzards circling overhead instead of watching where I was stepping. My foot slipped on a loose rock, and suddenly I was half-falling, half-tumbling down the canyon face. Somehow, I managed to grab a prickly little bush that was stubbornly growing from a crack in the rocks. I hung there, thirty feet of air between me and the rocky canyon floor. My hands were bleeding from the thorns, and I couldn't have climbed back up even if I wasn't scared out of my mind. Visions of quadriplegia danced in my head when I realized that the bush's roots were giving out.

But then George was beside me, holding onto the rocks with his legs and one arm while he tied a rope around my middle with his free hand. Then they hauled me up the face like I was a sack of flour. George saved my life – I don't think anybody else could have gotten down in time to keep me from falling.

"Liz got bit by the water snake," Carlie announced enthusiastically.

"It's just a scratch," I said. "But I hate that damn snake!"

"That's probably why he bites you," said George, smiling.

I noticed the cloth collecting bag in his left hand. "Hey, George, whatcha got?"

"I found a surprise on my morning walk." He cleared off a spot on the counter island and laid the bag down. We crowded around as he opened the bag and slid his hand inside. "But be gentle – he's just a hatchling."

George pulled out a tiny white serpent. It took me a second to realize it was an albino hognosed snake. It wasn't entirely colorless; the eyes were a light blue-gray, and it had faint, cream-colored diamond spots on its back.

"Oh, he's darling!" gushed Carlie.

"Hey, what's up?" asked Frank, the center's supervisor, as he came out of the office. "Oh, hey, would ya look at that," he exclaimed softly. "Where'd ya find it, George?"

"Beside the creek near my house."

"Good job, George. This thing'll be a heck of an attraction; I bet a lot of people haven't seen an albino *anything* before, much less a snake."

"It'll be hard raising this one," said George, frowning a little. "Albinos don't generally have good health, and he'll only be able to take tiny frogs. And it hasn't rained since May, so most of the tadpole ponds have dried up."

"Ah, we've got plenty of little frogs," said Frank breezily. "Liz caught a whole mess of 'em when she went out to the river last weekend. The little guy's gonna do just fine."

✳

Frank did an honest-to-God local media blitz. We had "Snake Mania" week at the center with the little albino as our spotlit centerpiece. There was a snake-naming contest for the kids, and at the end of the week the defenseless little guy was tagged with the moniker "Snowflake the Snake."

Flake was the perfect Show 'N Tell specimen. I could carry him around the center twined in the fingers of my hand. He didn't seem to mind being handled; I guess people's body heat felt good to him. It always amazed me how many kids, and even adults, came into the center thinking that snakes are slimy. In the pre-Flake days, if I brought out a snake during a tour, a few people would invariably scurry away and refuse to come within ten feet of the reptile. But people were always willing to touch Flake, perhaps because of his size, but probably because he was pretty. I even got one middle-aged woman, who wouldn't even look at our other snakes, to run her finger along Flake's back. I think she washed her hands afterwards. But she touched him.

The trouble began on the first Saturday of August. It was a feeding day, and I always started with the snakes. I fished a cricket frog out of one of the bait tanks and dropped it into Flake's terrarium. The glistening frog hopped across the gravel and landed *plit!* in the water dish. But Flake didn't even raise his head in response to the movement. Something was wrong. I gently turned him over. He barely moved at my touch, and a trickle of blood was oozing from his vent.

"Oh great," I muttered.

Then George and Frank came out of the laboratory, arguing.

"... but we have to release them now so they'll get acclimated before the first freeze," said George.

"I told you, we're not releasing any animals. They can hibernate in the center just fine," Frank replied.

"It's too warm in here for the reptiles to hibernate, and we won't be able to get live food for some of them. And we've already had most of them a year. We've never kept individual animals longer than that."

"Well, we will now. I don't see the point in getting rid of perfectly good specimens."

"Frank, you don't–"

"Not another word, George! They're staying here, and that's final." Frank turned on his heel and went to his office. George stood there and rubbed his temples. There were deep shadows under his eyes.

I approached George. "Still got that headache?"

"Yes, it's been on and off for most of the week. I wish I could shake it, but aspirin isn't helping. And neither is Frank. We really need to release some of the animals; they've been here far too long. I'm worried that their survival skills will atrophy so much that they *can't* be released back into the wild. And some of the lizards and turtles have become such picky eaters that I'm sure they're not getting a proper diet."

"Um, I have some more bad news."

"What?"

"Flake's sick...he's passing blood."

George went behind the exhibit and took Flake out of his tank to examine him. I noticed that his hands were trembling.

"What do you think?" I asked.

"Don't know...could be parasites, could be stress. Either way, I don't think he'll eat." George rubbed his eyes as though they wouldn't focus.

I asked, "So what do we do now?"

George didn't answer. He was leaning heavily against the back wall. "I don't feel so good."

His knees buckled, and he fell down among the buckets and junk that littered the floor. He lay there groaning. I stood there in a paralysis of stupidity for a few seconds, but then I jumped over him and dragged him out into the exhibit hall.

"Carlie! Frank!" I yelled. "Call an ambulance, quick!"

I had thought that George had a heart attack, but the situation was much worse. He had brain cancer. The doctors said the tumor was the size of a lemon. They helicoptered him to Evansburg and did emergency surgery, but it didn't go too well. A clot formed and George had a stroke that left his entire right side paralyzed.

I drove up to visit George three weeks after his surgery.

"Hey, how ya doing?" I asked softly as I entered his hospital room.

George lay motionless in bed, the sheets pushed down in a rumpled heap around his knees. The crown of his head was swathed in bandages, and his face was dark and puffy.

"Guess I can't complain too much." His speech was a little slurred. "There's not much pain, at least not now. They have me on so many painkillers I doubt I'd feel it if someone kicked me. How are things going at the center?"

"Okay, I guess. One of our hatchling box turtles died, but everything else is healthy. Except Flake, of course. He still bleeds sometimes, and he's not eating well. I hope the little guy doesn't die."

"What's Frank going to do if he does?"

"Frank wants Carlie to pickle him."

"What for? Frank keeps collecting preserved specimens, but no one ever looks at them." George stopped to cough weakly. "He should just let Flake go and let nature run its course."

"But he can't possibly survive in the wild."

"Better than dying a captive." George coughed again and turned his head to watch a mockingbird fly past the window.

"So...uh, what do the doctors think?"

"It's a glioma," George replied tiredly. "It'll keep coming back until it kills me."

When he said that, I felt as if somebody had slugged me with a sack of wet concrete. I spent the next few seconds trying to recover from the shock and trying to think of the proper thing to say.

"But...but they're getting better with chemotherapy," I finally said. "More and more people are surviving this kind of thing." My words sounded pretty lame to me.

George shook his head. "Even if it did go into remission, what then? I can't even go to the bathroom without help. Once I get out of here, if I ever do, Edna will have to hire a nurse to take care of me."

"But what about rehab ...?"

"I'm on the wrong side of the hill, Liz. If I survive the cancer, I'll just be waiting for something else to take me out." He looked out at the clouds that were leisurely cruising across the bright sky. "I can't live like this," he murmured to himself.

"Can...can I do anything for you?" I asked, desperately seeking the right words and not finding them. "Can I...get you anything?"

"Maybe." He paused, frowning. "Liz, you're old enough to drink, aren't you?"

"Uh, yeah...I turned twenty-one a few months back. Why?"

"I want you to bring me a bottle of Everclear. If you can't find that, then any other high-proof liquor will do. With all the pain pills they have me on...well, it shouldn't take much alcohol to do the job."

"Huh?" Then it sank in. "Oh wait, no—"

"Listen to me. I'm going to die, and I want to do it on my terms, not on the doctor's, and not on the cancer's. And I don't want my family to go broke trying to stave off the inevitable." He sighed and rubbed his eyes with his good hand. "Edna would try to stop me if she knew I was planning this, but I can't stand to be a burden to her." He paused, staring at me. "I would suggest that you buy the liquor and some assorted items at a store, then 'forget' your bag on my beside table."

S P A R K S   A N D   S H A D O W S

The door opened and a nurse came in. She was small and chubby and had big hair. Her candy-coated smile was so wide it showed her molars, and I wanted to smack it right off her face.

"Miss, I'm afraid you'll have to leave for a little while. It's time for Mr. Bloom's bath," she said cheerfully. "You can come back in an hour or so."

"Will you be back?" asked George.

"I...I don't know," I replied. I felt sick and dizzy. "Maybe. Look... I'll...try to come back later, I guess..."

"I hope you can make it."

My whole body seemed numb as I went down to the parking lot. I got into my car and drove away, not really knowing or caring where I was going.

Then an image of George drove into my mind like a knife. I saw him sitting alone in a wheelchair in a nursing home, dressed in an ugly green bathrobe. All his hair was gone but a few dry stands like spiderweb, his eyes sunk so far into his skull you couldn't see what color they were. His skin was a sickly white, looked like it hadn't seen the sun in year. The flesh was so thin on his face and hands that he looked like the men in the old photos of the Nazi concentration camps.

I started to shiver, and then I started to cry. I had to pull off the road at a little park beside the river that ran around the city. I got out and stumbled across the grass and sat down on a concrete park bench to try to get the chill out of my bones and my head. I closed my eyes and breathed in the warm summer air, trying to forget the hospital.

When I opened my eyes, I realized that the park was beautiful. The grass was a perfect emerald green. The nearby flowerbeds were a bright riot of pansies, chrysanthemums, and marigolds.

Then a flash of orange and black went past my face: a monarch butterfly. It fluttered dizzily to a nearby oak and landed on the rough bark. The monarch rested there, delicately folding and unfolding its wings.

I got up from the bench to get a better look at the butterfly. Startled, the monarch fluttered up into the safety of branches...right into an orb weaver's web.

Dismay washed through me. I stepped up to the tree to look at the butterfly struggling in silken trap. The monarch was caught spread-winged, the sticky strands pinning it as though the insect had been mounted for a collection. Black legs wiggled frantically and the web shuddered as the monarch tried to pull free. I almost imagined that I could hear it screaming.

I wished that the spider would hurry up, get it over with. But when I looked for the orb weaver, I saw a shriveled husk in the corner of the web. The spider had been dead for some time; perhaps it had starved, as the butterfly was going to starve.

I looked at the struggling monarch again. I knew it was just an insect, probably couldn't feel any pain, but still...it was beautiful. Beauty didn't deserve an ugly, slow death in a dead web.

I reached up to the web, tried to tear the silk apart to free the butterfly. I managed to free one wing, and monarch tried to fly off. It tore off the upper half of its other wing and fluttered to the ground like a falling autumn leaf. The crippled butterfly lay twitching in the grass, still trying to fly.

I stared down at it, feeling sicker and sicker with each passing second. I wanted to look away, walk away, but somehow I couldn't. Finally, I crushed the butterfly under my sneaker and went back to my car.

I drove to a little grocery store and bought some apples and an Anxiety Kit: Rolaids, Tylenol, M&Ms, and a flask of Everclear.

When I got back to the hospital, George's wife was in the room. I greeted her and laid the brown paper bag down on the bedside table, the mouth of the bag facing George. Then I sat down in the chair beside Edna and we all chatted for a long time. I can't even remember what we talked about – my heart was still hammering and I spent most of my concentration on keeping my voice steady. George was perfectly calm and almost seemed cheerful.

Finally, the nurse stuck her head in and told us visiting hours were over. Just as Edna and I stepped out into the hallway, she said, "Oh, Liz, you forgot your sack."

"Oh, yeah, almost forgot." I reluctantly went back into the room and picked up the paper bag. "Goodbye, George."

"Bye, Liz."

I went down to the parking lot with Edna. After I got into my car, I peeked into the sack. The Everclear was gone.

I ended up eating most of the roll of Rolaids on the trip back to Edgewater, and I played the car stereo at just below pain level. It was dark when I hit the city limits, but I didn't go home. I drove straight across town to the center.

After I got inside, I took Flake out of his tank and twined him in the fingers of my left hand. Then we went to the closet where Frank kept all the preserved specimens. I turned on the flickering overhead light and walked inside.

The collection seemed especially eerie that night. The fishy smell of decay and formaldehyde hung in the air. The metal shelves were loaded with an assortment of dust-covered jars. Dead, cloudy eyes stared at me from every corner. On the bottom shelf was the huge jar that held the remains of our python. It had been sawn into pieces before it was preserved, the once beautiful skin broken by jagged gray edges.

I looked down at Flake, who was tasting the air uncertainly. He was warm, warm from the heat of my own hand, and I could feel his sides rise and fall with every breath.

"You don't really want to be preserved for posterity, do you?"

Flake looked at me, startled by the sound of my voice. The gray eyes held no comprehension. His existence centered around little frogs and warm rocks. He could never care about how he died, or how his pretty skin and eyes would turn yellow and disintegrate inside a formaldehyde time capsule.

I tucked him inside a cloth collection bag and took him back to my house. I broke out my camera and arranged Flake on a sheet of blue construction paper. Then I took slides of him from every angle, as George always did before he released an animal.

After the roll of film was spent, I drove out to George's house on the edge of town. I got out of my car with the collecting bag and walked down to the creek that ran beyond his back yard. The night was warm; I guessed that we wouldn't have a freeze until October. Maybe Flake would manage to acclimate and go into hibernation. If not, he would fall prey to a neighborhood cat or perhaps succumb to whatever ailed him. But he would have died anyway – at least something would get a gourmet meal.

I lifted the little snake out of the bag. His scales shone pale and ghostly. I dropped him on the ground beside a thick patch of marsh grass. He didn't move right away. Instead, he looked up at me blankly, his

eyes black beads in the moonlight.
    And then he slid into the grass and was gone.

Afterword
by Nalo Hopkinson

I first met Lucy Snyder in 1995. We were both students at Clarion East, then housed at Michigan State University. Clarion is a six-week long workshop in writing science fiction, fantasy and horror. I had just had my first short story published in a Toronto magazine. I left Clarion mentally wrung out.

Whereas Lucy, within weeks of leaving Clarion, created the online fiction zine *Dark Planet*, which she edited for about seven years. She's been the fiction editor for a science magazine. She's done science writing herself, not to mention tech support, web design, research, bassoon instruction, and radio news editing. Her resume also mentions snake wrangling. Why am I not surprised? Through it all, she's worked at her own fiction and non-fiction, found her way back into poetry, and discovered her flair for short humour. ("Installing Linux on a Dead Badger" is in another collection of hers. Do go read it. When you do, don't have anything in your mouth that a surprised snort could catapult up into your sinuses. You have been warned.)

I remember the Lucy I first met as a pale young woman who had clothing in every shade of black. She would be responsible, several years later, for filling my miniscule one-bedroom apartment with goths when she and a few of her friends were in town for a convention. We were all pretty messy. Getting ready to go out on the town that evening was quite the challenge as we all tried to figure out whose clothing was whose. That was when I realised that I wear a hell of a lot of black, too.

The Lucy I first met was shy. I suspect all nineteen of us Clarionettes were, and far too many of us knew stanzas from Chaucer's *The Canterbury Tales* by heart. In the original old English. Lucy often looked serious; either unhappy or angry, it was difficult to tell which. Until she smiled, and you could see the friendly, sweet person that she really was. When writer Samuel R. Delany heard her responses to an autobiographical writing exercise that he had set us, he beamed and said, "I'm half in love with you myself, just from hearing that description."

He was right. Lucy was easy to like. Then you'd go back to your room and read the story she'd turned in for that week, and find yourself wondering whether you could manage to stay awake all night so that you could check under your bed every five minutes for the boogie man. Cause you know it's when you're asleep that he gets you. And the funny thing about it? Lucy was and has remained a sweet, gentle soul. It's just that you don't always see the impishness in that grin of hers for what it is right away.

Lucy didn't only write horror at Clarion. Her conception of how the baby in Lewis Carroll's *Through the Looking Glass* could have legitimately morphed into a pig fascinated me and had me thinking differently about biology than I ever had. I didn't quite understand the science, but I could picture it from her description, and I have never forgotten it. "A Preference for Silence," the story of the space-faring Cassandra, who "never lost her tea in zero gee," first showed up at Clarion.

One day, Lucy showed up for the critique session wearing a bandaid on her leg. I nearly didn't see it because she is that rare human being; her skin *is* the "flesh" tone of regular bandaids. I remarked on how unusual that was and how frustrating it is for this brown-skinned person to see the word "flesh" on boxes of bandaids when what they really mean is light pinkish-beige. And Lucy said the loveliest thing to me: "but don't they sell bandaids to match your colour skin?" (There are more now, but at the time, not so much.) To Lucy, bandaids that could match various skin tones was just so obviously the right thing to do that she hadn't thought to check whether that was in fact what was happening.

That sense of justice comes across strongly in her writing. Lucy's very aware that there are horrible people in the world, and oh, is payback ever a gleefully, terminally sadistic bitch in her stories! Some of her characters are the very embodiment of "I'm as mad as hell and I'm not going to take it any more." Lucy also doesn't forget for a minute that bad things can happen to good people. There were times I was afraid to turn the page while reading this collection, because I just knew that something more horrible than I wanted to imagine was coming down the pike for some unlucky soul. Man. And people think *my* writing is viscerally graphic. They don't know from viscera. Lucy does.

Is it sick and bad and wrong that reading *Sparks and Shadows* meant that I giggled my way through some of the most macabre fiction this side of the Seventh Circle of Hell? In fact, the last half of "Feel the Love" made me laugh out loud. It also shocked me. It's been a while. Lucy's one of the few people who can produce anything so irreverent that even I, who think that sacred cows are just perfect for tossing on the barbie (and enjoying with a fine Chianti), can find it blasphemous. Blasphemous in a good way, you understand. In a "sear the gloss off your illusions" way.

Lucy can write a poem about a one-horse twin. She can make Girl Guide songs kinky without changing a word. (Well, okay; perhaps they already were kinky.) But, not content with leaving it at that, she can spin off from the songs into a surreal futuristic feminine fantasy with a James Bond bravura. She's welcomed you, via this collection, into her imagination. It's a bacchanalia in there. And I must tell you; you may never find your way out again.

Lucy, I'm seeing blood running down the walls. Does that mean it's time to go to bed now?

Acknowledgements

The first edition of this book was published by HW Press in 2007.

"A Preference For Silence" originally appeared in *Lady Churchill's Rosebud Wristlet*, Issue #5,. It also appeared in the August 12, 2000 edition of *Dark Matter Chronicles* and in the February 2001 issue of *Writer Online*.

"The Monster Between The Sparks" (previously titled "Dark Matter") originally appeared in *Chiaroscuro*, January 2002.

"Through Thy Bounty" originally appeared in *The Midnighters' Club*, June 2001.

"Menstruation For Men" originally appeared in *Horror Quarterly*, Autumn 2004, and in the *Horror Quarterly Anthology*, 2005.

"The Dickification of the American Female" originally appeared in *Clean Sheets*, June 15 2005.

"Permian Basin Blues" originally appeared in *Lady Churchill's Rosebud Wristlet*, October 2000. Portions appeared in *The Indifference of Heaven* by Gary A. Braunbeck (Obsidian Press, 2000).

"Sara and the Telecats" originally appeared in *Farthing*, September 2006.

"... And Her Shadow" originally appeared in *Blood Magic*, Eggplant Literary Productions, October 2001.

"The Dogs of Summer" originally appeared in *Blood Magic*, Eggplant Literary Productions, October 2001.

"The Sheets Were Clean And Dry" originally appeared in *Masques V*, Gauntlet Press, June 2006.

"Photograph of a Lady, Circa 1890" originally appeared in *Lady Churchill's Rosebud Wristlet*, October 2000. Portions appeared in *The Indifference of Heaven* by Gary A. Braunbeck (Obsidian Press, 2000).

"Soul Searching" originally appeared in *Cosmic Visions*, Fall 1997. It also appeared in *Blood Magic* in October 2001.

"Flesh and Blood" originally appeared in *Blood Magic*, Eggplant Literary Productions, October 2001.

"Forgetting" originally appeared in *Jackhammer E-Zine*, April 2000. It also appeared in the *Best of Jackhammer E-zine Anthology* in Feb. 2001.

"Camp Songs: Innocent Fun or Diabolical Brainwashing Plot?" originally appeared in Full *Unit Hookup Magazine*, Summer 2005.

"The Dolls' Hearts" originally appeared in *The Midnighters' Club*, June 2001.

"So Lonely As The Grave" originally appeared in *Dark Lurkers*, Double Dragon Press, May 2004.

"... Next on Channel 77" originally appeared in *Guardian Angels*, Cumberland House Publishing, November 2000.

"Darwin's Children" originally appeared in *Snow Monkey*, December 1999.

About the Author

Lucy A. Snyder is also the author of the novels *Spellbent* and *Shotgun Sorceress*, the humor collection *Installing Linux on a Dead Badger*, and the Bram Stoker Award-winning poetry collection *Chimeric Machines*. Her writing has appeared in *Strange Horizons, Weird Tales, Hellbound Hearts, Chiaroscuro, GUD*, and *Lady Churchill's Rosebud Wristlet*.

She was born in South Carolina but grew up in San Angelo, Texas. She currently lives in Worthington, Ohio with a pack of cats and her husband/occasional co-author Gary A. Braunbeck.

You can learn more about her at www.lucysnyder.com

www.ingramcontent.com/pod-product-compliance
Lightning Source LLC
Chambersburg PA
CBHW071304250626
47159CB00004B/1306